The ... g

by
CJ Duncan

Contents

Chapter 1

Grey.

It was all grey.

Elongated forks of water streaked across dark glass as the car travelled through the muted landscape. The clouds overhead occasionally parted to let the light peer down for a moment before closing ranks again. The road twisted across the barren hills as the wind and rain continued its assault against the car, wipers beating back and forth, back and forth.

The undulating drone of the car as she worked her way up and down the gears was grey.

She was grey.

Her life was grey.

Beside her Marcus sat with his knees up against the dashboard. His head lolled to the left as he gazed emotionlessly out the window. Directly behind her, Daryl hummed softly as he focused on the Nintendo in his hands.

Her boys were grey right now too. She felt the familiar pit in her stomach as she chewed over this recurring theme: Were they going to be okay? Were they now forever changed? Forever broken; shadows of their former, happy confident selves? She squeezed Marcus's leg which was left unacknowledged before she put her hand back to the wheel, a long-left bend appearing before them. She eased her speed; the road was narrow and slick with rain and the weather limited her view of the road ahead. A sign showed that the ferry was another 20 miles away. She had thought they were closer than that. The ferry left at four giving her half an hour to make it. If she missed it, they would have to drive the three hours back to Glasgow and book it again.

Hazel gently pushed down on the accelerator and her Civic responded as the road stretched its back into an inviting dark grey straight line towards the horizon. She hadn't seen another car for hours and, as a seed of anxiety began to unspool inside her, she decided she was going to have to increase her speed to reach the ferry in time.

As the needle crept up, she could feel Marcus's gaze shift from the dull monotony outside.

They reached the ferry with ten minutes to spare. A man stood watching their approach, leaning inside the doorway of a small, weather battered hut. A bicycle leant to the side and she saw a small, bright orange glow, distorted by the water on the windscreen, followed by a plume of grey smoke which was whisked away by the wind moments later. He waved as they drew nearer and flicked his cigarette into the low, blood rust gorse that stained the land for countless miles in all directions. The cigarette disappeared despite Hazel's attention, and she raised her fingers off the wheel in reply, nodding in gratitude that he had come out on such a miserable day to ferry them to the island.

The ferry ran by bookings; and only at 10am and midday; it was only 25 minutes across the strait to the Isle of Mucach, but you still had to use the L & P ferry operator website to book the ferry. There was no app and definitely no turning up unexpectedly – there would be nobody here.

Mucach was a tiny island off the North coast of Scotland and, although island hopping using car ferries was popular, Mucach was such a bleak and forgettable island in an archipelago of countless others, that it was hardly worth the effort; it was, as Ronnie liked to say, *for completionists only*.

Mucach sported one road that ran the perimeter of the island. The only thing of any note was the outdoor activity centre on the Eastern side of Mucach and the mountain.

Her eye's drifted back to the hut and for a moment she hated the man within, the man who had so carelessly flicked his cigarette. *What worries does he have?* She thought, *I mean really? What was his life like?* He had to cycle out here among this beautiful, rugged scenery, drive a boat for an hour and go home. He had thrown that cigarette with such carelessness, such a lack of thought that it was forgotten before it even reached the floor. She would have agonised over that decision for an eternity – would someone see her litter and despoil the landscape? Would a bird or rabbit try eating it? Would it cause a fire, despite the constant rain, the damp terrain, frigid temperature? Would it somehow have found a small bed of dry, dead needles and begin to smoulder? How easy for him! Ride a bike, smoke a fag, chuck it away - without thinking or second guessing any of it and then go home! *God damn him* she thought to herself. *God damn his easy life! His fucking easy, no challenge, no conflict, no fear fucking life!* And, as she gripped her steering wheel a little too hard, she then scolded herself for this unwarranted venom. Who was she to judge? He could have cancer she reasoned. His mum could have it too. This might be the only respite he gets. This freezing, wet bicycle journey might be the one highlight of an otherwise bleak and tragic existence. Maybe it was just him caring for his cancer ridden parents. All alone. Maybe his wife had died from an incurable - "Mum," said Marcus, snapping her back to the present. "He's waving you on."

She eased the Civic down the slipway and onto the small ferry. She was surprised at how slight the ferry seemed against the rolling grey waves of the sea and, as she unclipped her seat belt, another bloom of worry flowered inside her, climbing snugly into the space that the relief of arriving on time had occupied so briefly. She glanced back at Daryl who was sitting up himself and looking around with bright eyes. "Are we there?" he asked.

"Almost love," she replied, "we're at the ferry." She opened her door and gasped as the wind tore it from her hands, yanking her hand violently. She winced as the door was flung outwards, convinced it had caused irreparable damage, but the door held strong, bouncing against the wind. "You coming out boys?" she asked. Marcus shook his head and tried to shrink further into his oversized hoodie as the warm, stuffy air of the car was replaced with the much colder, hostile air of Northern Scotland.

She climbed out of the car; back and legs aching resentfully at the sudden change in movement. Groaning she stood up and stretched her arms high and then fell into a range of tried and tested stretches and lunges that she had used most of her adult life. After a minute of this, she stood tall, legs straight, feet together and slowly bent forward, wrapping her arms tightly around her legs. Her back and hamstrings pulled pleasingly, and she held the position. The greyness seemed to fade for a moment as a calming black nothingness crept over her, leaving little room for anything else. Her jeans were restrictive, and she could feel the waistline biting her skin, but she held the position. Dimly she was aware of her hair dancing and flying around her head, but she was warm. Her coat was warm. The collar was warm. The blackness was warm, and she breathed slower and deeper. She squeezed her arms tighter and felt her spinal column pull in, felt her hamstrings tighten further. Slowly the sound of the wind and the waves hitting the rocky ballast shore grew faint. Her breathing slowed further, pulsing warmth against the denim of her legs, heat seeping through the fabric onto her skin beneath, louder in her ears. Her warm breath dispersed and melted across her face and she breathed deeply through her nose. And again. And again.

She straightened slowly and breathed deeply of the sharp, clean air. She opened her eyes and started when she saw the ferryman not less than two metres away from her, watching her with a wry, half smile etched on his craggy face. She was embarrassed and a car door slammed behind her, she turned to see Daryl pulling on his red puffer jackets, eyes wide at the cold wind jostling him, bright blond hair flapping.

She turned back to the ferryman who had not taken his eyes off her. "Hello," she yelled over the top of the wind. "Thanks for turning up! Was worried there would be no one here."

He gave her a thumbs up and walked past her to the ramp they had just driven up. He opened a small hatch and flicked a switch which in turn began to haul the ramp out of the water with a shuddering, juddering hiss of hydraulics, bringing it into a folding position and forming a barrier against the water. He returned after sliding a few locking bolts into place. "Won't be too lang getting over here!" He shouted. She nodded. "Ye may want to be back in ye car though," he suggested. "The wind is up," and he looked up expressively, indicating the obvious. "It's nae te bad but it will be choppy and ye will likely get a wee bit wet wi the waves ye know?" She nodded again, not really knowing much at all. She turned to see the route ahead. The sea moved briskly, small waves with tiny flashes of white foam and small, rolling peaks stretched out ahead, vaguely in the distance the brown-grey shape of Muchach could be seen.

"Is the sea not too rough?" she asked, hair whipping in a frenzy about her face. She clamped it back with one hand and said, "I mean, it's looking pretty rough."

The man smiled and shook his head, "We'll be fine. This isnae too much." He reached into his small cabin and pressed a button. With a clang and a low scrape, the ramp began to fold back up on itself. She looked at the ferry and was not reassured. The raft, for that is pretty much what it looked like to her, could have held maybe four cars in total. A small railing stood to the left and right, *port and starboard?* and the front and back *aft and...what was the other one?* were blocked by the two retracted ramps. Daryl suddenly ran into her from the side and wrapped two well insulated arms around her midriff.

"Want to get back in the car Dar?" she asked him. "We might get a bit wet out here!" Daryl grinned and shook his head energetically then ran to the front of the ferry. The ferryman took his position behind a small console with a steering wheel and a small, rather meagre looking control panel.

Hazel followed Daryl to the front, guiding him gently towards the emergency ring that hung near the corner. The ferry suddenly belched a black, diesel cough and she winced at the acrid stench of burnt oil and exhaust, despite the wind. There was a small scrape off the concrete ramp as the ferry put out into the sea. Waves slapped gently at the sides of the ferry and Hazel was surprised at how steady the boat was. An occasional wave, feeling bold, would sometimes hit harder, sending splashes of freezing salt water up over the railing causing Daryl to howl with delight. As they pushed into the main channel their speed gently increased, the waves slapping higher and splashes more frequent. Daryl kept turning excitedly, water running down his red, rosy face, eyes gleaming. "Did you see that one mum? I got soaked!" Another burst of water breached the barrier, and his screams of joy gladdened her. "It's salty mum!" It had been far too long since she had seen such pure pleasure on his face. He leant forward, screaming with glory into the spray as they cut the waves.

She leant onto the barrier, looking down as the grey waters parted, bumping resolutely towards their destination. Water beaded on her jacket and she took pleasure from the cold, misting spray that caused her dark auburn hair to cling and wrap itself to her face. She really hoped these next few weeks would allow Daryl and Marcus the time and the moments they needed to feel joy again. She knew Daryl would be ok, it was Marcus who concerned her. He had always been the quieter and more thoughtful of the two but, since the divorce, he had become a virtual recluse. Conversation was sparse and often like picking her way through a minefield, never knowing what word or action would be the one to draw a sneer of contempt or an angry word or early exit.

She felt a weight press in against the back of her arm; a weight she missed dearly and knew so well – Marcus. She felt an arm drape itself across her neck as she leant her head against the mop of curls she knew was incoming. They stood that way for several beautiful moments. Her head resting against her oldest boy's; golden light was beginning to push through the grey ceiling above in rays and the sea seemed to calm as flecks of blinding light bounced back from the rippling surface. The wind dropped for a moment, and, despite Daryl's howls of disappointment, Hazel felt for the first time in an age, that things were not completely broken, that there was light on the other side and that her two boys were not lost to her.

She reached up and squeezed Marcus's hand and smiled as she saw The Pig draw closer. The clouds above again grew dark and the wind picked up once more.

Chapter 2

The ferry slowed and softly scraped against the concrete ramp. The ferryman, Craig (according to Daryl who had always been able to illicit information from total strangers) walked to the barrier and repeated his earlier performance, lowering the forward ramp this time. A soft clang could be heard through the insulation of the car. He beckoned them onwards with a quick hand gesture and she lowered her window as she approached. "Hi. Um, can I check we have the return booked as well please?"

The ferryman grinned and pulled out a slip of folded paper from the front of his dungarees. "Yep," he said as he studied it. "25th yep?"

"That's right," she replied smiling broadly for no reason she could fathom, feeling the strangeness of the smile and how false she was sure it must look. "Umm, is it changeable do you know? Could we leave a week earlier or later if we wanted?"

The man shrugged, "Sure you could," he said thinking about it, "just do it all through the website. There's a number to ring to cancel and aw that so its nae bother. Just make sure it goes through the website like, as that's the only way I get told there's a booking," he waved his piece of paper as proof of this. His accent was a thick, West Coast brogue and, despite the two decades she had spent living in Scotland, she was still taken aback at how foreign the English language seemed so far up North. She was by now familiar with deciphering the accent and various dialects but still marvelled at the variety of new words she seemed to still be discovering. "I work at sea most days so if I cannae make that booking, it willnae let you make it, ken?" He smiled again, "Nae had any problems before. We'll plan for the 25th. If ye cannae make it, just go online and rebook." The man paused for a moment, "Youse have internet on The Pig no?" he asked.

"Yes, we can use the PC at the centre," she replied. "Anymore crossings this week?" she asked.

"Nope, just you guys. I haven't been out here in weeks." He smiled then nodded at her, waved her on and stepped back, allowing her to drive away. She nodded her thanks and pulled away, bumping down the ramp. Her foot slipped off the clutch a bit quicker than she intended and the car lunged forward, scarping the back of the ramp. She panicked before she forced herself to breathe slower, remembering her coaching. The fear slowly melted away as she looked out at the waving red heather and black rocks that stretched out before her. *Dry blood* she thought. *That's the colour of this landscape, the heather, in this light – dried blood. The whole island seemed stained with-* She blinked and shook the macabre thought away. She slowed her breathing, remembering the steps Basma her therapist had shown her. The mindful counting, the focus on her breathing, the slow smothering of those darker, upsetting thoughts until it was just her and her breath.

She pulled up to the junction and habitually checked both ways before pulling out. She felt lighter now. Just having the expanse of water at her back seemed to be another layer of protection. A further hurdle that he would have to navigate if he was to find them although, if he was determined, she knew he would.

The road was just one long unbroken circuit tracking the rocky coastline of the island. You could head left or right, drive for fifty minutes and wind up back at this spot. There was no chance of any cars coming, maybe a couple of wild campers somewhere on the island but at this time of year, in this weather, the odds were low. There were two Land Rovers at the centre, but Hazel had told them she was bringing her car, so she had the road to herself. She accelerated smoothly along the narrow road which was just wider than the Civic. The road hugged the coastline, and she began to speed up, the dread forgotten as the car responded to her heavy foot. Accelerating into the corners, Marcus gripped one of the overhead handles, "You enjoying yourself there?" he asked.

"No traffic. No police. No lights…. Yes Marcus, I am enjoying myself." She was. Arriving on the island had loosened something in her neck and back and she felt like she could smile. The smile never made it to her face but the fact that she was considering a real, genuine smile was encouraging.

They flew past a signpost for the centre and ten minutes later she was pulling into a gravelled turn off. A large pair of dark green metal gates stood open next to a large sign which hung from the iron fence – MUCACH OUTDOOR ACTIVITY AND MARINE STUDY CENTRE it said in white letters on a green background. Below, in smaller print, was a range of bullet pointed activities on offer as well as contact details. To the left was a faded picture of a grinning pig wearing a safety helmet. Unfortunately, the weather had taken its toll on the cartoon face giving it a rather unfortunate makeover. Paint had peeled from the sign, leaving vacant, eyeless sockets where she remembered two cheery blue eyes. Moreover, the peeling paint made it seem that the eyeless pig was screaming. It was a genuinely unsettling image and she made a mental note to bring it up with Ronnie when she saw her.

They trundled down onto the track, the gates were held in place with two large stones and she debated with herself whether she should be stopping and closing the gates behind her or not. If they had been left open for her, then they would need closing but there may have still been guests on site or Ronnie might have plans or…. She hated this about herself! The overthinking! It was ridiculous. Further back, in the dark corners of her mind, she felt the gates should be locked so others couldn't get in.

So Fraser couldn't get in.

He had no idea she was here and she was pretty sure he had no idea where to find it if he did but that didn't cure her of the wrench of panic that had twisted the moment she saw the open gate in her rear-view mirror.

She was tired and wanted a coffee badly. If the gates were supposed to be closed she could do it after she had parked. She made her decision. She continued down the gravel path and felt a wave of relief as a smile finally forced its way onto her face on seeing the low stone buildings of the centre.

The island had been used by many academic institutions over the years. The geology was unique with some of the oldest rock on the planet being available to study. Sea and marine biology was virtually untouched, the waters clear and pure and teeming with life. However, Muchach was also home to a historical monument which gained significant notice in the 70s and 80s. A ring of stone, similar to Stone Henge, sat perfectly in the middle of the island. It's official name was Mag Tul Storr but was mostly known as The Pig's Eye, or just, The Eye – in keeping with the porcine appearance of the mountain that stood beyond.

Some of the rocks had since toppled, much like its more famous counterpart, but the real mystery behind The Pig's Eye, was how it had been erected. The stone used was not local, could not even be found in Scotland, and many experts had been baffled with how the stones had made their way to this remote Scottish island – the distances involved, the journey across the sea – all research on ancient technologies showed that there was no way those stones could have made it to the Island of Muchach. Gavin had read much on the subject and was as close to being an expert on the subject as anyone. He had, for a brief spell, been caught up in the theories and speculation – Druids from the continent, Germania and such, was the most popular theory, but Pagan cults from Somerset and Wales were also considered. Aliens were always an obvious alternative but no one had ever landed on an answer. This delighted Gav as it was a great topic to introduce to guests to their island. In fact, Ronnie also took delight in introducing this mystery to new residents to the centre, fielding the usual questions, digging out the old books. In the early nineties the American Discovery Channel had filmed a programme here, before Ronnie and Gavin's time here, and an archaeology show once visited as well a few later when archaeology shows were a thing, setting up shop and digging in the usual spots. A much younger Ronnie and Gav had appeared being interviewed but, eventually, interest in the island tailed off with all research being inconclusive and it remained a mystery.

She loved it here.

She had been here several times over the years, always telling Fraser it was for scientific research essential to tie in with her research, using a different field study centre each time, never mentioning Muchach. This was her place. She had always had to provide proof of her visit and photographic evidence to show she was actually studying water purity levels or tidal patterns, which she diligently produced using equipment already on the island, but what the photos didn't show was Ronnie sitting behind the camera with a wine glass and a sad smile at the necessity of the charade. It was the one act of defiance and bravery she had given herself and it was the brief and rare visits to The Pig that had kept her sane.

She loved Ronnie and Gav. She loved Ronnie's expressions and expressionistic face. She loved the fact her best mate had bought this place and made a go of it with her husband. She loved the isolation. The ruggedness. The wildlife. The exposure. The mystery. She loved that you had to physically make yourself be here. To actively exist. Back home, days seemed to blur and weeks became months without ever really feeling that she had done anything of note. Her existence was a cosy one, but an existence devoid of any depth. An existence of large, soft sofas, thick carpets, woollen slipper socks, commutes in a modern car with heated seats and air conditioning, ergonomic chairs with wrist supports for typing. An existence without effort, without challenge; and, now she was able to recognise it, an existence of unspoken misery.

Young Hazel, no, Original Hazel had always been active; from childhood she had always been first into the fray. If there was a tree to be climbed or a river paddled in, Hazel would be the first. As she grew older, she took the opportunities to explore and go on adventures when they presented themselves, completing her Duke of Edinburgh Silver award and participating in a four day trek of the Andalusian Mountains in the sixth form.

However, it was in University where she really developed a taste for the outdoors and challenging herself, and it was here that she met Veronica, the woman she could see now, waving frantically running towards the car with a huge grin plastered across her face.

As she pulled her jacket tight against the biting wind she remembered how much she loved this feeling: the effort of pulling her coat closer because she was cold, reacting to discomfort. This was a place that didn't want you, that invited you to leave and head back to safety. The irony being of course was that this place was the safest place in the world that she could think of.

The hug the two women gave each other was enough to bring tears to Hazel's eyes. God she had missed this woman. She laughed and almost sobbed as she hugged her friend who had been there for her through everything. Who knew the silence and unreturned phone calls, the one word replies or weeks and months of nothing was not Hazel's choice. Just the smell of her frizzy hair brought back so many good memories and a feeling of warmth and safety she had never felt with another person, not even her husband when she loved him. She squeezed her tighter until Ronnie wheezed, "Good grief woman, I can't breathe!"

Hazel laughed again and held Ronnie at arm's length. She was looking older since they had last seen each other but she was still the picture of health and she wondered what Ronnie thought on seeing Hazel's pale and strained face as they looked at each other. Hazel saw the laughter lines that were creeping further out from those warm eyes. Grey crept from Ronnie's temples, curly white rivers in her thick brown hair but she could still feel the strength in Ronnie's arms through her warm, purple fleece and was so thankful to have this woman in her life. "Should I...D'ya want me to close the gate Ron?" she asked.

"Fuck the gate," said Ronnie. "Let's get you guys inside and get some wine in you!" She ran to the car and shrieked when she saw the boys! "Oh god! Look at them Haze! Marcus! My god! Come here you!" Daryl was grinning as his older brother jumped from the car as Ronnie ran around it, reaching for the older boy. He took off running but Ronnie was in full flow and caught him before he had a chance to stretch his long legs. She wrapped him up from behind and squealed louder at the size of him. Marcus did not fight too much and eventually turned round giving her a proper hug. They were too far to hear what was said but Marcus was smiling and seemed happy to see her but then Ronnie had discarded him and was bellowing for Daryl. He laughed and kicked as she dragged him out of the car and pulled him into another fierce hug. "My god Haze! What are you feeding these boys! They're huge!" Ronnie had only seen the boys a handful of times but her love for them, and their happiness at seeing her didn't seem diminished by this.

Hazel laughed and then burst into tears.

"Oh god Haze. No no no," said Ronnie, taking her friend in her arms again as the smaller woman sobbed.

"I'm so sorry Ron," cried Hazel. She tried to speak again but the emotions were too strong to fight. The fear, the relief, the love, the misery – it all swirled inside her and the only way out was this unstoppable outburst of emotion.

Ronnie held her silently and closed her eyes softly, beckoning the two boys over who also joined the embrace.

"Shhh now. Let's get you inside." She led Hazel by the shoulders and indicated to Marcus to bring Daryl. They walked for a spell down a gravelled thoroughfare. Hazel gathered herself together and brought her head up, pushing her hair away from her face. She was exhausted and trembled as they walked. To either side set squat buildings wearing rooves of dark slate, ancient stone covered in no less ancient looking white paint, ancient moss clinging bravely to the first few inches from the floor. Each building had a heavy wooden door painted black with a small wooden sign attached – Drying Room and Stores were the first followed by the various dormitories named after Scottish islands – Jura, Arran, Skye and the like. At the far end, joined to the last white building on the right, labelled Canteen, stood a two-story cottage, just as solid and clad in the same green moss and grey stone but missing the white paint of the other buildings, exactly as it had always been.

A large stone building stood further away; stone walled with a tiled roof but no front. Two Land Rovers which had seen better days stood parked looking out at her. A small 6-seater dinghy which Gavin insisted on calling a rib sat with one outboard engine ready to go on its trailer with twenty or so kayaks lying in a neat row next to that. Behind the kayaks, three jet skis lay hidden under tightly wrapped tarpaulin. On the wall hung wetsuits and dry suits, ropes of all sizes, huge shelves held archery sets, helmets, scuba tanks, all neatly stored to Gav's idiosyncratic system.

A wisp of grey smoke could be seen escaping the chimney that sat atop the grey tiled roof of the cottage and Hazel found comfort in how little it had all changed.

They entered a side door and the warm smells and heat emanating from a large range was further balm to Hazel. They were led through to a living room furnished with deep, worn sofas and covered in colourful knitted blankets. A giant wood burning stove lazily ticked over, orange flickers could be seen through dark, soot-stained glass. A black and white collie lay dozing before it. "Boys, you haven't met Hamish have you? This fellow here is the laziest dog in Scotland. He's an old man now right enough, but he was like that as a pup. Complete fraud." Daryl fell to his knees next to the dog and began stroking, causing the dog to stretch out in pleasure. "Sit down guys," she instructed. "Who wants a drink? How long did that take you from Glasgow then? Juice lads? Fizzy?" She looked at Hazel and arched a questioning eyebrow, "Vodka?"

"Can I have fizzy please?" asked Daryl hopefully.

"We have coke, lemonade and cherryade," she answered.

"Cherry please," replied Daryl, waiting for his mother to shut it down and insist on water, but it never came. He turned back happily, continuing to stroke Hamish.

"Coffee please Ron," said Hazel. "I'll have something stronger later if that's ok?"

"Course it is," said Ronnie.

"Could I get a coffee too please Ronnie?" ask Marcus, taking his cue from his younger brother and seizing an opportunity. When she didn't say anything he added, "two sugars?" Hazel raised an eyebrow at that but stayed quiet as Ronnie headed back to the kitchen.

"Gav is about. You'll see him throughout the day I'm sure," she called back as she rounded the corner.

Daryl looked up at his mother and mouthed, "Who's Gav?"

"Ronnie's husband. He's lovely. Very mellow guy. Nothing like her," she replied. Daryl grinned.

Marcus fished his phone out of his pocket. "Can we get the Wi-Fi d'ya think?" he asked.

Hazel shook her head, "Don't think they have Wi-Fi sorry boys." The noise of appalled disgust that came from Marcus made her grin. Daryl spun round; Hamish's soft fur momentarily forgotten at this travesty. He clawed his phone from his pocket and howled in anguish as his fears were confirmed. "They do have the internet, but it's still wired in through the phone line. Think the computer in their office has it for bookings and emails and all that. No good for gaming though sorry boys." Marcus looked as if he was about to cry. "I don't have it either. No internet, no signal....but that's a good thing! We can talk and play games and reconnect a little bit no?"

"Oh my god!" barked Marcus.

"Oh my God!" repeated Daryl, aping his big brother's dismay.

"What?" said Hazel? "We won't need them here. We'll be busy enough. There's so much to do here, its not as if you'll have time and it's only a few weeks. It's not like-"

"Weeks!" yelled Marcus echoed almost instantly by his younger brother. "Weeks mum?" He was about to begin one of his rants when Ronnie walked back in with a tray of drinks and a small plate of biscuits. "You said days, not weeks!"

"What's this?" she asked at the loud voices and pained expressions.

"The boys have just found out there's no Wi-Fi. They haven't taken the news too well."

"And we're here for weeks!" said Marcus. "I thought it was a week max!"

"I didn't say anything about time Marc, and who knows. It might still only be a week. Let's just see eh?" Hazel was relieved when Marcus resentfully grunted acquiescence and, despite his teenage tendencies, had manners enough to withhold one of his bitter attacks as they were in company.

Ronnie smiled as she placed the drinks out for people. Daryl said a thank you and rolled back over to continue his discovery of Hamish and to investigate the merits of cherryade. Marcus was also momentarily distracted from his laments by the huge mug of coffee now steaming before him. "Don't get used to that," said Hazel as she reached forward and lifted her own mug. He rolled his eyes and reached for his.

Hazel leant back and looked at Ronnie who was sitting on the arm of the opposite settee. "How's life on The Pig then?" she asked. "You're looking really good Ron."

"Thanks Haze," she said with real sincerity. "It's great here. Its really good. I mean, its not, obviously. We're on a rock in the middle of nowhere surrounded by bird shit and the weather's fucking awful and we're pretty broke" She gestured around her head as if to point out every aspect of the island, "It isn't Monaco, but, I still love it. I wouldn't change a thing, you know?" Hazel smiled at her pal's soft East Coast accent. "Well, I would obviously, like more money and maybe more staff so me and Gav could maybe have a few lie ins together and fix a few things but nah. Loving it." She paused and sipped at her tea. "How are you getting on Purp?" Hazel smiled at the use of her old university nickname given to her by some pot head she had bedded for a couple of weeks. He hadn't lasted but his nickname for her, 'Purple Haze' had, and Ronnie had been delighted with Hazel's new name and still wheeled it out from time to time.

She sighed. "Bit shit Ron," she said. "Pretty bad the last few months. Most of the year actually." She closed her eyes and sighed before looking back at her friend, "Well, the last few years have been tough but then the split and the police and that. You know about all that though. But then lockdown hit so we were stuck in for ages and then he would just turn up randomly, knowing that we would be in. We were trapped. And he would just turn up, no warning." She was aware that both boys had slowed what they had been doing and were listening intently so Hazel changed tact gently, they didn't need to hear the shit their dad had actually ended up doing. The violence and hate filled messages that had made her feel sick on reading them. They didn't need to relive those scenes where their father had been screaming and shouting outside the house, the drunken violence to the garden and car, the police visits, the constant ringing. "It's been very intense," she said instead. Ronnie knew most of it anyway. Knew about most of the incidents anyway, either through tearful chats or screeds of text message.

What she didn't know about were the crippling panic attacks Hazel had been suffering from for the last five months.

She didn't know about the heart stopping fear that would slowly worm its way into Hazel's stomach as she sat watching The Antiques Roadshow on catch up or some other equally banal activity; or the way she would stifle a panicked sob as she eased herself out of her curled position on the couch as Daryl bashed away next to her on his phone or coloured in his homework task so she could tiptoe to the bathroom surreptitiously and lock the door so she could collapse to the floor as her legs buckled, sucking for a breath that never came.

Her chest would wrack painfully, her body feeling like it was being vacuum sealed and scalding tears would squeeze out of her bulging eyes. Desperately she would fight for air and when it finally and painfully exploded into her she would howl hysterically into a towel or a dressing gown or whatever she could claw to her face so as not to alert her boys. She knew it was irrational. That her husband of 14 years wasn't really coming with a crowbar to split her fucking head open or with a can of petrol to burn her alive in her bed whilst he and the boys watched but, in that moment, as her heart raced and her adrenalin poured through her, she was sure he was there. Or nearby. Watching. Planning. She had never felt an emotion as strong as this fear that gripped her during these moments. Not the fraught birth of Marcus, not rafting down the Colorado

River or getting lost on a Scottish mountain one evening, or that bungee jump she did – nothing came close to this paralysing dread that would occasionally just ambush her.

She would eventually be able to push herself up into a sitting position, back to the wall or door. Occasionally she would see that she had lost control of her bodily functions and then would have to strip down and take a quick shower, shame covering her as effectively as the water. No, Ronnie knew the causes, but she didn't have a clue about the effects.

The worst part was that Hazel suspected that her husband, *no, ex-husband* she told herself, knew exactly the effect it was having on her. Hazel had always been an explorer, an adventurer, but Fraser Chapel, a software engineer from Paisley, had slowly and methodically stripped her of those attributes. So slowly and cleverly had he dismantled her sense of independence and confidence that it took her ten years to realise that she was nothing like the person who Fraser had met in university all those years before. That she was nothing like the person who she *believed* herself to be. She had thought of herself as an outdoorsy person. A hill walker. A kayaker. An Adventurer! Confident and independent and it was only when after a chat with Ronnie and a brief foray into her Facebook page that she realised that she hadn't done anything like that for almost eight years. Not one single adventure. What's more, as freezing realisation dripped into her consciousness, she realised she had no real life to speak of. She worked. She came home. She prepared food. She laundered clothes. She cleaned. She slept. Most nights would finish on the sofa watching a show of his choosing until he would announce it was time for them to go to bed.

It hadn't happened overnight. It had been a culmination of small, microscopic changes. Missing work functions because he would miss her too much, cancelling meet ups with friends because Fraser had double booked, avoiding certain friends because Fraser didn't like them and that should matter to her. Once, early into their marriage, he had asked her quite innocently if she had always been so selfish. She had been planning on kayaking down the River Spey with some old university pals and had been looking forward to it for weeks. He had watched her planning the route, the stopovers, the equipment and watched her pack the night before. She had been humming as they ate breakfast together and quite calmly has had asked her that. Shocked, she had stammered that she did not understand. "You have two young children at home and who you seem quite happy to abandon," he had said calmly over the rim of his mug. She had protested but he had pressed on, "and what if something happens eh? It's not shopping is it? There's risk attached. What if something were to happen Hazel? You would leave those boys without a mother."

"My God Fraser," she had said incredulous. "You knew I was going! Why say this now! This is nothing! Perfectly safe I swear. Been doing it for years. The Spey is calm. Nothing is going to happen-"

"You're not going Hazel," he had stated. And instantly she knew this was true. She knew that no matter how much she argued, he would have his way. And she had argued. And he had gotten meaner, the name calling had crept in, *selfish bitch* was used an awful lot and when he had said, *and when the boys ask where mummy is and I have to say I don't know boys, she's left you both* she knew that not only was it this weekend away cancelled but any future trips as well. Yet, at that point, she still hadn't fully realised the trouble she was in. He was very clever and made her feel wanted. The fact he always wanted her home, that he wasn't willing to share her was a compliment, wasn't it? Didn't it show how much he loved her? Women would give anything to have as committed a man as him. They would kill to have what she had. *She was lucky* she told herself.

She had slowly lost her friends as Fraser had manipulated and bullied her into giving them up and over the years they gave up inviting her. It was only because Ronnie was the most stubborn bitch Hazel had ever met that they were still friends. Ronnie had seen through Fraser pretty quickly and had continued to stay in touch with Hazel despite the years of silence and one-word replies. Ronnie had been her port in a storm without Hazel ever realising it.

She sipped at her cooling coffee and gazed deeply into the eyes of the only person on this planet, aside from her boys, who she knew genuinely gave a shit about her. "How about that booze?" she said.

Chapter 3

The fire crackled warmly in the wood burner, its doors wide open, bathing Hamish in a warm glow as outside, rain spat loudly against the windows. Night had arrived quickly, and they had all returned to the sitting room after gorging themselves on a delicious stew that Ronnie had had bubbling away all day in preparation. The boys had each eaten several bowls between them as well as half a loaf of crusty bread. Even Hazel had eaten what she had been given, rather than pushing it about for several minutes before abandoning it like she usually did at mealtime. Gavin had burst in halfway through the meal, throwing his dripping coat on a hook behind the door and making his way round the table: a kiss on Hazel's head, a manly pat on the back for Marcus and a handshake for Daryl before giving Ronnie a squeeze from behind and a longer kiss on her head and then settling himself on the end of one of the benches, informally pushing the two lads higher up the bench. "I've parked your car at the bottom Hazel, next to the garage," he said. She thanked him and watched him hang his, and her own keys, onto a kitsch little key hanger, made to resemble the tails of cats, each showing their arseholes to the world.

Marcus groaned and held his hand up in defeat as Ronnie came back into the living room, a tin of biscuits in one hand and another bottle of red in the other. She offered the tin round, heading to Marcus first who instantly thought better of his initial reaction and reached in for three chocolate looking affairs. He carefully balanced the chosen biscuits on his knee which was draped over the side of the armchair he had chosen whilst, with surgeon like delicacy, he picked up his second coffee of the day; with his other hand he picked up the book Gav had given him about the history of the islands. Ronnie continued her circuit as Daryl pulled himself away from Hamish and adopted the posture of a meerkat as he strained up on his knees, craning his neck to see what particular biscuits were on offer. He deliberated for so long that Hazel snapped at him and he hurriedly snatched three at random. Gav watched all this with a bemused grin, stifling a laugh as Daryl convulsed in silent despair on realising he had inadvertently selected a biscuit which had the dreaded dusting of desiccated coconut. "Hamish will have it pal," he said, giving Daryl an escape from the uncomfortable social torture of selecting a biscuit you don't actually want to eat.

Gav made a move for the tin next but Ronnie glided past him, putting them on a table, far out of his reach, then approached Hazel and, with the use of a stern frown, made Hazel offer up her almost empty glass for a generous refill. She then poured another for herself and shuffled back in her oversized slippers to her side of the sofa, next to her husband. Gav gave her a small nip for denying him his biscuits and then reached to a small table next to him, retrieving a large glass of port he had been nursing for an hour or so. As Ronnie lowered herself into the seat, he beckoned wide eyed at Daryl who deftly threw him the unwanted biscuit which Gav quickly devoured before his wife caught him.

"You guys gonna be ok in the dorms Haze?" asked Gav. "It's just easier for you all." Hazel, her glass to her mouth mid-sip, tried to gesture that it was fine but Gav pushed on, "It's just we have the one bedroom here in the cottage and I know you normally take the couch when you've been here before; but with there being the three of you and-"

"Its fine. Honest Gav. We're here for a week or two. We can't have the boys on your couch every night. The dorms are fine. We have our sleeping bags and toiletries. I'll take one room; boys can have the other. Showers and all that will be easier. It'll be great. It's all fully stocked. Freezer is full, so's the larder. No fresh stuff though, but help yourself to what's there."

"That's what we thought," he continued gratefully. "They've all been deep cleaned as has the canteen and the kitchen so use this place for cooking and chilling and all that, so we won't have to do it again when we reopen yeah?"

"Thanks Gav," he was being so friendly, but she could tell underneath his tanned and well-worn face he was actually quite worried about leaving his centre to her care.

"And all the equipment? You know how to use it? How to check it? Store it?" his wife nudged him with her foot.

"She knows more than me Gav," said Ronnie. "I told you we did a lot of the qualifications together."

"Yeah. Over a decade ago," he said. "A lot's changed."

"Gavin, trust me," said Hazel. "I am a bit rusty, but I used to do this stuff too and I know what I'm doing. We'll be doing a bit of kayaking, climbing, paddle boards probably. Might do The Pig at some point, couple of jumps and a few treks but nothing crazy and it's just the three of us. I'll look after your gear. I promise. I just really need to get back out there you know?"

"I get it Hazel. Just know we're just not insured for this. If it was you bringing your own gear then that would be fine but seeing as you're on site using our stuff without us, we're liable. Any damage done, gear broken and that – we won't be able to claim as its outside our operating window. We are officially shut so they'll ask why people were using it. I just have a few concerns. We've never let anyone stay here on their own before. The timing is bad. Wish we were here too but we do the boat race every October. Always just lock this place up tight. We open for the odd Christmas and New Year party booking but it just feels weird leaving it open when we're not here."

She understood. Gavin had put his heart and soul into this place. He had sold his small roofing business and house that he and Ronnie had bought together for the chance at living on a remote Scottish island and living the active and outdoors life they had both dreamt of. And it had worked, the gamble had paid off and 26 years later they were still here, ticking over. They had bought the farm house and out buildings at a knocked down price – no farmer was choosing this place as a viable operation and had converted it to the activity and residential centre it was today, adding to their facilities year after year. They housed their mostly teenage staff over their open months which was usually March till October and took school groups, corporate team building exercises, scientific research expeditions and the odd private party and they got by. Gav was savvy with his money and was able to make their income stretch pretty far. Most of the gear they used was second hand but all in great condition. He and Ronnie were able to get away on their yacht on slow weeks and had a few trusted long-term staff who could run the place blindfolded. Ronnie and Gav still personally led groups out onto the freezing water and rain lashed cliffs partly to keep costs down and partly because, like Hazel, they loved that kind of thing although she imagined it was getting harder and harder for them, they looked older.

"Hey Gav. Its alright. Its Hazel. We did Colorado together, and The Appalachian and –"

"I know. Sorry Haze. I do trust you. It's just weird letting someone else-Just…. this is our baby you know? No kids. This. I do trust you. I know it'll be fine." He raised his glass to her as if to say, that's settled, and took a long sip of his Dow's.

The conversation lulled and only the occasional snap from the fire peppered the silence.

"Hey Gav? Did I ever tell you about your mum taking a crap in some old lady's handbag?" asked Ronnie looking directly at Hazel. Hazel almost spat her wine out, her eyes bulging.

Gav smiled and answered that she had, at exactly the same time as Daryl and Marcus shouted "No!" Ronnie clapped her hands with delight at their shocked expressions and then gurgled in delight at the outrage on Hazel's face.

"Ron!" yelled Hazel in shock.

"I've heard it before Haze," laughed Gav, "don't worry. It would be weird if you pair hadn't been caught short out in the wild. That's part of the job. That's the *fun!*."

"Tell us Ronnie!" pleaded Marcus. "Please?"

"Did she really Ronnie?" yelled Daryl on all fours now.

"She really did Daryl," replied Ronnie. And despite Hazel's protests, Ronnie continued. "We were three or four days into our Bavarian adventure weren't we? You guys weren't born yet. Awesome trip. We were just romping about Germany and Austria – mountains, lakes, biking, rapids – you name it, it's got it all there. Anyway, we had had a bit of a night the night before. Ate too much, drank too much. Met some Dutch lads didn't we Haze?" Hazel glowered back at her in resignation. "And so we left this hostel and had been trekking to this cable car station, the *cabelstation*," she said in her best German accent, "and as we approach I notice two things. Hazel has upped her pace, walking much faster than normal and there are lots and lots of mountain bikers about the place.

"Turns out your mum needs a…. movement," she saw Darryl's confused face. "A poo." Darryl beamed expectantly at his mum. "So she is powerwalking to the nearest toilets at the next cable car place a mile away, but, when we get there, the place is absolutely rammed with bikers. It's a mountain biking festival on that weekend and your mum looks at me and says 'Ron, Im not being funny, but im about to shit myself'" The two boys laughed, looking at their mum with a look that says this is a side to their mum they've never known.

"So?" asked Daryl. "Did she poo herself?" he giggled.

"Oh no Daryl. It gets better," laughed Ronnie. "So the toilets are all heaving yeah? The station we arrived at had this mini-festival going on. Music, food stands, seats and that. Gorgeous day, blue skies. It. Is. Mobbed. Loads of Austrians and Germans and all sorts, all downing pints of water or pints of beer and the queue for the toilets was unreal. And your mum, even though she has a bit of crazy in her, is still far too British to push in front of people, even in an emergency as bad as this yeah?" The boys nod, understanding this. "So your mum sees this small clump of trees and runs into it and does her business. But, Hazel being Hazel, couldn't possibly just do a dump on the floor so she sees a bag on the floor and used that." The boy's eyes were wide with anticipation.

"In my defence boys," blurted Hazel, "It did look like an old bag. It was this battered woven plastic thing that looked like it had been there since the seventies."

"But!" interrupted Ronnie. "It wasn't an old bag, it was this rather posh woman's bag, and she sees Hazel standing in the trees holding her bag and Hazel, being Hazel, gives it to her!" giggles Ronnie. "She actually said thankyou to her."

"Who did? The old lady?" asked Marcus.

"No. Your mum! She thanked the old lady as she gave this lady her own bag with a turd in it!" she shrieked. The boys looked at their mum in equal parts disgust and amazement.

"You gave it to her, mum? Why?" asked Marcus, appalled.

"I don't bloody know Marcus, do I? It was hot. I was bursting. I panicked. I didn't want to just run away. It's such a beautiful country and here comes the English leaving their shits all over the floor. I don't know. To this day I don't know what the hell I was thinking." She was grinning now. Trust Ronnie. "I'm standing there with this bag and this lady comes out of some trees and asked what I was doing with her bag. I couldn't say, 'oh I just did a crap in it. Here you go." She was bright red remembering the encounter but pressed on, "So I just thanked her and walked very quickly away."

"So what happened?" asked Daryl.

"I don't know love," said Ronnie. Your mum took off running like a streak of lightning the moment we got out of sight. She ran for about an hour straight, in the boiling sun. She left me for dead, I thought something terrible had happened. I caught up to her about two hours later at this bar in the next village and..." She beamed at her friend, eyes twinkling, "Oh my god Hazel, I still haven't laughed like that since. When she told me what had happened, I actually pissed myself boys. I'm not ashamed to tell you. When she told me she had shat in that woman's bag I full on pissed myself laughing. Had to go and change! It was amazing. Best holiday ever that. She got proper drunk that night your mum I can tell you. She kept looking at the door every time someone came into the bar expecting it to be the woman!"

"I'm just picturing that woman's face when she found what your mum had left for her in that bag," laughed Gavin. "That's a nasty, nasty surprise that."

"Mum!" said Daryl incredulously. "Did you really poo in someone's bag?"

"I didn't know it belonged to anyone!" replied Hazel. "I thought I was being really clever. Poo in the bag, bag in the bin. No harm done."

"Gadz mum, that's disgusting!" added Marcus. "I can't believe you did that. You're sick!"

"Sick!" parroted Ronnie clapping her hands in utter delight. "You're sick Haze!" She rolled back in her chair, revelling in the memory and Hazel's poor attempt at being angry.

They spoke some more. Marcus returned to his book and Daryl alternated between playing on his Switch and playing with Hamish. After some time and several generous glasses of wine, Gav finally finished his port. "Right. That's me guys," he proclaimed, standing to his feet. Hazel stood also.

"And us," she stated. "Come on boys, say goodbye. We won't see them tomorrow, will we?"

"Afraid not," Gav replied. "Heading south tomorrow so we'll be leaving super early. Won't wake you up." The boys got to their feet and gave small awkward hugs to Gav and the slightly unsteady Ronnie. The wine had raised her affection levels even further and she kept pulling them back for one last hug.

Hazel wasn't feeling too clever either. The heat and the wine combined with the six hour drive had made her incredibly lethargic, and she almost fell into Ronnie who yanked her into a smothering embrace. "You look after yourself Purple," she said, holding Hazel's face and staring directly at her. "Relax and remember who you were, and who you are and who you're going to be!" She hugged her again and Hazel was thankful that the tiredness also stopped the waterworks from turning back on. She squeezed Ronnie's hand as she left.

The three of them trooped through the kitchen and left the cottage via a red fire door with a small window with safety netting trapped between two panes of glass. The door opened into a corridor which linked the cottage to the rest of the centre and the rest of the accommodation plus the canteen for staff and visitors. They passed through another set of safety doors, white this time, walking past the double doors which led to the canteen. They passed doors leading to male and female toilets and a small staff room, this was where adult visitors and teachers attached to school groups could retire for the evening after a day out on the island. A small TV and coffee area was installed as well as a variety of battered couches and armchairs as well as a small electric fire. They reached the dorm corridor, a small light blinked on above them as they entered through another fire door. The hallway stretched away into inky darkness.

Hazel knew that there were rooms branching off at opposites to each other the whole way down. There were twenty rooms in total, ten per side. She was taking the room to the left, Room 1, the boys were having Room 10, across the hall from her own. Each door had rules and safety warning stuck to the front and a small fire extinguisher hung from the wall.

She showed them how to input the door's unique code for their room and wait for the door to unlock, 1011, it hadn't changed in all this time. She ushered them in and grimaced as their breaths plumed in front of them. "Sorry it's so cold boys," she said. "I got the extra blankets and I'll switch the radiator on, should have done that earlier, you'll be toasty in no time. It takes a while, but these are really warm rooms when the heating kicks in." The boys, to their credit, didn't make much of a fuss. Daryl climbed into his sleeping bag and was asleep before she had finished pulling the well-used but clean duvet over him.

Marcus was climbing into his bag as Hazel came over and perched on the side of his bed. "You ok Marc?" she asked gently.

"I'm good," he said, twisting himself sideways and zipping the bag up tight. "Can you get that blanket on me mum?" he asked.

"Uh huh," she replied, pulling his own duvet up and over him. "Thanks for being so great Marcus," she said gently. "About everything. Its been a horrible year and I know you don't really want to be here but I honestly think it will be good for all of us."

"Its ok mum. It'll be good. As long as you're ok." She leant over and planted a small kiss on his forehead.

"Thanks love. Get some sleep mate," she said. She squeezed his leg gently and left the room.

Just as she shut the door he asked, "Do you think Dad is alright? Do you think he's still angry with you?"

"Probably," she said. "Night Marcus."

She looked down the dark corridor, mentally preparing herself for her own freezing room and shivered. It was cold and the silence in the corridor was unnerving. She hadn't lied, the rooms were pretty snug once the radiators had had a chance to kick in, she was annoyed she had forgotten to turn them on earlier when she had brough the bags down and set up the sleeping bags. As she made to open her door she frowned and looked down the dark corridor.

A light was on at the far end.

A small square of white light shone brightly through another red fire door window which led to the drying room and from there to the outside.

Her heart lurched – why the hell was that light on? Nausea swept through her and she felt her bladder loosen as the red door opened. Fear grabbed hold of her tight and a low moan escaped her as a large figure stepped through the door, silhouetted against the light beyond. She took a half step backward, pressing her back up against the wall. The figure moved quickly towards her and her heart began to jack hammer. The figure grew closer and Hazel began to gasp. "Hazel. Hazel?" It was Gavin. "Hazel?" He whispered again as he drew closer. It took everything she had not to collapse and wail in relief. "You ok Haze?" he asked, concern written across his face.

"Ha, yeah. Fine." She managed. "I… You just gave me a fright Gav."

He looked back around him frowning, unsure at what he had done. "I didn't know it was you," she explained. "The light was on and I didn't know it was you. I thought it could have been…someone else or something."

The concern on his face remained, "Jesus Haze. Are you sure you're up to this? It can get a bit spooky out here alone and…well." She put her arm on his shoulder. He smiled, "Sorry Haze. Was just checking something in the drying room that's all. That's where the boiler is remember? Came in from the outside door." He looked awkward, "Just remembered as well, the netting is pretty frayed on the assault course so leave that, plus we have spares of everything in the drying room if you need it." He paused then said, "Really sorry I scared you."

"It's ok Gav. It's me. Nothing to apologise for. I'll be fine. Thanks again. Enjoy your adventure," she gave him another big hug and bid him goodnight before accessing her own room. "Can you switch off those lights please Gavin?"

She sat on the edge of her bed and bit her nails as she weighed up the need to lock her door against the need to be able to exit quickly to reach her boys. Her heart had not slowed down particularly, and the adrenalin was taking its time leaving her system. Trembling, Hazel slowly climbed onto her bed, door unlocked, and pulled her sleeping bag over her. She curled up tightly and began noiselessly sobbing into her pillow.

Chapter 4

The following morning had a bright, loud sky. Hazel wasn't sure if it was the blazing paleness or the remnants of too much wine but she found herself squinting and looking down at the dark grey stones as she headed to the car.

They were officially alone now.

Anxiety had made its familiar place at home in her stomach.

She had woken early with a lurch and had scrambled mindlessly out of her bag, lunging across the corridor and bursting into the boy's room. Both had been sound asleep. The room was stifling now. She had silently made her way across the room and turned down the old radiator, mindful not to wake them. She made her way back to her room glancing at the red door at the other end of the corridor – the small window was black.

It was just past five in the morning. She had gone to the loo before nestling back into her bag. It was still warm, and daylight was still a good few hours away and so she had no choice but to stew and think about her choices and the paths she had taken. About 40 minutes later she had heard low voices and car doors opening and slamming shut. Low chuckles could be heard, and Hazel smiled as she pictured her friend loading up the Land Rover. Moments later an engine coughed into life and light has danced beneath the curtains as Ronnie and Gav departed, heading to the small dock on the East of the island where their yacht was moored.

She had expected to feel happiness, a sense of liberation as they left, a sense that she was now free to do as she pleased but, instead, she had felt the cold, unwelcome hand of fear begin to caress her. She closed her eyes and willed herself to sleep rather than focus on how isolated she now felt.

She hadn't considered how she would feel when Ronnie and Gav left the island and it was unsettling to realise how horrible it actually felt. They were the only three people on this island.

There was no backup.

Any accidents or emergencies would have to be dealt with by Hazel. There would be no one to lean on. In her previous life she would have relished this but her confidence was low and she had her boys to think of. Was it irresponsible of me to bring them here with no access to trained medical staff? She breathed deep, this was Fraser's legacy. This self-doubt. The questioning. She breathed slowly, trying to spin it. This was a good thing surely? She didn't need anyone! This was half the reason she had decided to come here! If there was an emergency, she could use the landline to contact the mainland. There was also a radio and the PC. She could reschedule the ferry via the internet and she had the car, a Land Rover and bloody canoes and kayaks if needed. There were first aid kits all over the place. There was nothing to worry about and yet, as she lay there in the dark, she could feel that queasy, sick feeling growing in her tummy. She curled up tight and tried not to think of the dark expanse that lay between them and the rest of civilisation.

The feeling had eased as the charcoal grey beyond the curtains gave way to light. She had gone for a shower and abused the hot water, cooking herself until she began to think more positively about the days ahead. Her therapist had told her to break up her planning into small, achievable blocks. She focussed on today and the range of possibilities.

She had padded through the corridors and doors to the cottage kitchen and put some bacon in the George Foreman and sausages in the oven to cook. She had made a proper coffee and sat as the bacon had sizzled. Food cooked; she switched off the appliances before trotting back to the rooms to wake the boys.

They had sat round the kitchen table eating quietly, Marcus glowering at his mother over his breakfast. Her refusal at his request for a morning coffee had not gone down terribly well. "What are we going to do today mum?" asked Daryl.

"Not sure love. We could just go for a walk today, go to the coastline and pick round so you can see where we are. Could also check the sheds, take some bikes out."

"Yeah!" said Daryl enthusiastically. "Let's go on the bikes!"

They had set off after breakfast, thirty mountain bikes were kept in a large storage shed away from the main buildings. She had checked the tyres and repair kits before heading out. She had unlocked the padlock that was used to secure the large double gate and then relocked it after they were through. "Why are you locking it mum?" asked Marcus. "There is literally nobody else here."

She had thought a while and then said, "Just in case."

"In case of what?" asked Marcus.

"I don't know! It's just a good habit. The chances of anyone coming are very slim but who knows? It isn't our place; we need to look after it."

Blue skies had begun to make an appearance and a stiff, bracing breeze had soon got their faces rosy as they sped along the smooth, flat, empty road. The tarmac hugged the coast and again it was disconcerting to think that they were the only three people on that island. The boys were racing on ahead of her and as she had cycled, she had gazed out to sea, lost in the vastness of the ocean, speculating where the next land would be if she were able to cycle in a straight line from that very point across the surface of the sea. How long would it take her? Physics permitting, how many nights would she have to camp on the surface of the sea? Could she still dangle her legs in the water if she chose to? Would it be weeks till she hit America? Canada? Would it take months? Could she- "Mum!"

She jumped and almost went straight off the road. She braked and span round, heart pounding, furious. "Bloody hell Daryl! I almost crashed!"

"Mum, there's an island there!" He pointed to a small outcropping of rock, maybe four hundred metres out.

"There's a few love," she replied.

"Why do you all call it The Pig?" he asked.

"You'll see. Keep on going. When we get to the far side you'll see. He had shot off then, shouting for his older brother to wait, legs pumping furiously.

The road had started to climb and Hazel had been forced to stand and pedal harder at the more steeper parts. The wind was picking up as she rounded the most Northern point and, in the distance, Ben Storr came into view, clouds shrouding the peak. The Pig started as a collection of hills becoming a small mountain on the Western edge of the island. From this distance it looked very much like a pig lying on its stomach. There was an extra outcropping, the snout, lower down on the northern face, that looked like the snout of the pig and was called that very name. The 'snout' had always reminded Hazel of a suckling boar, prepped on a Lord's table and every time she saw it, she wished there was another feature that could resemble an apple lodged in its mouth. The mountain itself was a good height, just under 1000m with 'the ear', a column of rock which took the total height to 1042m which officially made it a Munro, those mountains of Scotland over a certain height – she forgot the exact figure, only that The Pig was one. It did have an official name, Ben Storr, but almost everyone who had climbed it referred to it as The Pig. Gavin had explained the Gaelic word for the isle, *Mucach*, also meant *pig* so even hundreds of years ago, folk had also recognised the shape.

She had climbed it several times, clambering up the scree covered slopes and picking her way along the boulders and heather towards the summit or following the longer path that had a tendency to just disappear at times. Visitors to the island would lament the lack of a clear route and it was usually only die-hard Munroe Baggers, those whose goal it was to scale every one of the 300 or so Munroe's dotted across Scotland, that would venture to the Isle of Mucach to take on The Pig. There were several books on Munros which spoke about their location and routes to the top and each one, to Gav's joy, put The Pig into the very hard category although she suspected this was as much to do with the location as it was the difficulty of the actual climb. Some Munro's had well-worn paths and simple ways to the top with spectacular views to be had and ample parking. Other Munros had virtually no discernible path; some were covered in treacherous scree which could shift and give way with little warning and others had such unpredictable weather with fog and cloud cover a real danger, especially in colder months, that it was all too easy to lose your bearings and get lost, roaming the wrong part of a mountain as light and heat departed. The Pig had all three of these hazards and several climbers over the years had had to be rescued from The Pig as night closed in and temperatures dropped, some due to injury, some to exposure and some to a complete loss of bearings. Hazel had walked the Pig several times and done The Ear twice, using climbing gear to traverse the rocky chimney that sat at the highest point. She knew the best way up and had camped on its slopes twice.

She caught up with the boys who were waiting for her and pointed out the shape of the hills, explaining the name and the difficulties some people experienced. "Can we do it?" asked Daryl hopefully.

"I suppose we could," she said. "But we would have to leave really early and on a nice, sunny day. Ill check the forecasts but the weather can turn really quickly up there guys. I once set off in shorts an t-shirt and by the time I was at the top I had four layers on and was soaked to the bone. When I got back down, it was still sunny, and the ground was dry! It had rained up there and nowhere else!"

"Wow!" said Daryl in awe, he looked again at the mountain. "And you know the ear? Can we climb that?"

"Not this time love. We would need Ronnie and Gav with us too. The equipment is here but I wouldn't be happy. If someone got hurt or something, it would be a long ride back to the centre and the phone. Not worth the risk Dar." He nodded at this sagely, sober thoughts occupying his mind as he pictured himself lying, broken on a dark magic hill with its own rain.

"Right," she said, "let's crack on. We'll stop there for lunch." Darryl air jabbed at the thought of lunch and set off down a gentle slope towards the brooding hills. Marcus kicked off parallel to his mother.

Forty minutes later they sat beneath a huge dark slope of rock. Half way out, a massive ceiling of rock jutted out casting a black shadow, the 'snout'. Admittedly, it looked nothing like a pig's head this closely, but the imposing wall of rock still dominated. They sat on a raised peninsula that could be the Pig's legs as they jutted out into the Atlantic. The sea smashed cheerfully against the black rocks as they ate. There was the odd clattering rumble as rocks slowly rolled back and forth against each other. Boulders of various sizes dotted the rocky shore and the sea seemed eager to reclaim them. "Where we are sitting now will be under water in a few hours," she said. There is a real drop off here and it will be over our heads soon. See the seaweed? That's usually hidden."

"Can we camp here mum?" asked Darryl.

"Don't see why not," she returned. "I mean, not right here Dar, we'd drown, but a bit back from the sea will be fine. I can check where the camping gear is. Bound to be some at the centre." She looked around her. It was saddening that even here, at the edge of the world, litter and plastic could still be found.

"There's loads of tents mum," said Marcus. "They're in the storeroom. I went exploring whilst you were doing the bikes," he added defensively at her questioning face.

"We could camp and then do The Pig the next day," suggested Hazel. "Have a fire and all that. Ghost stories?"

Both boys grinned at the idea, "No ghost stories though," said Darryl. This place is freaky enough."

"Well, there are stories about what people used to do at this place you know?" Daryl paled and she jumped up and began to pack her bag, regretting her comment, Darryl didn't do well with ghost stories and the like and some of the tales she had heard from Gavin about The Pig were quite upsetting. She set off, the boys struggling to catch up and Marcus pleading for more details.

"Gadz, look at this stone mum," Daryl said, he held a dripping rock aloft. "It looks like a baseball. Look at the white line going around it. Don't it look like a baseball Marc?"

"Aye it does," agreed his brother. "But I'll find one better!"

They arrived back at the centre by late afternoon. After finding a variety of interesting rocks of varying hues and shapes which Hazel had ended up putting in her pack, they had stopped twice more. Once to sit on the pebble beach on the South Western edge of the island just before the ferry point. They had thrown stones for the best part of an hour, something all three of them had always enjoyed. The second stop was for another snack. They had polished off the sausages and fruit she had packed and arrived back at the centre, the sun smearing oranges and reds across the empty sky as it made its way from the day.

Hazel ached pleasantly and waved Marcus off who had immediately begged to be allowed to go to his room and use the toilet. She had locked the gates behind them and Darryl had helped secure the bikes and had found an old football in the storage shed and was busy kicking it against the wall. Hazel twisted the old key in the lock and called for Darryl to hurry, light was fading and she had still to figure out what they were going to have for dinner. She could heat up more of that delicious stew Ronnie had made. There was-

Her thoughts died as she glanced up the main thoroughfare towards the gates.

There was somebody at the gate.

Chapter 5

She walked as casually as she could towards the main gates, her stomach was in her mouth at the idea of a confrontation with a stranger in the middle of bloody nowhere. As she approached, she could see that it was more than one person. A collection of shadows silhouetted by the beams of torchlight. Lots of torchlight.

Bags were piled high and a large group of people, all teenage boys as far as she could tell, were milling around. She moaned loudly. Drawing closer still, she heard one of the boys shout something then spit and a moment later a man made his way towards the gate. He raised a hand in greeting as she approached. "Hi there, any chance you could let us in please?" He had black hair streaked with grey which ran just past his ears and he ambled rather than walked.

Hazel wanted to run. "I'm sorry. Who are you?"

"Hi. Yes. We're from Porthverry Boy's Home near Aberdeen. We're expected."

She breathed, thinking of her mindfulness training. Breathed again. "I'm really sorry to tell you this, but it's closed. The owners are away," she answered calmly. She adopted the voice she used at work, calm, slow, deliberate.

"Yeah, no, I know. That's expected. They always let us stay when they're away. The name's Sol." He held up his hand in greeting. Behind him the youths had quietened and were listening intently.

"Well, I'm really sorry Sol, but it's just me and my boys here looking after the place and I really wouldn't be comfortable letting, you know, you guys in. You know? It isn't my place and it's been deep cleaned, and Ronnie and Gav didn't say anything..." she shrugged helplessly.

"That's fine. We just need the grass to be honest with you. You know the island's all rock. Just somewhere to pitch our tents that'll take pegs, and maybe use the loos you know?" He smiled eagerly as if his enthusiasm would sway her. He had a nervous energy and kept brushing his hair back up over his head, his whole body seemed to move as he spoke.

"Well it isn't our place and I'm really sorry but I just wouldn't feel comfortable-"

"You wouldn't be comfortable letting some boys sleep here for a few nights?" asked Sol. Hazel opened her mouth to answer but he cut her off. "We come every year- I'm sorry, what's your name?"

"Hazel," she answered without thinking. She was squirming inside and wished he would just leave. Take his group and leave.

"Well, Hazel, we come here every year. These lads don't have much and look forward to this each year. We have our own gear. We won't be in your way. We'll pitch tents out by the assault course." He gestured towards the site. The assault course was at the back of the complex and could not be seen from this position, so he obviously knew the place. "We have our own food; we won't be any trouble and we'll be away Saturday morning I promise!" He smiled and, in the twilight, she caught sight of a brown, dead tooth nestled amongst his straight, white teeth. His accent was English and had some of the West Country about it. The way *I* sounded like *oi*.

"It's really not up to me. I'm sorry," she said. Her stomach was in knots.

"Well, it absolutely is, isn't it?" Before she could answer he said, "They your lads?" Hazel turned and in the distance near the buildings, stood Marcus and Daryl. She couldn't see their expressions, but they stood close together. On seeing her turn, Marcus made to approach but she held her hand up and told him to stay there.

"I'm really sorry. I am, but you can't come in. It isn't my place and-"

"Aye, you said that. So, what are we supposed to do then? Sleep on a fucking beach for two nights?" there was an edge creeping into his voice now and Hazel closed her eyes and fought back the panic that was threatening to creep into her voice. "The ferry is longgone. It took us forty minutes to walk here. Our bus is parked up on the other side." Behind him she could hear the gang muttering and thought she heard the word 'bitch' muttered. "It's getting dark," he added. "Let us in!"

"You have tents," replied Hazel. "And food. It re-"

Sol shook the gate hard, checking to see if it was locked. The noise was loud. "Look Hazel. We were expected. Veronnica must have forgotten to tell you. We come every year. Kayak on the loch for a couple of days – climbing wall and bit of orienteering and that's that. Highlight of these lad's shitty year. Last chance for most of them as well. We only take up to 17-year-olds and some of them are too old to be with us much longer. We can't sleep on the beach! Where will they go to the toilet? How will they wash? These are young boys and I know they look tough but not so tough that they can sleep on pebbles and rocks! Please Hazel. Have a heart! Two nights. Camping out the back? No harm. Please?"

A part of her wanted to say yes. To just agree to whatever he wanted so that this painful exchange could finish and she could go back to the warmth of the cottage and have done with it. What harm would it do? A bunch of kids camping out by the assault course wouldn't hurt anyone. But of course, it wasn't just that. It was the risk! What if they broke the canoes? Damaged equipment? Made a mess? What if they slipped on site and sued for damages? What if they wanted to be in the building? Use the facilities? Who would tidy that up? How would she explain the need for another deep clean to Gavin? What if they damaged something in the building? What if they drank? What if they attacked her? Attacked her boys? They didn't look like nice people. Some looked older than the 17 Sol claimed, although there were a few younger boys mixed in. No. This was her sanctuary and there was no way she was letting them in. She felt her resolve stiffen, a new Hazel waking up, and she looked him in the eyes. "It can't happen Sol. It isn't my place.

"The boiler isn't working either so you couldn't shower," she regretted the lie the moment she said it but she was getting desperate, he didn't look close to accepting her answer and she was getting angry.

"Look Sol, maybe you could get the ferry back tomorrow?" He pulled a face at that but she pressed on, "Get the ferry back tomorrow and send Gav an email and get another booking sorted. It's just... I can't open the gates. And I'd appreciate you guys leaving now." He shook his head, his black hair swaying back and forth. He wore a grey jumper and olive cargo trousers and looked a little in need of a shower himself. She swallowed; her stomach was in ropes. This kind of confrontation was what she lived in fear of, but she also felt a growing tide of indignation. Who was this man to just keep badgering her? She had said no, and she was done with being railroaded by men who felt that because she was small and a woman that they could just do as they please.

All of a sudden, he smiled and again she noticed the dead tooth to the left of centre on his upper row. "It's alright Hazel. I completely understand!" She made to talk but he pressed on. "I would do the same thing! Middle of nowhere, two boys and all of a sudden we rock up! Even though I said we won't be any trouble how are you to know?" She made to protest but again he gestured and cut her short. "These boys have had a rough life. Excluded from most of what normal kids take for granted. They don't get much to look forward to, so that's why I was getting all het up. But I understand. Ronnie or Gav has dropped the ball somewhere and it's the lads who will pay for it eh? But, oh well eh? Not much to be done." Hazel gave a weak, conciliatory smile and wrung her hands despite herself. "We'll head down to the beach. If you could book the ferry for tomorrow, that would be appreciated." He nodded and then spun on his heels, gesturing to the boys who glowered resentfully at Hazel and the gates. "C'mon boys, pick your bags up. We're sleeping on the beach tonight! Let's move quick before its pitch black!"

Hazel smiled again and attempted another token apology knowing it wouldn't be heard or accepted. She began walking slowly backwards. It was almost fully dark now and she knew they were in for a time of it trying to pitch up on the beach. But why the hell were they here? And at this time? The ferry was at 10 or 4 but why book a 4pm ferry? Plus, hadn't the ferryman said he had no more bookings? It was all wrong. It would still have been locked up, even if Hazel and the boys weren't here. She doubted that Ronnie and Gav would have forgotten to tell her about this which meant that Sol had been lying and that they *were not expected*. She would email Ronnie straight after she booked the ferry. She realised that Sol had not offered to pay for the ferry crossing but right now, she just wanted them gone. She could reclaim the cost from the boy's home at a later date if need be. She walked slowly backwards towards Marcus and Daryl.

Suddenly she heard a small cheer, she turned back to the gate but couldn't see anything past the blinding light of all the torches aimed at her. There was the sound of a metal clink and an even louder cheer and with horror she heard the gates swing open. There was another cheer and she heard the audible crunch as the groups trainers found the gravel. They drew closer and she could see Sol holding a pair of bolt cutters aloft.

"Oh fuckin'- " whispered Hazel under her breath.

"Mum? Who the hell is that?" shouted Marcus, running towards her, Daryl behind him, eyes wide.

"Just...I don't bloody know Marc. They just turned up. I told them no. Said they couldn't come in, and they've just come in anyway!" Panic had her now. She knew she should go and confront them and demand they leave but she was genuinely scared. Her voice was trembling and she was clutching her arms. She could hear their steps approaching and raucous laughter. "Follow me please boys," she ordered and marched into the drying room. Her heart was pounding and the panic in her chest was forcing unwanted tears to her eyes - she wanted to scream. She burst through the doors and strode past the dorm rooms, past their own quarters, past the canteen , through the two sets of fire doors and into the cottage. She went to the office and switched on the PC. As it booted up, she picked up the ancient rotary phone and began to dial, she was on the verge of hyper ventilating and she focused on the numbers on the phone and deliberately slowed herself down. As the dial whirred back into position after each number, she recognised that the silence in the receiver indicated no dial tone. She toggled the handset but no tone. She slammed the receiver down and leant over the PC, sighing in frustration as an outdated Windows logo shimmered on the screen.

"Are you phoning the police mum?" asked Daryl.

She pondered and then said, "Yes, I bloody well am. I couldn't care less if they have permission or not. I am in charge here. Even if they were booked in which I'm sure they're bloody not because they have a bloody great chain snapping thing with them. I told them no and they ignored me and broke onto private property. They do not have the permission of Gav and Ronnie to be here! I'll email the police and Ronnie and Gav and let them know what's happened. This might spoil the trip boys but there's nothing I can really do. I don't think they do have permission and I think they thought this place would be empty and that's why they had bolt cutters."

"Are you worried mum?" asked Marcus.

"No. I'm not. I'm bloody angry and that fucking arsehead better watch himself. Hopefully the police will be here by tomorrow and they can sort it." She saw Daryl's shocked expression and added, "sorry for the language mate."

The PC was taking an age to load, so she walked to the living room and peaked out the curtain. They were all there, milling around, backpacks on, and she could see Sol organising the boys into pairs to start pitching up. He looked up quickly and saw her peeking. She dropped the curtains quickly, feeling guilt at being caught and then felt another flush of anger. "No!" she hissed. "Fuck this! Fuck him!" She hadn't felt this kind of anger in a long, long time. She paused before opening the door, "Get the internet up please boys!" She yanked open the cottage door and headed towards the gang. A wall of Adidas and Nike tracksuits greeted her, all looked grubby and very well worn. "Sol!" she shouted. He looked up and trotted over, hands held high, half mea culpa, half placating and the roguish grin he adopted only served to incense her even more. "What the bloody hell are you doing Sol? You are trespassing. The lot of you. You have caused criminal damage and right now are trespassing! I'm calling the police so you need to get your stuff and clear off!"

"Look Hazel, we both know we couldn't have made it down the beach." He lowered his voice, "These boys know fuck all about camping, the light's gone and this whole bloody island is rocks." He saw her stony expression and tried again, "I promise we'll be no trouble Hazel. You won't know we are here. One full day tomorrow and we'll be gone. We'll use the showers once each and the toilet block. Not the dorm showers, the ones there," and he pointed to the toilet block that stood opposite the main dorm block that lined the main drive, again demonstrating his knowledge of the site. The block was connected to the rooms named after islands. These rooms were only used for large parties when the main dorm wasn't enough. These rooms were in need of an update and shared a communal toilet and shower block which Sol was gesturing to now. "We have our own food. We'll pitch up on the grass, away from the buildings." He gestured to the boys. "We'll be gone before you know it. Look, these lads have hard lives. Let them have a good weekend eh?"

"But I don't even know why you are here," she said. "This place is shut every October. Why have you come here? It doesn't make sense."

He looked surprised but said, "I promise you; we were booked in to come this week. Gav had okayed it and gives us a discount as we're a registered charity. We come every year. Hit the climbing wall, kayaking on the loch and orienteering on The Pig. I swear Hazel, I wouldn't mess about, not when I'm responsible for these lads." She heard the clatter of the letterbox behind her as the door shut. Marcus and Daryl stood there failing to hide their worry.

"You can't use the equipment here," she said, conceding. "I need your word you'll be gone on Saturday. If not, I will be contacting the authorities. I'm really not happy about this. I will book your ferry tonight and will be letting Ronnie and Gav know you are here. I will also email the local police and tell them what is happening."

"I would expect no less and it is a credit to yourself as a mother," he said. She wasn't sure if he was mocking her but he seemed earnest enough. "And Inchard is the nearest police station, if you're wondering," he added. He walked towards the boys, "Pritch, Conal, come here." He turned back and approached with two teenagers either side of him, equal to him in height, their eyes were cast to the ground and only looked up when they stopped before her. "This is Pritchard," he said, gesturing to the taller boy. The lad had the beginnings of a moustache and his hair was shaved down to the skin, mostly hidden by a black cap. "And this is Conal," he said, gesturing to the boy on his left. Conal nodded a greeting. His skin was oily and his white hoody was grubby and stained. Both boys wore trainers that had seen better days and Hazel felt a flash of sympathy which quickly turned to guilt as she pictured her own boys bedecked in brand new designer gear. "They're good boys these two. Will do whatever they are asked and always happy to help. Aint that right lads?" They both grunted agreement, desperate to retreat to the sanctuary of their peers. The three of them turned back and finished sorting what they needed.

40

Marcus and Daryl joined her in the middle of the driveway. "You won't even know we're here Hazel. Many thanks." He humped his backpack higher up his back then shouted for his group to follow. They made their way towards Hazel and the boys. "And who are these fine fellows?"

Hazel wished the boys had stayed indoors. She didn't want them to have anything to do with this. "This is Marcus. And this is Daryl."

Sol looked them both up and down, the rest of the boys barely acknowledged them. "Say hello boys," he commanded. The group nodded scant greetings then pushed on, swamping the three of them as they passed by them on both sides.

"Sorry pal," said the tall youth.

Within moments they had gone, disappearing round the side of the cottage and the grass beyond. Hazel sighed and rubbed her left arm with her right. It was dark now and she was hungry. "Come on boys, lets get something to eat. You both hungry?" They both nodded and as they made their way back inside, Hazel noticed Daryl holding his right hand. "What is it love?" He looked at her then, eyes brimming with tears.

"Nothing," he said.

"Show me," she insisted. He let her take his hand and she gasped at the bright red scratch on the top of his right hand. "Daryl? Who did this? How? Who? One of them?" Her blood was racing and she felt sick. He was only 12!

"I don't know mum. It was when they all pushed past. I think it might have been one of their bags! I was in their way anyway."

"No Daryl! This isn't your fault! One of those bloody yobs did this to you! And that wasn't caused by a bag!"

"They didn't mum. I promise. Sure it was an accident! Sure it was a bag that caught my hand. Please don't go out there and say anything. Honestly, it was an accident." She sat down and looked at the nasty looking mark. His skin was torn in several places and blood was beading where he hadn't smudged it already. She signed and looked at him. He was tired and his eyes shone with the possibility of tears.

"OK love. But I don't want you near any of them okay? They are only here for tomorrow so we'll make ourselves scarce and they'll be gone Saturday morning. Just stay away from them ok boys?" They both nodded mutely. "Go get a wipe from the first aid bag Daryl." She walked through to the living room and switched on the TV before lighting a fire. She couldn't believe this was happening. The boys flopped into their chosen seats. In the kitchen she got a second tub of Ronnie's stew from the fridge and transferred it to a large pot then lit the stove. In the office the PC was ready, and she clicked on the email icon. The little round loading circle began its rotations to show her that it was thinking about her request. She sighed and tried the phone again: nothing. She would have to check that out tomorrow. "Fuck," she breathed out. She couldn't stay. They couldn't stay. It wasn't safe. Fifteen, twenty young men outside. That just wasn't a good situation. She decided to book the ferry. She would get in touch with Gav and Ronnie as soon as possible and get a ferry booked for Saturday morning for them to leave first thing. She would go straight to the police and let them handle it. No matter how earnest Sol had seemed, she didn't trust a word he said and she just wanted to be gone.

She returned to the kitchen and stirred the stew before checking on the boys and heading back to the office. The email system was open and she sat at the desk and composed a message stating everything that had happened that evening. She copied both Gav and Ronnie's addresses in as well as Police Scotland's email which was conveniently placed on a poster warning about computer fraud above the desk. She opened another tab with a view to finding if Inhcard police station did exist and, if it did, did it have an email address. Inchard was a lot closer than Glasgow but still, not as close as Hazel would have liked. Again, her nemesis, the little loading circle appeared, and she sighed and returned to the kitchen. After finishing the stew and boy check, she returned to the computer. The little round icon was still spinning so she brought up the email tab deciding to send the email without Inchard's address, but this page was frozen too. She clicked the mouse several times and the page greyed with a message that it was not responding – the most pointless message in existence in Hazel's opinion – and tutted several times. The pages stayed frozen, so she tried to close them and start again. She growled when nothing happened, so she returned to the kitchen and instead ladled the stew into three bowls. She cut generous slices of bread and placed it all on the solid oak table that sat at the far end of the kitchen. She called the boys through who burst into the kitchen seconds later, jostling and pushing to be first to eat.

When they had finished eating, she asked Darryl to tidy away and for Marcus to do the dishes – there were no complaints. She made her way back to the office only to see the same grey pages she had left. She switched the computer off at the wall, then switched it all back on again. The Windows logo appeared briefly then vanished, then appeared again. A small loading bar informed her of its status. She stood there for a few minutes, counting down to ten in her head, her infallible system of getting gadgets to work, but the blue bar stayed shimmering and refused to go any further.

Hazel muttered a silent but poisonous curse at Bill Gates and decided to check the temperature of the bedrooms and, if she was being honest, a surreptitious check on the new guests.

She visited the boy's room first – more to convince herself that this was the reason she was here, rather than to satisfy her dread curiosity. The radiators had been on low all day and the room was warm. She then checked her own which was similarly cosy. She kept the lights off and slid over to the window.

Peeking through a gap she could see a forest of torch beams, twitching and dancing in the darkness. The tents were mostly up, and she could make out Sol bent over, pegging in one of the small, bright orange, 2-man tents. They had set them up in a circle and a fire was burning away in a metal fire pit in the centre. Two lads leant against a wall laughing and others could be seen either in their tents already or helping others. She sighed loudly; this was awful. She hoped that it would be fine, and that Sol was true to his word but the way they had gained entry suggested he was not a particularly good or trustworthy person.

As she was about to leave she heard Sol call out and they all stopped. He said something else but it was inaudible but the boys had heard perfectly and stopped what they were doing and approached the fire. As they walked Sol said something else and, as one, the boys all turned and looked directly at her. The multiple torch beams blazed through the gap in her curtains. She fell to the floor gasping. Had Sol seen her watching them? Had they sensed her? She began to panic and had to bite her hand painfully to bring her thinking under control. She crawled on her stomach towards the door, not daring to take another look. She opened the door from the floor and, when through, finally stood up and made her way back to the cottage at a small run.

She added more wood to the fire and opened the doors allowing the heat to flood the room. Marcus sat in his preferred armchair reading his book. Daryl lay along one of the couches, headphones connected to his Nintendo, humming along to Mario.

The PC had loaded and sat compliantly as if had never taken close to an hour to work. She sat at the desk, patiently clicking the requisite buttons until her emails had sent, she gave up on the Inchard site deciding to drive straight there the following morning. She then logged into the L & P website to book her ferry. It would be here in two days. She also booked one for Them, for Sol and his gang, but she was under no illusions – Sol wasn't going anywhere. After paying for both trips on her card, she checked her email and printed off the confirmation email, pinning it to the notice board. She switched off the computer, hoping the messages were delivered and that, despite Sol's saintly ambitions, the police turned up tomorrow and threw them all out on their ears. She had sympathy for the young boys she supposed, but she was still fuming at the violation and unease which she was now experiencing.

She sat back and went over the events. She was rather surprised at how assertive she had been and that she hadn't caved in, but the fact that Sol had completely ignored her stilled galled her. She pulled out her mobile and tried to ring Ronnie and Gav but there was no signal so she recorded a message on her messaging app and sent it to the group chat. At any point, if her phone picked up a signal, the message would send.

She spent another ten minutes locking every door and window she could find before finally collapsing onto a sofa in front of the fire. Daryl remined focussed on his game, Marcus craned his neck round to look at her. "You ok mum?"

"Not really Marc. Really not happy with those boys out there. Just. I don't know. It just doesn't feel good. They shouldn't be here. I know for a fact they weren't supposed to be here and I don't trust that Sol one bit."

"Did you contact the police?" he asked, shifting round to see her better.

"I did, yes. Contacted Police Scotland. Used the email. And Gav and Ronnie. The internet seems a bit unreliable but it said messages sent so hopefully we'll hear from them and they may just send someone tomorrow." She tried to sound hopeful, but she did not believe it for one second. She sighed heavily for a moment wondering if there was another way she could have gone. If she had been sterner, more assertive, would Sol and his band have backed off? Or could she have lied more? Threatened him? She went over and over the exchange in her head. The angry shaking of the gate had scared her more than she had let on at the time. It had taken her back to her life with Fraser and a slammed door or hurled glass felt the same as a physical attack. Sol had shown that same burst of temper that had scared her for so much of her adult life and she was exhausted of being afraid of these men, these bullies who used aggression and violence as a means of getting what they wanted. What was worse was they were right outside her window. She was going to have to move rooms. She wasn't having all those boys on the other side of her curtains.

She closed her eyes and tried to think of the day before the visitors had shown up. The bike ride had been a great start and the boys had enjoyed it. The weather had been great, and they were fired up for camping and hiking and now everything tasted sour. She really could cry she thought to herself. If she could radio an airlift right now, to take herself and the boys off the island, she would take it. Whilst that lot were outside doing God knows what, the place was tarnished and despoiled. It had lost its purity and status as haven.

"Mum?" asked Marcus quietly. She turned to him and smiled, "What did they used to do to people out there on The Pig?"

She sighed again, "Marcus...I don't really want to-"

"Come on mum! Daryl can't hear us. I just want to know."

"Please don't speak over me Marcus," she said flatly. "I am sick of men doing that to me and I would prefer it if my own son didn't do it as well." The look on his face told her she had wounded him. The suggestion that he was being lumped in with men like Sol and his father obviously didn't sit well with him. She sighed again. "Sorry Marc, just, please don't speak over me."

"Sorry," he mumbled softly but sincerely.

"Gav said there used to be sacrifices out there. Out by the sea. On The Pig," she said.

His eyebrows rose, "Really?" he asked. "Like proper human sacrifices?"

"My god Marcus. I don't know. I don't know if was even sacrifices." She remembered the chats round the fire when her, Ronnie and Gavin were much younger, and he was elbow deep in the lore and mythology of the place. Some of the details were pretty shocking and she was loathe to go into too much detail. "Might have just been killings or executions or something. Gav told me about it years ago. He said you can still see the blood stains on the rocks so much blood was spilt there." She wrinkled her nose at that. "Don't believe that. Not in Scotland. Our house paint only lasts a year."

"Oh my God!" exclaimed Marcus both equal parts horrified and awe-struck. "Is there still bloodstains mum?"

"Gav has a book somewhere, old photos and that showing the bones they found here. Apparently, there are thousands, and they can still be found on the shore. All these broken bones. Smashed and worn smooth so you wouldn't notice them unless you were looking but this book shows illustrations of what they used to get up to. Burnings were common, drowning, dismembering, disembowelling, mutilation. Gav said they would cut people to look like pigs – snip their ears and chop noses." He blinked at that. "That's what Gav said. I'll dig the book out if you like?"

"Find that book please mum!" He laid back on his armchair, feet dangling back over the arm rest.

"Gadz." He lay there for a moment, lost in his gory imaginings. "And all for a hill that looks like a pig!" he exclaimed. "Unbelievable!"

"But people are still killed today because of what others believe. There have been wars because of what gods some people follow."

"Yeah…" he agreed. "Just. Bloody hell. Getting thrown off that ledge onto those rocks… Bloody hell."

"Who was thrown off rocks?" asked Daryl, eyes wide, one earbud held in his hand.

"No one man," snapped Marcus. "Stop listening!"

"Mum. Who was thrown off rocks?" redirecting his question.

"Back in the olden days love. The Celtic, Gaelic tribes and that. They would throw people off the ledge we were at today to please their god."

"Ha," he said. He returned back to his game.

Marcus and Hazel exchanged a grin. "That could have been much worse," Hazel stated.

Afterwards, with both boys in their room and her gear from the day unpacked, including several rocks which now decorated her windowsill, she lay back in her bunk and considered her options. She would not move rooms, not yet. She wanted to keep an eye on them. She dared to hope that maybe Sol was just going to take the boys out and leave the next day.

The night was peppered with cheers and laughter drifting through her double glazed window.

It was a very long time before she was able to drift off to sleep.

Chapter 6

The rain whipped sideways and plastered their hair to their faces as they clambered up the rocks towards the small patch of dune grass that clung to the grey, lichen covered rock. They had been kayaking around the northern tip of the island before the wind had picked up and the sea had become too choppy. Parking the Land Rover just off the road, they had launched their kayaks under blue skies onto a calm sea. Within an hour the sky had blackened, and the chop had risen considerably. Hidden currents had provided a nice scare for Hazel as they had made their way back towards the shore, but the wind and rising waves had forced her to head westwards, away from their launch point. Maybe she and Marcus could have made it, paddling furiously against the current but Darryl had tired quickly and she was beginning to panic. Twice, a large swell had caught Daryl by surprise. Both times he had managed to stay upright but the shock of the cold water and the speed of the current had given them all a good scare and she had called it quickly after that, aiming for the shore at a diagonal to the current. It had still been a hard slog, but she was proud of them all as they finally dragged themselves onto the light grey shingle shore. The weather had worsened much quicker than the forecast had suggested. Despite being only a short foray out onto the sea, and the layers and layers she had clad them in, the cold had bitten deep and Daryl's lips were already blue. She was not looking forward to the walk back to the Land Rover.

They collapsed onto the grass leaving their boats at the foot of the dunes. Hazel dug through her drybag, searching for the thermos of soup she had prepped that morning. She poured generously, giving the boys a mug each before using the cap for herself. Steam billowed out and away, "Don't let it get cold boys, drink it up. It'll really help." They all tentatively sipped at their mugs and for moments they sat quietly, enjoying the heat the soup gave each of them holding their mugs at an angle to prevent the wind and sand gaining access.

"So? Did you enjoy that then?" she asked. They both nodded, although Daryl's shivering suggested he wasn't haven't the best time. "Sorry about that boys. I thought the weather was with us but it shows you how quickly it can change here. Was warm when we set off wasn't it?" They both just grunted agreement again, more focussed on their warm soup. She regretted her decision now. The weather had not been as good as she had wanted to believe and it had been a real risk knowing there was wind and rain forecast and if Sol and his troupe had not been here, there would have been no way she would have taken them kayaking today.

She had chosen the kayaks purely to prevent Sol's group from using them and, she realised, to probably get as far away from them as possible. *Them*. She was surprised at how vehemently she disliked them. She had never considered herself a snob or middle-class, but she could feel the prejudice steeping inside her. The truth of it was that this large group of teenagers scared her. Pure and simple.

Was it worth it though? She, in turn, had now scared her own children and it would take a good deal of persuasion to get them back out here on the sea.

She had awoken to her phone alarm blaring at 7am and jumped out of bed quickly to switch it off. Creeping silently across the corridor and into room number 1 she had peeked between the curtains to see…. what exactly? She didn't know, she just knew she had to check. It was still dark at that hour and there wasn't much to see through the glass. There was no movement at all.

After a quick shower and getting changed she had walked to the cottage kitchen and made herself a coffee, chewing over possible courses of action. She had slept poorly, playing out hundreds of different scenarios and situations and how best to handle these. Her thumb was chewed ragged and throbbed from the skin she had peeled from it. Some of the situations she had imagined were very credible and would probably happen whereas others played with the utmost worst-case scenarios. There were no situations, she realised, that had a good outcome, for instance, there may come a moment when the group wanted to start using site gear. What should she do in that situation? She considered her options. She could lock as much of it away as she could in one of the storage sheds – the life vests, the helmets, harnesses, wetsuits, oars etc. But, she knew how Sol dealt with locks. She could also confront him, just actively block access and argue the toss but it was a fight she did not have the energy for and his potential aggression scared her. Ultimately, as she sat there nursing her coffee in the silence, she decided she would best help Gavin and Ronnie by documenting everything as best she could. She suspected Sol and his crew would have been here regardless, what Boy's Home travels with bolt cutters? But had they actually planned to break in and just use the site or were they planning on stealing it or destroying it? She had no idea but what she could do was record everything she could before her and the boys left tomorrow morning. She would leave voice messages and email everything she witnessed and hopefully, when all was done and dusted, Gav would be able to pursue the necessary prosecution and restorations when Hazel and her boys were not stuck in the middle.

She washed her coffee mug and had quietly left the cottage clutching her mobile phone tightly. She had quickly began filming, stating her name, date and time clearly and then verbally documenting everything she could think of whilst she filmed. She filmed the Land Rovers that still sat in their garage, the Rib on it's trailer, the kayaks; she went to the storeroom and filmed the harnesses and helmets, the waterproof all in ones and wetsuits. She had oh so quietly tiptoed round to the exterior of the canteen where the group was based and quietly took several photos. She then uploaded it all to her messaging app and cloud storage although both apps replied with 'no connection available' messages. Nevertheless, hopefully it would all auto-upload the moment she had a signal.

Hazel had returned to the cottage and began preparing a large pan of soup to take with them that day. She had decided they would go sea kayaking.

She had been the first to finish the soup and had begun packing everything back into her dry bag. The wind was fierce and sand stung their faces as it screamed across the beach. She was picturing the long walk back to the Land Rover, dragging their boats behind them. "Come on boys, finish up please, I'd like to get back and have everything stowed before it gets much wilder. This wind is bitter. I'm bloody freezing."

"You have started swearing a lot," said Daryl. "Since we arrived here you have sworn loads. You don't normally."

"Sorry love," she said. "Shall I bloody stop?"

The boys grinned. "I like it actually," said Marcus. Means that you're more normal than you want us to believe."

"Shit Marcus! I'm not bloody nor-

Daryl shouted, "Look! Its them!" He was pointing back up the beach, the way they had come from. In the distance, about half a mile away, Hazel could make out the group walking on the beach towards the sea.

"No way....Do they have their tops off?" asked Marcus.

"I... It looks like doesn't it?" she replied. She leaned forward to try and make out the distant shapes better and marvelled that it did indeed look like they were naked. The white of their pants as the boys stepped out of their tracksuits, leaving them on the shore left her in no doubt that the group was totally naked. Several of the group seemed to be carrying oars.

"Lie down lads," she whispered. "I'd prefer they didn't know we could see

them." They squirmed onto their fronts and slid backwards, just their heads over the brow of the dune, obscured by the spiky grass.

"What are they doing mum?" asked Daryl.

"No idea Dar. I think they might be going swimming but those waves are a bit high and the water must be freezing. Plus, the wind. If they had wetsuits that's something but that is some seriously cold water! They wont last long." The group continued to walk in a disorganised clump into the water. Several had kicked off their remaining clothes and, as one, they broached the freezing sea, waves leaping and splashing and, what was particularly unsettling, was that they didn't seem to be reacting to it. Young men and women, kids, pensioners...everyone she knew, everyone would be screaming or yelping or laughing or howling or reacting in some way to that shockingly cold water! She thought it would be almost impossible to enter that water without convulsing in shock and horror and, yes, laughter. If they were friends then surely there would be some horse play and splashing each other but there was nothing. Sol seemed to be towards the back of the group, maybe shepherding them in, but apart from that there didn't seem to be any order or pattern to their behaviour.

They watched, mystified for several minutes, the group going in deeper until they were all in up to mid chest level. The waves were coming more regularly and some of the boys were struggling to stay above some of the larger swells.

The pat patter of rain started, hitting their waterproof gear and reminding all three of them that they were lying on their stomachs on a remote beach on a remote island in Northern Scotland. The rain began to pick up and Hazel decided to break cover. They couldn't lie there much longer and who knew how long those nutjobs would be out there in that sea? "C'mon boys. Lets get back to the jeep. We'll have to drag our kayaks. Stay on the sand. I don't want them to get scraped and broken on the rocks ok?"

Marcus and Daryl rolled down the soft dunes to their kayaks and began hauling them. Daryl was shivering and Marcus picked up the other end of his, helping his younger brother.

"Mum?" yelled Daryl over the wind and rain.

"What?" she yelled back. The wind was unrelenting, and she had to keep averting her face from the stinging sand and rain.

"What are they doing?" he yelled.

"No idea!" She looked up towards the group. White breakers crashed onto the shore and the group seemed to be closer together now, standing still as the waves pushed and pulled and swamped them.

She walked another hundred paces, eyes focused on the wet sand beneath her before looking up again. Her hair clung to her face like a desperate octopus, the wind screamed and the sand biting her face was incredibly painful, but she tried to focus on the boys in the sea. *What were they doing?* It was maddening! One boy, closer to the shore, seemed to be kneeling in the water as the waves crashed around him. The others moved in bursts, hidden by waves momentarily then ominously closer to the boy until they surrounded him. A particularly angry gust of sand stung her cheeks again and she had to lower her head. Doggedly she tilted her head back and squinted harder. One boy seemed to approach the one kneeling and raise one of the oars high above his head. She gasped as she saw the tall boy bringing the stick down hard towards the kneeler before a large wave obscured her view and sand made its way into her eyes.

She panted and wiped frantically at her face, cleaning the hair and sand back from her eyes. She looked up again and saw nothing. No boy on his knees. No sticks held aloft. No vicious blows. Just the group standing still in the sea like broken remnants of pier, dark against the bright grey of the day. She turned to see if Marcus had seen it too but both boys had their heads turned against the unforgiving storm.

Her heart was racing. Had she actually seen that? Had that boy struck the other? She grunted with effort as she pulled and tried to quell the queasy dread.

Dread.

That feeling of utter hopelessness and helplessness in the face of terror. That closed door in a room filling with smoke. That moment when you hear something in your house that you shouldn't have. She was stuck on an island with these people. These boys who what? Who killed each other? Who didn't act as they should? Who didn't feel the cold? It was nothing. She hadn't seen anything yet the fear she felt at this moment, as she dragged her kayak and her boys towards who knew what was terrifyingly real. She didn't want to be anywhere near *them*. Could they get some tents from the stores? Camp elsewhere? Away from the centre? Ridiculous, they would freeze. They had to return.

Furthermore, and what had tipped her panic and unease into full blown fear was the fact that no ferry was sailing in this weather. The booked ferry would remain where it was. The waves were high, white explosions of spray burst from the peaks. The breakers were roaring and crashing now, the wind was violent and the rain was heavy. There was no way off this island in this weather. Her skin was crawling and she felt like she was mumbling to herself but wasn't sure. But she knew the feeling of dread all too well.

They were still a fair way from the van, and she could see the procession of young men leaving the sea, maybe half a mile away. All in a straight line. No talking or turning to each other. They stopped midway up the beach, and some put on their clothes they had discarded earlier. None of them seemed hurt or suffering from severe head trauma.

By the time they reached the car, the group were nowhere to be seen. She had veered closer to the sea to try and spot anything, *like a floating body,* but there had been nothing of the kind. And why would she want to find it? Have her fears confirmed? That they were sharing the site with a group of killers? No, she had been glad when the sea yielded no pasty corpse. They had reached the car and seen the footprints that had veered both right and left around the car. Why had they came to this spot? *This was where the road met the sand, no coincidence here*, it was why she and the boys were at this spot too, easy access to the beach for the Land Rover.

But the group hadn't arrived by car.

They must have walked here. But why this spot? It was two miles plus from the centre. Why not go to a closer beach? As she had walked round to the driver's side chewing this over, discomfited by how close they had walked to the car, her stomach had lurched again.

There was a symbol carved in the sand by her door. She had never seen this symbol before but she had no doubt it had been left for her to see. An odd-looking symbol, it seemed to her to be a stick figure but with slightly malformed appendages, trapped in a circle with odd marks and shapes around. It was over a metre in diameter, and she hated it and scuffed it out with her boot, irrationally worried that her boys would see it.

Together they had wrestled the kayaks onto the roof which the howling wind had seemed determined to prevent and, once ensconced within and the heaters blasting, she let out a huge, shuddering breath. She clutched the wheel and focussed on her breathing for several minutes. "You ok?" asked Marcus.

She was beginning to doubt what she thought she had seen. It was a ridiculous suggestion! To think that they had wandered out into the sea and attacked, or even killed one of their group was preposterous but, nonetheless, her unease was quite real and, again, despite her rational assessment, her old friend panic was making an attempt to seize control. "I'm fine," she'd managed before shutting her mouth tightly to stop a whimper that threatened to squirm out. *They were completely cut off!*

They had no way of getting off this island. "Cold Marcus. Really cold," was her voice wavering? Was it hidden by the collective chill they all felt? *They were marooned here with a bunch of fucking thugs who could be here for any number of dark reasons. Who could do whatever they wanted to them with nothing to stop them.* She closed her eyes and felt hot tears welling beneath. She had lived in the shadow of this inevitable moment for so long; the moment where she collapsed before her boys. The moment when they saw the fragile, hollow shell she had so diligently painted to look real and three dimensional, where the props holding all the fake scenery disappeared and the whole illusion fell apart. She clenched her eyes shut, panting silently and shallow. If she broke now, they would never forget it. They wouldn't understand and what's more, it would scare them to the core. The screaming, sobbing mess in the car with them would not be their mother. It would be a monster. Something that resembled their mother but the screams, the contortions, the gasping, rasping, sucking face would not know them, it would shoot blank, desperate socket stretching looks at the two frightened boys and it would not know them, it would not even recognise them. But they were in real trouble, and she couldn't deal with it.

She could recognise that neither Marcus or Daryl were comfortable sharing Mucach with Sol's band either, but the cheap, alpha coated masculinity that had been bestowed upon them by their father prevented Marcus, and by extension Daryl, from voicing their fears and misgivings. It was hidden beneath a thin veneer of male pride and contempt which prevented them from saying, 'Mum, I'm worried.' They had always felt, and had always been told, that it was their job to look after their mum. To not 'act like a girl' or be a cry-baby. Numerous visitors, their dad and yes, even her, especially since Fraser had left the house, had all spouted the same old shit – *you look out for your mum, you're the man of the house now Marcus, you're in charge now big man,* all that shit. All that poisonous shit; that shit that had spun its insidious webs which now wouldn't let a boy tell his mother he was worried. A spell that made his little brother do likewise in fear of appearing...what? Weak? Like a girl? Weak? It was all fucking bullshit and now, when it actually mattered, it was so clear to her that all along it was her job to look after them. They owed her nothing. This whole adventure was to help them! They were kids! And now, more than ever, they needed their mother. She knew, without a scrap of doubt, that if she caved now, in front of them, it would harm them irreparably and do damage that maybe she couldn't fix. And she wasn't talking about letting them see her upset, *never let them see you cry darling,* crying was fine. Everyone cried. No, upset was one thing, but seeing their mother's complete mental disintegration on an island where no help would be available, that would be too much. She would not subject them to that. She let out another, ragged breath, sobs desperately scrabbling to be released. The total conviction that if she did, if the walls crumbled, then they would be lost, somehow stopped those sobs from escaping.

She eased the pressure off her aching eyes, opening them gently. Marcus was hunched forward but his head was turned left and he was looking directly at her, as if waiting for this long awaited collapse.

"What?" she said.

"Nothing," he said smiling.

"What you looking at Marcus? I'm bloody freezing! Stop looking at me."

"Sorry. Am I making you cold by looking at you?"

"Shut up," she muttered, turning back to the controls and putting the Land Rover into first.

On the way back to the centre, she veered to the far right as they caught up on the group, jogging along the road towards the centre. The rain was falling in sheets across the island and she marvelled that they had chosen this as an activity. They were so under prepared. Thin tracksuit tops, trainers and not a waterproof in sight. For a moment she considered pulling over to check on them. "How many are in that group?" she asked innocently.

"No idea," said Marcus as they shot past the group, kicking up spray as they went.

"Fifteen I think," said Daryl authoritatively.

"Daryl," said Marcus, "How did you come up with that number?"

"I counted them," he replied defensively, instantly aware of his older brother's contempt for his answer and already scrambling to justify it.

"Really Daryl? When? Last night in the dark or this morning when they were miles away in the sea?"

"Shut up Marcus!" said Daryl.

"Did you count them though Daryl?" asked Hazel. "It's actually quite important and if the police get involved later on, it needs to be right."

Daryl thought about it for a second and eventually shook his head, "I didn't count them. It just looked like there was fifteen of them."

"Hey, do you know what? At least you owned up. Prefer you are honest now than keep digging away at a lie. And you," she said to Marcus. "Don't be so mean to him. Its been a long day, we're all tired and cold. Just be nice. OK?"

"OK," replied Marcus with a goofy voice.

They pulled into the centre fifteen minutes later. Despite a barrage of protests they stowed the kayaks which proved again to be a much harder job in the wind and the dark and she winced as one of them fell to the floor with a bang. They then trudged to the Drying Room where they disrobed. Hazel was in her underwear and despite the layers, water had inevitably gotten in and some of it now clung to her body in places she preferred it didn't and she suddenly became aware of the time. How long had it taken them to pull the kayaks off the Land Rover and stow them? How long before the group arrived back? She could imagine the scene as they burst into the room with her standing in her underwear. There would be leers and comments, of that she had no doubt.

"Hurry up Daryl," she commanded, an edge in her voice. There was no reason why she thought they would even come to the drying room yet she was convinced they would all burst in at any moment. She felt Marcus averting his eyes and wondered if she should get back in her wet suit just in case. She peeked out the Drying Room window towards the main gate. The sun had set recently and the sky was a metallic navy blue, turning darker by the second. There was no sign of them.

"I am mum," he replied, hopping on one leg, waterproof dragging behind him.

"For God's sake," she snapped and pushed him roughly back onto a bench. She began tugging away at the waterproof and, even though Daryl fought back, she yanked it off. She flapped it about the right way and hung it over one of the lines that covered the wall.

"Mum!" Marcus exclaimed.

"Just hurry up boys! Please!" she begged. She felt herself getting frantic but this time she could feel the control slipping away. She could not be caught like this. She began to tug roughly at Marcus's suit and when it finally came off, she flung it in the corner of the room and yelled at them both to get moving. Daryl was on the verge of tears, but she felt Marcus understood her panic.

Out of the drying room the lights blinked on up the corridor which led to their rooms and she felt her heart rate begin to slow as she moved quickly away, the course red carpet rough against her sodden, wrinkled feet. She calmed her breathing and slid into her room. She threw her wet gear into the corner of the room and quickly threw on some warm clothes. She was absolutely freezing.

The panic she had felt was subsiding. She would grab the boys and they would head straight to the cottage and light a fire. Have something good and hot to eat – maybe put a DVD on. She had seen a handful of films on a shelf in the cottage; there was nothing as fancy as Netflix here, much to the boys' chagrin. She was shivering; stick thin and was feeling the cold. She peeked her head out of the door; there didn't seem to be any movement from the drying room and so she went to peek out at the tents to see if they were back yet.

They weren't. In the fading light she saw the tents billow and bend in bleak synchronicity as the weather continued its assault of the island.

She knocked on the boy's door and Daryl opened. "Are you both changed yet?" she asked.

"Well, I am," he replied. "I just need my socks. Marcus is still down there." She glanced down the corridor again but saw nothing through the glass window.

She swallowed a curse. She had whizzed up the corridor assuming both boys had been following her. Bloody Marcus! "Ok love. You get your socks and shoes on; I'll go get him." She set off back to the drying room and within moments heard voices coming from beyond the red door. She closed her eyes and forced herself on.

She pushed harder against the red door than she intended and it flew open, banging off the wall. She saw Marcus still sitting on the bench where she had left him, surrounded by at least seven or eight youths him whilst others stood looking at her and her dramatic entrance. She had been gone at least ten minutes and she wished she had checked he had followed her out. She kept her tone light, not acknowledging the young men that surrounded her in various states of undress, for some reason thankful that Sol was absent, and looked directly at Marcus. "You coming love?" Her voice wavered ever so slightly but she hoped it was unnoticeable. Wet tracksuits and trainers littered the floor and the benches, some thrown over drying racks and radiators, others abandoned in wet clumps on the floor. "I had no idea you were still down here. You OK?" The energy of the group was palpable and it was hard to not look at the strong, glistening bodies that stood before her. The room was warm and steamy. Condensation trickled down the dark windows and water beaded on their young skin. She could feel their eyes on her, looking her up and down. Some with contempt, others with barely disguised adolescent hunger. They seemed to range in age, but all looked to be about Marcus' age or older. One of them did not take his eyes from hers, he had white hair and a pinkish tinge to his eyes -an albino, and his gaze was making her feel incredibly self-conscious and made her feel like she was wearing nothing at all. He was tall and muscular but something about him made her even more on edge, as if an any moment he could leap forwards at her. The others, although focussed on the scene, were still moving and slowly getting their gear sorted – not him, he was immobile, just watching her.

She tried to convey her dire need to get out of that room to Marcus by a look but it drifted to nothing as he replied, "I'll be up soon. I'm not ready yet."

She died inside. He had left her with nowhere to go.

"But… you're hungry Marcus. Come on, you need to eat. I've made food." She struggled to hide the desperate, pleading tone she felt and she could see his face harden as he made to argue.

"What y' avin then?" asked a youth who stood before Marcus. She recognised him as one of the boys who Sol had introduced but for the life of her, she had no idea what his name was.

"What?" she said.

"For tea. What you made'?"

"Um….I-" her mind was blank. Why had she lied? She ignored him and continued to speak to Marcus directly. "Marcus-"

"Don't be rude mum. Answer him," he told her. "This is Pritch," he gestured towards the half-naked youth who stood before her. His hair was cropped closely to his scalp, and he looked a very unhealthy shade of pale. He had several tattoos which were already faded with age and lacking detail, scattered across a pale, blue veined torso. One tattoo, looking older than the rest, more blurred than the others and nestled in between many others looked very similar to the symbol she had seen scrawled in the sand earlier on. Red spots dotted his chest, but she also saw wiry, lean muscle underneath the white skin. Pale blue eyes watched with amusement as she scrambled desperately for an answer.

"We have'nae got much to eat," said Pritch. "What did you make? Enough for us I hope?" Some of the boys grumbled and grinned in mock agreement.

"Sorry…no. Not enough. Sorry. Just three meals I'm afraid." She started walking backwards towards the door. "Where is Sol? He not getting you something?"

Pritchard shrugged, "No idea."

She was getting too warm. She could feel a flush creeping up her chest and neck.

It was too warm.

"Please hurry up Marcus, and make sure they are all out and the door locked please," she said and turned and left the stifling room. She closed the door behind her and heard an eruption of laughter moments later. She walked calmly back to her room and sat on the edge of her bed. Her heart was racing, and she slowly willed her hands to unclench. She was furious with him. *That little shit!* She thought. *He fucking abandoned me! He fucking...* She took some slow breaths and eased herself down on to the floor, crossing her legs as she did. She closed her eyes and focused on her breathing. *He had no real choice* she thought. *He was surrounded by them, and mummy comes in calling for supper and what? Was he supposed to come running? He may have been threatened.* Her breathing continued to slow. *Yes. But he shouldn't have been there. Why had he lingered?* Her back straightened and her breathing evened out. Her breathing became slow and rhythmical, in through the nose, out through the mouth. *He betrayed me. I needed him to help me there and he didn't.* Several minutes passed until a small knock on the door opened her eyes. She rose quietly and opened the door. It was Daryl.

"Let's go eat," she said.

She glowered at him over her sausage and chips. He remained deliberately unaware, talking to Daryl about trivial shit that he would never have asked him about on any other day had he not just betrayed his mother to a bunch of louts on a remote fucking island. "Have they all left?" she finally asked.

He looked away. "Yes."

She gripped her fork and replayed the scene again and again in her head. "What the hell was that back there?" she blurted.

Daryl's eyes widened and he looked terrified until he realised she was speaking to his older brother. "What mum?" came the reply. "What was what? I was speaking to people," he replied a little too calmly, a trait his father had passed on. "Should I be sorry I was making friends?"

"They're not your bloody friends Marcus," she replied trying to add a coolness of her own that she did not feel. When did it become so hard to tell your children off. At one point you are their Heaven and Earth and then, very quickly, you are the most tiresome, boring, repetitive creature thay have ever met. Old tricks and tones no longer worked. "They're a bunch of bloody thugs and thieves and they have no business being here and no bloody business talking to you! I don't want you mixing with them."

He clapped mockingly and rolled his eyes towards his younger brother then shot back at her, "Thugs and thieves? Are you serious right now? What's your problem? You and dad always moan about me not going out.

About me gaming all the time. The moment I talk to anyone you shit your pants about it and embarrass me. Is it because they're poor? Because they haven't got nice families? God's sake. Just be fucking chill." At that last part Daryl's eyes widened further, and he grinned as he looked back at his mother.

"I will not be just fucking chill," she hissed. "We're on an island in the middle of nowhere with a bunch of fucking god knows whats, bloody neds, who have broken in, who brought bolt cutters and shouldn't be here Marcus and you're acting like they're your pals. They're not your pals. They're criminals who shouldn't be here! They could have drugs. They probably do. They could do whatever they wanted to us! To me! I'm the only bloody woman for a hundred fucking miles Marcus! And there is nothing to stop them! Nothing. They can kill us if they want. They could-""

"My God," he yelled. "Are you trying to terrify him? Stop talking like that!"

She looked at Daryl and closed her eyes as she saw the horror on his face. "Are you serious mum?" he asked, tears forming. "Could they do that? Oh my god-"

"No Daryl, no no no. Of course not," she began.

"Well done Mum," said Marcus clapping again. "Well done, good job." He put his hand on his younger brother's shoulder and squeezed it gently. "It's fine mate," he said. "Don't listen to her. She's losing the plot." Her heart clenched at this, she desperately wanted to stop him speaking to her like that, for reducing her and dismissing her but right now she needed his help with Daryl. She could see she had scared him badly and right now they both had to try and remedy this. If this meant taking a few barbs from Marcus, so be it. Maybe she was losing the plot. But it was partly his fault for god's sake. If he hadn't-

"But she's right Marc," said Daryl. "They could burn us alive if they wanted. Stab us or something and there's no police. Mum's right. No one is here. They could kill us, and no one would even know!" Fear had a hold of him now and his face was pale.

"No mate, no," soothed Marcus. That's not gonna happen though, is it? Because its 2021 and things like that don't happen anymore, do they?" Daryl looked at his mum and she nodded in support, allowing Marcus to continue. "When was the last time you read about someone getting sliced up in their beds?" She balked at the phrasing, but he continued. "It just doesn't happen. And why would they anyway? Plus, they'd have a fight on their hands, it wouldn't be worth it. And there is nothing to gain. We have a shit car and no cash. Why risk prison for that? Plus, mum has already contacted the police."

His words were having an effect and Hazel added, "I'm sorry Daryl. I was angry with your brother and just wanted to shock him. I felt he let me down earlier and was angry with him. I shou-"

"How the hell did I let you down?" snarled Marcus. "I was talking to them and I said I would come!"

"Cos I thought you were already with me and Daryl and you weren't. And I had to go back down there, in front of them, into the room, when they shouldn't even have been in there, and make sure you were all right. And you showed me up. You could have said 'OK' but you didn't!" She sighed and pushed her hair back over her head. "It's stressful, I could have done it all differently and much better if I could have but it's a horrible situation and I'm freaking out and making poor choices. I'm sorry Daryl. I didn't mean all that stuff."

"See?" added Marcus, "she's sorry and made a mistake. You're ok. We're ok. There is nothing to worry about. Pritchard is quite funny as it happens." He looked at his mum. "You should get to know them instead of judging them because they're from a boy's home. They know the place well. Told me some stuff about the history of the island. Good stuff. I'll tell you about it later Daryl," and he had winked at his younger brother. She made to argue the unfairness of that statement when a muted crash and then a roar was heard vaguely from behind them.

"That was from the canteen," said Marcus.

Chapter 7

She pushed through the second set of doors which led to the main building after leaving the boys with instructions to get the fire going and a film ready. She couldn't stand this. The nausea and anxiety that was gnawing at her stomach slowed her steps and she considered just heading back to the cottage but she was determined to document everything and deep down there was a small, leaden ball of anger that insisted she find out what on earth was happening.

How the hell had they got in? The doors were all locked and there was no access unless they had all come from the Drying Room and even then, it had been locked, or so Marcus had said.

She turned the corner and headed towards the blue double doors of the canteen. Laughter and cheers could be heard and she steeled herself for whatever lay beyond. She set her phone to record and placed it in her top pocket and then pushed into the room. The boys were all sitting up beyond the serving area atop the counters and steel work surfaces of the kitchen. Sol stood at the industrial cooker with a big pan of something steaming away. She could see the door to the larder standing open, as was one of the lids of the chest freezers.

She made her way slowly towards them, aisles of upturned chairs hanging off outdated but well-maintained plastic-coated tables, hiding her and her all-seeing eye from the group and, again, she wished that she and the boys were anywhere else. She pulled out her phone to film specific areas which would no doubt be used as evidence at a later date.

They spoke loudly, some standing, others sitting. Knives and chopping boards were out, though what they had been preparing was a mystery as there was no veg available and everything else was frozen solid. She thought she saw blood running down the side of one white cupboard door but this was obscured by the moving bodies; many of the boys held steaming mugs. The air was peppered with swearing and the raucous banter which seemed the sole privilege of men. She grimaced at the mess and disrespect as she slowly backed away. The language and general air of testosterone and aggression was enough to persuade her to leave. She had what she needed. "Alright?" the voice came from behind her. "Getting some good footage there are ye?" She spun round and was met with a grinning, insolent face.

"I...-"

"Sol!" Sol turned and he grinned as he saw Hazel! He waved and said a few words to one of the other lads who nodded and stepped up to the stove. Sol was grinning as he walked around the gleaming counter tops towards her. Several boys jumped down from their perches and followed. Hazel's heart was beating hard and she was painfully aware of the young man standing between her and the exit.

"Sol," she began, "how did you get in here? And why are you in here? You said you wouldn't be using the building. This has all been deep cleaned and will need it again now. I mean..." she gestured futilely, her hands slapping loudly against her legs.

His grin never faded and his eyes never left hers as he held up his hands in supplication, drawing closer. "Hazel, come on," his voice was warm and friendly, "have you seen the weather? There's no fire being lit in that! It's torrential!"

"You shouldn't be in here! Any of you," she replied. "The fact that you are and that you're causing this mess is just awful Sol. Who's going to clean this? This was all spotless." She found herself running out of steam under his constant grin, as if he was aware of something she wasn't. He remained silent. "And how on earth did you get in? All the doors are locked." Her voice was beginning to rise. "Sol-"

He stopped in front of her, brought his head back slightly then spat in her face. "Get out," he said quietly.

Her shock was total. She gasped loudly. The humiliation and disgust she felt as his warm spittle slowly ran down her cheek towards the corner of her mouth was almost numbing. The boys around him also seemed taken aback. She turned away, wiping thoroughly at her face with her sleeve, bumping past the young man behind her who she had been so nervous of just moments before.

As she walked, the emotion she felt transported her back to her life with her husband. Although he had never done anything as outrageous as this, the feeling inside was terribly similar. Often he had left her feeling empty and powerless. Once, at the start of their marriage, after spending over an hour getting ready to go out, she had been given a glimpse of what her future was going to be. She was wearing a new dress she had bought in the January sales and her favourite shoes. Although they had ridiculously high heels at the back, they were also really comfortable. Never had she had shoes like these. She had rushed getting ready as she was keen to see some old friends she hadn't seen since her wedding day. Nevertheless, she had scrubbed up well and had admired herself, and her shoes, in the mirror before trotting down the stairs into the living room clutching her coat and purse. The sight that met her had stopped her on the last stair. Her husband lay on the couch, shoes off, browsing the TV listings, suit jacket draped over the arm of the chair. "Why aren't you up?" she had asked. "Let's go. Taxi should be here."

He had looked at her then. Looked her up and down and his coldness had caused her to swallow with uncertainty. The look he had given her, the lack of a smile or a compliment was unsettling and unlike any he had shown before. He had then turned back to the TV, "Well, you obviously think its ok to keep me waiting so now it's my turn." She had protested, how had he been kept waiting? They weren't running late she explained, the table with Ally and Debs was much later and they still had time for drinks beforehand, she could feel her frustration and anger and her hurt creeping into her voice as she tried to reason with him. Fraser Chapel had cooly replied that she had kept him waiting for over twenty minutes. Every argument she used, he ignored, idly skipping through listings, eyes fixed on the glowing screen. She explained how quick she had been, how she had rushed and, what was worse, was that she found herself apologising. She supposed it had been rude to keep him waiting. Maybe she could have put simpler clothes on or spent less time fussing with her hair, but Fraser was watching an old episode of Top Gear now and had said he wanted to finish it first. She had sat down on the opposite seat and began to text an apology as to why they were running late, citing car trouble, all the while anxiety chewed away at her.

As she had texted he said, "Let's not go out now Hazel. You're obviously not that bothered about it if you rushed. You don't look like you made much of an effort." She stood up clutching her purse to her, hurt as he continued, "I mean, these are your friends Haze, and if you can't even be bothered…" and he had shrugged, turning back to the TV. "I know I don't want to go out, not now."

"I have…Fraser. I have made an effort," she had stammered.

"Hang on," he had said and jumped to his feet, heading upstairs. Moments later he returned wearing blue knee length shorts and a faded grey t-shirt and trainers. "There. Now we match."

In the end, they hadn't gone out. She had phoned her friends who could see her fabricated tale for what it was but were still too polite to say anything despite having travelled from Edinburgh. When she had suggested she could go on her own to see them, he had simply said no – they didn't do that. "We are married Hazel, if that means anything to you."

As the months and years had gone on, the social occasions had dwindled to nothing. The apologies had increased. Sometimes Fraser would re-enact tonight, finding a reason why the night shouldn't go ahead – Hazel had neglected to tell him times or he wasn't feeling up to it; other times he would go out and then call the night to an abrupt end before it had even started. On these occasions Hazel was often happy to acquiesce as his surly behaviour and monosyllabic answers to conversations were more embarrassing than not showing up at all. Hazel would come to dread his reactions and performances around these social occasions, so much so that she would decline invites on the spot, citing babysitter shortages, illness, prior engagements, anything that headed off any questions and pre-empted Fraser's scathing criticism, his-

She snapped back to reality as a pain shot up her wrist as she slammed open another set of doors, misjudging their weight and her outrage. She walked back to the cottage in a daze and headed straight to the bathroom, running the tap to scalding before soaking a flannel. She pawed heavily at her face with the scalding cloth, barely noticing the pain in her face and hands. She had to get the feel of that cunt's spittle off her face. She welcomed the pain. It was cutting through the haze she found herself in, the nauseous pit that swirled with memories of her husband, of Sol, the grinning faces.

It was curious though she thought, that she wasn't sobbing. Something like this should have launched a full-blown panic attack and yet here she was, focussing on what she needed to do. The emotion that had her now wasn't misery.

It was anger.

She scrubbed harder.

Chapter 8

She opened the door canteen slowly. She had barely slept and light was still hours away. She had lain awake in the darkness, eyes bright as she had heard them returning to their tents. The noise had been minimal, the weather forcing them into their shelters and the voices and yells of laughter had fallen silent quickly, yet she had still not slept. The humiliation and anger, fear and aggression warred inside her and she had finally decided to get up and survey the damage they had wrought in the canteen.

The lights blinked on, one after the other, and she slowly walked towards the kitchen area, scanning for damage.

It was spotless. Everything seemed clean and the heavily scoured steel gleamed under the lights. Except…

On the furthest counter was a small object. She couldn't make it out and so she slowly approached it. It was brown and an irregular shape. Drawing closer still she saw it was a rabbit's head, lying on its side on a wooden chopping board.

It was bloodless, not a speck of crimson anywhere, not even on its fur, and as she grew closer, she could see bundles of small twigs had been forced into each of its eye sockets. Its mouth was stretched open as if screaming, but what was keeping it open she could not see. Her stomach rolled. It looked dry and as she peered closer, she saw small markings made inside the rabbit's ears. Tiny, neat cyphers carved onto the inner ear where there was less fur. The marks made her feel sicker still. She looked about but she was alone. Why the fuck had they done this? She peered closer, into the rabbit's mouth and saw something dark and wet, further up towards the back. It glistened and as she peered closer she could see slight movement as the blackness curled ever inwards. It was a slug. Or several. Slowly writhing and twisting in the rabbit's mouth and throat.

She made a disgusted face and reached out to pick it up by one of its ears and the head twitched. She made a high-pitched shriek, short and sharp and her hands flew to her mouth, she jumped back. It had only been the slightest movement, but it had definitely twitched. Hazel began to back away, her breathing quickening and her heart beginning to thump. The hairs on her arm were up and she moaned softly. She caught herself and stopped, taking a deep, calming breath. There was no one else to deal with this. She began opening drawers and found what she needed. She turned back, her stomach knotted and she inched closer, yellow gloves on. Without thinking, she quickly swept the head into a binbag, wrapping it tightly and made her way quickly from the canteen.

She strode into the cottage, heading for the fire and as she opened the cast iron doors, she ignored the moving, writhing thing she could feel in her hands through the gloves and the thin plastic. *It was moving! It's fucking moving!* She flung the bag onto the orange embers and slammed the door, opening the vent and breathing out as the contents flamed bright.

Later that morning they had sat watching gentle, swirling snowflakes as they ate their breakfast in silence; tiredness and lack of sleep aiding the lull. "Can we have a lazy day today mum?" Daryl had eventually asked. Hazel had agreed quickly, her aching muscles and unease not up to the task of organising another adventure into the unforgiving Scottish weather just yet.

She had added several logs and gone through the selection of DVDs with them finally settling on the original Matrix film followed by Jaws. Occasionally she had popped back to her room and sneaked a peak at the tents but of the group there had been no sign. She had not heard them leave nor had she spied them in the tents or anywhere on the grounds.

At the same time as one of the characters was advising his crewmates that they were going to need a bigger boat, she heard a *thunk* somewhere deeper in the cottage. On investigation, she had found nothing. Snow whipped across the grounds and small dusting covered the floor but the skies were now clear. Later, she had braced the biting wind to load the coal skuttle and again, a small bang had been heard but she paid it no mind. She believed the group were out on the island somewhere and she did not have the energy to find out the source of the noise.

She had made bacon sandwiches that afternoon as they each found something to get lost in. She had found the book with a whole chapter dedicated to the island entitled *Celtic Lands: A Look at the Life and Lore of Celtic Scotland* and given it to Marcus. Daryl continued to achieve level after level on his gem destroying game. Hazel had opened an old Jigsaw of some gentle countryside idyl she doubted even existed which she had found in a cupboard and had spent a few blissful, mind-numbing hours sorting the edges and corners, stockpiling different colours and details ready for her campaign but, despite the absorbing distraction, she still felt uneasy. She had gnawed worriedly at one thumb cuticle, something she had stopped doing as per Fraser's command, but now found herself doing more and more often. She had been worrying a piece of dry skin until she finally gained purchase and tore it away, blood welling quickly. She had gazed at the deep crimson dome as it grew before gravity broke the bubble and a thick line of blood ran down her left hand. She snapped to, moving quickly to the sink before blood dripped everywhere. The sting of the water was a surprise, and she was shocked to see the damage she had done. Her thumb throbbed and she berated herself as she wrapped a fabric plaster around and around.

Later, as the day had faded, she had taken Gavin's keys and double checked every door and window, rattling all deadbolts and unlocking and locking every door. She locked the Drying Room, the canteen and all fire escapes and exit points.

It was dark now. The fire crackled and her and Daryl were watching some good-looking people fight off a wave of Egyptian mummies – Ronnie's film collection was sparse to say the least – but Daryl was enjoying it. His head lay on her lap and she was idly twirling locks of his hair through her fingers whilst her gaze flitted from the fire to the film and back again. "Jeezo," murmured Marcus, long legs still dangling over the arm of his chair and he continued to read. The snow had continued to fall that day but it was thin and insubstantial and she was not worried about getting snowed in. It was still Autumn and the serious weather was still weeks away although it was absolutely freezing out there tonight.

"Book any good?" she asked.

He looked across to her. "I wouldn't say good," he replied. "More like freaky." He sat himself up, "It's just mad to think it happened on this island. I mean, some of it is really boring but some of these tribes were proper messed up." He turned the book to show her the page he was on. "It's mad. Some of the stuff they used to do."

"Like what?" she said.

"Well, this island was like a holy site. Lots of the islands were apparently. Not many tribes lived on the islands as it was hard to contact and that and no supplies and that," he said. "But all the tribes used to come to The Pig every few years or so when things were going wrong, when the land needed it. Things like crap harvests or fall outs with other tribes and that. Even diseases and stuff. If things were going bad enough, then all the tribes would agree to come to the Pig. And make sacrifices," he added grinning.

"What kind of sacrifices Marc?" asked Daryl, pausing the movie, his grisly curiosity aroused. "Animals?"

"Yes….." replied Marcus teasingly, "but also people. Human sacrifices."

"Really Marc? On the island?"

"Yep," came the reply. "Actually on the Pig. They would come in their thousands, they had loads of boats that went back and forth, was always a month or so long, all building up to this one day, and it was always on the longest day of the year, and everyone would bring food and they would bring stuff to make shelters and that and they'd all get mashed up on booze and mushrooms and have massive parties and that. They'd gather at the Eye and then on that one day, they'd climb the Pig and….." he trailed off, leaving the unsaid floating between the three of them.

"And?" insisted Daryl.

He looked at his mother, "Well, Pritchard told me some of this stuff. It's not in the book and it's pretty grim some of this."

"Oh my God Marcus! I'm almost thirteen! I think I can handle it!" Marcus looked at his mother who nodded for him to go on but with a look that managed to say *go ahead* and *be careful* at the same time.

"Well," he began, a macabre grin on his face, "the whole idea was it had to be a bad death Daryl. It had to mean something. They thought that if they just died in their sleep or from an overdose or something then the Gods, well, the earth spirits or something, wouldn't be that impressed, and nothing would change." He looked meaningfully at his younger brother, "It had to be painful." Daryl's eyes widened. "It had to be horrible."

"Like what," Daryl asked quietly.

"Like," Marcus said, "like being taken up onto the snout and having your guts pulled out and tied to a log or to a stone and then having that stone thrown off the edge while you're tied up."

"Oh my god," whispered Daryl appalled.

"Bloody hell Marcus! Snapped Hazel.

"Sometimes they did that, pulled out their guts I mean, but then they would just leave them. Everyone just went back to the camp and left a few of them tied up, guts hanging out, to die. Pritch says all flies and stuff would come and lay eggs and that and that it could take some of them days or even weeks to die."

"Weeks?" asked Daryl again.

"Marcus!" Hazel interjected again

"That's what it says," said Marcus, ignoring her. "Doesn't say if they kept them alive. If some people would bring them water or what but yeah, weeks. So, people must have kept them alive I suppose."

"How does he know that then Marcus?" Hazel challenged. "I mean, this is hundreds, no, thousands of years ago yeah? How on earth does he know this?"

"I don't know. Gadz. Don't have a go at me. I'm just telling you what he said. And the book says there were human sacrifices, so it probably is true. It just says tradition and word of mouth has been passed down and they know that these rituals took place in key areas across Scotland and that The Pig was a really important one. It even said that some people still practice these religions or whatever and live in small communities in Scotland but there is a whole chapter of this book dedicated to this island. It was really important to the Celtic tribes and they got up to all sorts here. It didn't happen regularly like, just when everything seemed to be going shit- sorry. When things were going wrong. It says it would take months and months to plan and get everyone sorted to make it there at the same time. There used to be stone buildings and stuff. Permanent buildings as well. People lived here and just kept an eye on everything so that when another gathering happened, it was already halfway to be being ready."

"Jeezo," murmured Daryl. "That's harsh though eh? Imagine being tied up with your guts hanging out and flies and that eating and pecking you."

"And birds," said Marcus. "Birds would come and peck at you. Carrion birds. Pulling your guts out and pecking your eyes out."

"Alright enough Marcus," said Hazel. "Think we need to change the subject eh?"

"Yeah okay," he said. "It's just that, well, want to know the really crazy thing?"

"What?" asked Daryl.

"This book says that it worked."

"What?" asked Daryl.

"Yeah," his brother replied. "It said that after a gathering, the results were always good. The diseases eased off, the harvests were good or whatever."

"Well, again Marcus, that's all speculative and unprovable and totally clouded by superstition and story telling," said Hazel.

"Aye. Maybe," he said. "This has been researched though mum. And, if it didn't work, why would they keep doing it? For hundreds of years they did it. Pretty sure they would have stopped if nothing changed but, it always seemed to work."

"Who were the people?" asked Daryl. "The people they killed?"

"The victims?" asked Marcus.

"Yeah. The tributes."

"Well, that's another odd thing," replied Marcus. "I think a lot of the time they were volunteers."

"No. Way."

"Think so."

"Shit."

"Daryl!" said Hazel.

"I know. But why would you volunteer for *that*!"

"Apparently it meant more. It doesn't say volunteers, but it never mentions people being forced into it either. It seems it was worth more, you know? Like when mum says if she makes you say sorry, it doesn't mean anything, but if you say sorry yourself, then its believable. Think it's the same thing. They went willingly."

"Well, the apology thing is true," said Hazel with a meaningful grin.

Later that evening she wandered through the cottage as the boys watched what was possibly their sixth film of the day. Marcus had put the book down and had settled down in front of the fire which popped occasionally. She had replenished the logs earlier that day and, after popping more wood on the fire, had started to tidy up. After collecting the limitless number of mugs and glasses dotted around the place, she had busied herself with putting a wash on and folding the clothes from the drier. She passed the office and decided to check and see if the internet was back up and running. She double clicked the Chrome icon on the desktop and was met with the now familiar white page of No Connection. She clicked refresh a couple of times and then typed in her outlook account but no luck there either. She wondered if her message had reached the police and her mood soured instantly. Today had been a nice oasis of calm and safety. There had been no sign of Sol and his 'boys' and for a brief moment she had forgotten their vulnerability and isolation. Now, recalling the message she had sent, it all came back in a surge. She slammed her finger down on the return key several times, but nothing happened. She-

A yell of pain from the living room made her jump in shock, her heart lurching. She dived through the door, sprinting in the direction of the noise, fearing the worst. What was happening? Were the boys okay?

On arrival, she found Marcus sitting on top of his brother's head on the sofa, a cushion smothering him. Daryl bucked and writhed beneath his older brother, his blond hair sticking out but Marcus sat quite comfortably atop.

"Marcus? What's going on?" she asked.

"I wanted to turn this film off. It's shite," he replied. "And Daryl forgot who was in charge and tried to rise above his station." A furious, muffled howl could be heard from beneath the cushion and Hazel couldn't help but grin.

"Get off him Marc," she said. "He can't breathe."

"I know that mum. But I will only get off if he promises to never try to rise above his station again. We'll have no revolutions here." Below him, Marcus flailed and tried to punch Marcus but this only served to amuse Marcus further. "Brother!" bellowed Marcus, as imperious as any Caesar. "Do you promise to accept your station in life?"

A muffled, defiant scream could be heard and so Marcus applied a direct and painful finger to one of Daryl's ribs and asked the question again. Daryl convulsed but Marcus continued his torture until Hazel tried to grab him and pull him away.

Marcus had looked at her then, smile growing as he realised her grip and strength were in no way a match for his own. He shook her free and then grabbed her arm. *My god he's strong* she thought to herself *When did that happen?* He held her away with one arm and then continued to administer his poking to Daryl but Hazel's intervention had done enough. With a strangled howl, Daryl managed to pull his head slowly and painfully from beneath Marcus. Hazel, seeing a window as his balanced shifted, launched herself at Marcus and threw him back onto the couch. Daryl reacted quickly, hair as crazy and wild as the demented, furious rage on his face and he jumped onto his older brother, arms swinging as Marcus brought his legs up in defence. Hazel also jumped, landing heavily onto Marcus' chest who wheezed as her weight hit him. He laughed in shock as the two of them tried to pin him down, Hazel sitting on him, trapping his arms as best she could as Daryl began a brutal and systematic campaign of revenge, jabbing Marcus in any and all available and unguarded areas that he could find. Marcus laughed and screamed in equal measure as Hazel asked, "Marcus? Do you promise to never try to rise above your station? To never turn your hand against mother and state?" It was his turn to buck and fight now but he kept dissolving into laughter as Daryl hit critical spot after critical spot.

"Please get off," he begged. "I'm gonna piss myself!" Tears leaked as he laughed and shouted and fought and even Daryl was laughing now, furious retribution forgotten, but enjoying delivering the torture, nonetheless.

Marcus had gone to the toilet and Hazel has straightened the cushions and throws that littered the living room. After what seemed like an eternity he finally returned. She had reminded them of the following day's schedule. "We're climbing tomorrow. Want to do The Pig?"

"Yes!" Marcus had shouted far too loudly.

"Well, we need to be up early. If we stick to the path it's an easy three and a half hours but there could be a bit of snow so may take us a bit longer. It's an easy enough route. Few scrambles but fine. Route to the Snout may be covered but that doesn't matter. We won't climb the ears either, but want to be up there by midday, so that means an early start. Ill pack a lunch and we'll eat on the way. Bike from here to the bottom and set off. Sound good?" They both nodded in agreement. It had been a valuable day. The laughter at the end had been a balm to her worries and she didn't want that feeling of family and closeness to end.

"Why can't we do the ears?" Daryl had asked.

"We need climbing gear. The ears are about 40 foot high, and you can't climb without the gear and we need to be safe and that so, no ears, especially in this weather. They nodded, both now fuelled by the prospect of visiting an actual site where who knows how many grisly deaths- no, *murders,* had taken place. She wished Marcus had kept all that to himself, but it was too late now and –

Thunk

That sound again. She sat up and went to the window, but it was pure black out there beyond the glass. "Did you hear that boys? I've heard it a few times now..." she trailed off, her unspoken fears hanging in the air between them. The snow had eased off earlier and it had vanished in the evening's rain. She double checked every window and door, but all were still locked. A vague uneasiness had stolen over her though, the warm fuzzy feeling all too easily pushed aside and she had wrapped the night up quickly after that.

The boys had headed to their room, and she had spent a further half hour tidying up and then preparing food and drinks to take on their hike. She was in her pyjamas now, her favourite ones. Light cotton button ups which she had had for countless years. Time and use had worn them thin and smooth, and she was looking forward to an early night. She liked having a plan to execute.

That noise though.

Like something slamming shut. She had heard it a few times and had looked several times trying to identify the sound. She was still unsure as to how the group had gained access to the canteen and she wasn't sure that this place was as secure as she once thought.

The backpack was full now. Three empty flasks sat on the table awaiting their bounties: sugary tea, sugary coffee and one of soup which she would make in the morning. The flasks stood next to three Tupperware's of sandwiches and three packets of crisps. The pack also contained a first aid kit, flare gun, foil blanket, water and portable battery pack. She rested against the table and checked the route. She had walked it many times and, although it was a broken and challenging path, it was no worse than some of the other hills and mountains she had scaled in her youth. What did give her pause was her fitness, she was out of shape and hadn't walked for more than an hour in any direction for over ten years. She also had no doubt that the weather would still be challenging. Muchach was windy at the best of times and the temperature had dropped. She was hoping the rain would keep off and she was tempted to pack a tent to stay the night there as well and probably would have, if not for their unwelcome guests. She sighed in frustration. Whenever she was in any danger of relaxing, the thought of *them* ruined it. She wished again that they were off the island and somewhere else. Somewhere safer.

Again, her thoughts were dragged back to the gang of men who had forced themselves into their world and ruined their chance to heal. She was constantly on edge, unable to relax and Marcus was feeling it too, her tension, her fear. There had been no sign of them today. Several times she had checked their tent area, peeking through her curtains which she now just kept closed, another testament to the negative impact they had wrought. The area had been deserted and she had even gone back to the canteen to see if they had gained access again. She resolutely ignored the desire to question the twitching rabbit's head she had burnt – that way led to questions she knew she could not bear the answers to, not right at that moment, but try as she might, the image of Sol hawking his spit at her was engrained and had been playing on a semi regular loop for the duration of the day. That fucking bastard! That outrageous, aggressively Cro-Magnon fucking ape. What a fucking coward – doing that to her! She hated him then. Another bully in her life. Another example for her boys to learn from. She walked from room to room, switching off the lights as she went.

When she reached the dorms, she typed in the code and pushed open the boy's room and wished them both goodnight; Daryl seemed to be already sleeping whilst Marcus read his book. Hazel punched the code to her own room and switched on the lights and gasped, the room was freezing, and the curtains billowed gently as the wind, invited by the wide-open windows, gusted in. She quickly began to close each one, locking them and double checking them as she went. The windows were one of the bigger outlays Ronnie and Gav had invested in. Every window was double glazed and had the same handles and locks that were commonplace in millions of houses and buildings across the country. Not only were they much more efficient at stopping heat loss and thus, keeping their bills down, but they were much more secure and could only be opened from the inside by pressing a small silver button where the key went and twisting the handle. One window open may have been explainable but all of them? No, it had to have been them, *them!* There was no other explanation, but her door had been locked and she hadn't seen anyone all day. Marcus and Daryl were above suspicion. She cranked the radiators and grabbed the laminated list of room codes that Gav had given her and then left to check the other rooms. She went methodically, checking all the rooms on her side then all the rooms on the boy's side. All were dark, all were secure. There was no suggestion that anyone, *or thing,* had been in these rooms, yet her windows had been opened and opened *wide* and she knew that something was deeply wrong.

Several minutes later she was standing back in front of Room 01, yawning as she typed in her own sequence of numbers and pushed open her door. Hazel knew before seeing them that the windows were open again. She could feel the wind on her face and as the door opened fully, she saw all the windows that she had only just shut and locked were now wide open again. Her skin broke out in goose bumps, the fine hairs on her arms and nape of her neck standing on end which the cold wind had nothing to do with. Her stomach slowly flipped and her legs began to shake slightly as she glanced quickly around. Had someone been in her room? How? It was locked, and she was certain that no one had been nipping between rooms. All the other rooms had been locked and she had merely poked her head into each one. How had this happened? *And how had that fucking rabbit's head been twitching and moving with no fucking brain and no fucking heart and no fucking anything to –* "No," she sobbed out loud and began once again to close each window, twisting each small silver key, pressing the button to check and then pulling the key out and placing it on the window. *Maybe I hadn't locked them? Maybe I had opened each one instead?* She thought, almost pleading, *Really Haze? Why on earth would you do that? But if not, did the wind open every fucking window? Maybe they weren't locked, but they were definitely closed and the fucking wind was not opening them.* She propped the door open and went to the boy's room, punching in the code and opening the door slowly. "Marc?" She whispered into the warm gloom. "Dar?"

"What mum?" came a low rumble from her left.

"Have you guys been out? Been in my room?"

"No," came the reply. "Why?"

"My windows are open. All of them. Did you open them earlier?"

"No mum," came Marcus' reply. "Why would we do that?"

"I don't know. A prank?"

"No mum. That's not funny."

"I know. I didn't think so."

"You ok mum? Want me to come and look?"

She smiled at the half-hearted offer and knew he would if she said yes. "No, it's ok love. Get some sleep Marcus." He mumbled an agreement to that and went back to his book as she closed the door softly.

She walked back to her room, determined that this would be the last night she spent in this particular room and prepared her sleeping bag. The radiators were doing their job and the room was already warming up. She stripped off and changed into her light blue plaid shorts and button-down pyjama set. These were warmer than her favourites and she was glad she had picked them, although she wished they were long legged just for this night. She had a thing about her legs in bed and something about long bottoms in bed just didn't sit right and many times she had found herself kicking them off in a manic attempt to get comfortable. She was also one of those people who had an irrational need for one foot to be free from blankets etc. and it had been a fine balancing act between having her foot sticking out, having it at the right temperature and not waking up Fraser who would tut and moan as she attempted to find said balance. Over the years she had learned that even just her toes facing towards the gap in the blankets was enough for her odd habit to be sated but she still struggled with sleeping bags and again, every night so far, she would wake up in a blind panic, fixated on unzipping her bag and releasing her foot!

There was an ancient lamp next to her bed but Gav, ever the eco-warrior, had fitted every lamp with an energy saving bulb which protruded inelegantly from the top of the small white shade. Although ultimately fine, these bulbs took several minutes to reach full brightness and, when first switched on, offered a very dim light. Hazel had no intention of being awake for that long and instead, she switched off the main light by the door and used her phone's torch to find her bed. She clambered into her sleeping bag and zipped it up, then pulled the duvet that was folded at the bottom of her bed up and over her. She plugged her phone into the charger and switched off the torch. The blackness was absolute, and she yawned again. As sleep crept quickly over, she dimly heard a *thunk* from somewhere in the building, but her eyes were closed, and she was warm and sleep had her now.

She surfaced hours later, aware that something was wrong.
Her feet.
Her feet needed to be free.
She was still half asleep and muttered something inaudible into her pillow as she tried to turn and find an empty area of her sleeping bag which would suffice before her awareness sharpened and she had to waken fully and start finding zips and all that carry on. She moved her legs and felt something utterly alien down there at the bottom of the bag. Something that brought her instantly up through several layers of sleep, something was terribly *wrong*.
Something was in her sleeping bag.
On her feet.
She moved her legs again carefully and again, the sensation that she could feel brought a terrified whine from her. There was a wetness down there. A lumpiness. Down near her ankles, near her shins where they were rubbing together but far too easily. They felt lubricated. They slipped against each other too easily, too slickly.
She was awake now and she could feel her heart thumping hard in her ears. The room was black. There were no external lights on and the ones that did come on were motion triggered – nothing moved outside on the island and nothing was moving in the room. Christ, she was terrified. She felt woozy as well, dizzy, but adrenalin was bringing everything online quickly and her heart continued to thump loudly in her head. She was frozen she realized. Caught between fear of the unknown and fear of seeing.
She lay there immobile, desperately trying not to move any part of her. Whatever was in her bag with her, was that moving? She was too hot and she needed the sleeping bag open. She needed the duvet off her but she was terrified of seeing what was in the bag with her.
She felt clammy, it felt as if everything was sticking to her, the soft, polyester sleeping bag, her pyjamas, her hair, which clung across her forehead. The duvet seemed heavier and she was aware of its weight, of the layers of heat it held against her and she was convinced it was getting warmer. Her feet were still. She refused to move them, but she could still feel the wrongness down there. The wetness. Maybe it was just sweat.

She remembered doing a three-day hike with the University and many of them had slept in Bivvy Bags, giant orange sacks of plastic which you put your sleeping bag in and which allowed you to sleep where you lay, without a tent. In the mornings, many sleeping bags were wet through with sweat and condensation and she hoped that this was the case. She was hot enough. Ever so slowly she brought her right hand down and slithered it into the bag and felt around her body, gently clutching at her pyjamas and arms but they were dry.

She steeled herself and groped slowly in the dark and found the smooth reassurance of her phone. She fumbled it on, pulling it from its charger, and switched on its torch function. She squeezed her eyes against the light, it was blinding in the darkness. Her heart was even louder now and her breathing was speeding up, and she had an overwhelming urge to pee. She began to tug at the duvet, slowly peeling it across herself, piling it onto the floor as she held the torch in her spare hand.

She found the zip to her sleeping bag and slowly began to unzip it. The torch threw long, dancing shadows across the room and she realised that she was panting. The urge to pee was agonising, her stomach was in knots and she just wished she could rest her head back down and go back to sleep. The zip kept snagging in the soft fabric, needing tension to glide smoothly but it was two thirds down now and that was enough. Gingerly she lifted the bag back, angling the phone to best illuminate her legs. As first it was hard to discern what it was that she was looking at then a wave of sheer repulsion swept across her.

Slugs. Her legs were covered in slugs.

She let out a short, high gasp of pure disgust and began kicking and thrashing in a bid to get away. She fell off the bed, kicking the bag from her and lunging across the room. She slammed on the lights and grabbed a towel that was sitting on the desk opposite her bed. They were huge. Plump, brown slugs, over ten at least on each leg. She wailed and began to brush them off using the towel. They fell away easily, retracting and curling up on impact. Her breathing was ragged, and she was close to hyper ventilating. She scooped the whole lot up in the towel and then wrapped the towel up in a knot before throwing the entire, slimy mess into a plastic carrier bag that was being used as the liner to the small bin in her room. She tied that also and flung the sack out into the corridor.

She walked shakily into the bathroom and turned on the shower before sitting down to pee. Her breathing was slowing but she needed something, she was about to break. Hazel snatched a small white hand towel from the rail and began to wail into it. Softly at first, sobbing, her eyes screwed tight against the material and then louder, and longer. The sobs wracking from her, painfully. The stress and the fear escaping her. She screamed then, into the towel, a muffled, almost inaudible scream but a scream nonetheless and a scream that seemed to strip her throat and tear her neck muscles. *What was happening?* If either of her boys had walked in at that moment, they would have struggled to recognise her. The bright red face, veins strident across her temple, her neck muscles and tendons corded and pronounced. If they had recognised her, they would have been terrified at the look of anguish writ across her face. She sat there for God knew how long, shower running fierce as steam billowed, shorts pooled around her ankles, white hand towel clutched tightly in her lap, sporadically rising to cover her face and catch the next burst of tears that were forcing their way to the surface, slug slime now dried against her pale, slender legs.

Eventually her breathing slowed and the tears dried up and the internal debrief began, ever so slowly, to unpick the night's happenings. She stepped out of her pyjamas and climbed into the scalding shower and, not for the first time that week, began to methodically scrub at her skin, ridding herself of unwanted residue.

Chapter 9

The day was brighter than anticipated and pockets of blue could be seen nestled between ice white clouds. The wind, however, hadn't disappointed and it battered them as they walked, heads down against the gales, across the moorland towards the mountain. Speaking was hard as the wind ripped the words from their mouths and they had to yell at each other to be heard. Nonetheless, the two boys grinned every time she checked them and they were making rapid progress. The Pig loomed in the distance. *Loom*, she thought to herself, *what on earth does loom actually mean? Who came up with that belter? The mountain is looming.* Her mind wandered aimlessly, focussing on banalities and small details lest she thought about the previous night too much. She was hoping she could rely on some old cliché, *the memories of last night are but a distant memory,* or even, *everything seems better in the morning,* but she knew this was not true. She remembered every part of it vividly and, if she began to pick at it, she would panic. The memory of those slugs on her bare skin; that moment of realisation of the black shapes glistening in the torch light, the warm sludge at the bottom of her bag. It threatened to engulf her if she allowed it.

She had discarded her sleeping bag and all traces of slug had been scrubbed from the room and she had hastily moved all of her gear finally out, setting up in the room next to the boys, but the sensation remained a potent memory. Nothing about last night made any sense but to contemplate the why and the how flicked a switch in her and she began to breathe too quickly, and her hands bunched up and she would squeeze her eyes shut and- no. Down that avenue were beartraps and pits and she would not emerge. Instead, she had focussed on the processes of getting ready that morning, actively aware of the here and now. Rousing the boys, prepping the bags and meals and extra kit which no one would ever need, adding weight to their packs – that's what she had done, mindful of keeping busy, blocking out unwelcome questions and memories. She had also managed to access the L&P website and booked the ferry for herself and the boys and also for twenty others at £3.95 each. No car meant it was considerably cheaper to book and it was how most tourists visited the island. The confirmation e-mail with the QR code came instantly and they were all booked for 10am. She screen-grabbed the code on her phone as well as printed off the confirmation and pinning it to the cork board in the office. This was their last day and they would be out for most of it, packing in the evening and then away. The relief she felt on seeing that message had lifted her spirits considerably and she bounced along the road.

They had set off around eight, the sky less dark to the east. Torches bobbing, they had headed out the back gates, and made their way north on the road before taking an abrupt left onto the footpath that bisected across the island.

Of the group, *Them*, again, there was no trace. The darkness not allowing her to confirm her feeling that behind the main building, twelve empty tents sat gently billowing in the silent breeze.

Two hours later they had stopped at the Eye, Mag Tul Storr, the monolithic stone circle which Gav claimed proved their were ancient technologies that we still aren't aware of, remnants of ancient gatherings and which gave testimony to the claim that there was a settlement on the island at one point. They sat on one of the fallen stones and drank some tea and ate some biscuits before pushing on. Daryl had talked the entire time.

An hour later and they were onto the gentle slope which wound lazily up the southern and easterly slopes of The Pig. It was a notorious climb for the uninitiated, the path fading before your eyes but Hazel was no novice and knew the way markers and clues that always kept them on the right bearing. She relayed these to the two boys who lapped it up. The only challenging aspects in Hazel's opinion were the mountain's remoteness; the often-foul weather that frequented the island of Muchach and deterioration of the path which often just disappeared amongst the underbrush and scree but which was not more treacherous than she remembered. The Pig had a series of false summits which could be demoralising but it was always a morale boost to spot The Ears which sat close to the peak and were officially the highest part of the mountain.

The path had materialised again and they had ambled ever upwards. "You guys ok?" she yelled. They both gave her the thumbs up, Daryl turning to show her a big smile peeking out from his bright blue knitted hat and she felt a wave of love at that rosy cheeked face quickly followed by a wave of sadness that all loving parents must feel; that keening pain of awareness that the rosy cheeked child before you is a temporary thing, that age and life will pull your child away from you.

She looked ahead to Marcus and remembered him at a younger age, his boundless energy and manic high-pitched songs he would croon when truly happy. She recalled a time when he had cavorted around their living room wearing a bin bag and nothing else, legs poked through either corner. He trudged ahead of her now, broad shoulders hunkered down and that sadness washed over her again; that little boy was gone forever, she now had a young man in her life and she felt she barely knew him.

In the distance the path wound left and right quite steeply before meandering onto the eastern slope where it zigzagged gently upwards but for now, they pushed on with the trail taking them westwards towards the sea. The wind was less here with the mountain taking the brunt of it, but it was still pretty noisy. Daryl pointed down at something off the path, towards the western slope and the ocean beyond and shouted something intelligible to her. She shook her head not understanding and moved closer to him.

"What's down there?" he shouted. She could barely make out his words and moved her head closer still. Her eyes followed where he pointed and she saw a small animal track leading down off the path.

She shrugged with an exaggerated manner to compensate for her bulky clothing, "No idea! Rabbit track!" she yelled. "Never seen it before. Let's keep going." He shook his head and pointed again at the track.

"Look!" he shouted, and she saw it this time. The footprints in the dark mud that branched off from the main path.

It had to be the others. *Them.*

"No Dar-" but he was gone, hastily picking his way along the sloping path which was barely visible. Ahead of her, Marcus had turned and performed the universal gesture of *Where the fuck are you all going?* He stomped back towards her, and Hazel beckoned him to follow and took off after Daryl. She yelled for him to stop several times, but the wind snatched the words from her mouth, casting them out to sea. As she trotted to keep up, she saw many footprints in the path, not as fresh as the ones Daryl was making and bigger. She had no idea where this path lead to and she had never heard Ronnie of Gav mentioning anything on this side of the mountain.

She caught up with him as they came down onto the rocky shore. Huge boulders stood among other stones and there was very little room between the sea and the sheer wall. "My god Daryl, where the bloody hell do you think you're going?"

"I'm following the tracks mum! Look!" And again he pointed and again she followed the direction and this time saw what seemed to be a cave, about 100 yards further down. Her heart sank.

"Daryl, absolutely not. Now come on!"

81

Marcus arrived behind them then. "Marcus, sure we can get in that cave over there?" yelled Daryl. Marcus grinned and pushed by them both, heading towards the cave.

"Marcus!" she yelled at his back, but the dismissive gesture was all Daryl needed to go hopping down over the rocks after his older brother. "Fuckin'-" she hissed under her breath as she began to follow. The cave *loomed* closer, and she had to bite back a small, hysteria laced giggle. *This is crazy* she thought. *I'm heading into a fucking cave on an island in the middle of fucking nowhere with my two children and there's a very real possibility that those fuckheads are already in there and there is nothing I can do to stop it.* It was all beginning to feel slightly surreal and a wave of light headedness swept over her and she was forced to sit down before she stumbled. "Boys!" she gasped but it was nothing more than a whisper against the wind and the waves. Marcus and Daryl continued on and she forced herself up, swaying slightly. "Come on Hazel," she said to herself. "Get going."

She caught up to them at the mouth of the cave; it was bigger than she had first thought, about 20ft high and pretty well hidden from the island. Seaweed covered the floor and grew halfway up the walls and she knew the tide would be coming back in at some point, hiding it once again. "Boys, can we-"she began, but then she saw the symbol painted on the wall in what must have been white paint. It was the same as she had seen by her car on the beach a few days ago – a crude stick figure perhaps, surrounded by a circle and symbols and glyphs she did not recognise. Again, she felt sure it had been left for her to see although why she felt that, she could not say.

"Look at that graffiti mum," said Daryl, pointing at the wall. "What does it mean?"

"No idea love," she replied. "I don't like it though. And I don't like it in here, and the se will be coming in soon so we should leave eh?"

"It is cool though isn't it?" asked Daryl.

"It is cool," she replied. "But-"

"Whoah!" came Marcus from deeper in, "this is mad." He had picked further into the cave where the slick rock rose and escaped the wet, clinging green of the seaweed. She could barely see him back there. "I think people live here mum." Although she couldn't see him, she could hear a note of panic in his voice. "There's a lot of rubbish back here. And more symbols, and beds I think. And..." his voice trailed off.

"And what Marc?" shouted Daryl, his excited voice echoing all around them. It was so dark in there and she seemed to be riveted to the spot, eyes constantly drawn back to the symbol. Daryl had reached his brother now, "Gads!" He exclaimed, "It stinks up here mum!" Hazel barely noticed, the sound of the sea in the cave and the way the figure was drawn, it all just seemed wrong and she could not stop looking at it. "Plus, there's cans here. Beer and coke and that." She was dimly aware of Daryl chattering away but it wasn't important.

What was wrong with that thing on the wall? Why did it offend her so much? It just didn't work. The symbols surrounding it too, what did they represent? Why was-

She came too, freezing water swamping her feet. The tide was coming in. She turned and gasped as the seaweed floor swayed and swelled. How long had she been standing there? Where were the boys? Another shock of freezing water engulfed her boots and she scrambled back towards the rear of the cave. "Boys!" she called.

There was no answer. She scrambled up the slippery rocks, grabbing fistfuls of cold slippery seaweed, and made her way higher into the gloom. Up ahead she saw what looked to be more symbols painted on the rocks, the white paint stark against the black rock. Crudely drawn and hastily done the symbols offered no meaning to her but several seemed explicit and, if asked, she would not have been able to say why. They did not look new and in some places lichen had obscured some of them. Litter was strewn everywhere and in the dark it was impossible to make it all out but there seemed to be sleeping bags laid out and, as she pressed onwards calling for her two sons, she heard the empty metallic clank and cling of aluminium cans rattling in the far distance. They weren't alone! "My god," she mumbled. "My god," her voice was low and she felt sick with panic. "Boys," she said again but the terror prevented her from raising her voice any louder. Where the fuck were they? Who was in here with them? Oh Fuckin' "Boys?" she hissed again. It was black in there now, the final wisps of daylight brushed the rocks behind her but ahead was sheer darkness. She fumbled her phone out of her side pocket with trembling fingers and managed to bring the home screen up but her shaking prevented her from drawing the code needed to unlock it. The dim light was not much better and only seemed to accentuate the darkness but at least she could see where she was putting her feet. She kept shuffling forwards, stopping every so often to scan the area with the light from her phone but the cave showed no sign of getting narrower and she had no idea of the size of space she was in, apart from her echo which only served to tell her the space was much bigger than she thought. "Boys?" she asked the silence. "Marcus? Daryl?" Her voice was feeble and hitching with attempted sobs, the fear was all consuming and her legs were beginning to wobble badly. She thought about just sitting down. Folding onto her knees and just resting for a bit, maybe waking back up at home; waking up anywhere but here. Anywhere but this fucking rock.

"Mother." The voice came from deep, deep in the cave, far ahead of her and as sure as any mother knows the sound of her children, Hazel knew that what had uttered that word was from no child of hers. Her bladder loosened and her legs almost gave out. A soft, deep voice but unlike any she had ever heard and, although faint, was unmistakable. She screamed then. A short burst of terror escaping her and then she ran. She span around, phone held out before her like a talisman to protect her from whatever lurked in this place. Her feet ran blindly and she tripped, landing hard and letting her phone skitter out of her hand. Was it footsteps she could hear over her panicked breathing? Footsteps coming at her from all directions? She lunged forward, grasping for her phone, her backpack threatening to topple her again, but she regained her balance and ran, ran towards the faint glimmer of light ahead, ran towards the sound of the sea. It was lighter now, but the sound of feet getting closer was all she could hear. The detritus of the cave's lodgers, the cans and wrappers could now be seen, and she ran harder still and then suddenly she turned her head to one of the sleeping bags.

Oh my dear Christ what the hell is that?

A figure could be seen in a sleeping bag, lying back on one arm, a figure made of pure blackness. Two white eyes and a big crooked white smile was all she could see.

It uttered something but Hazel's scream drowned it out and she ran out into the relative brightness of the cave entrance. The sea was further in now and at the mouth of the cave she could see Daryl and Marcus beckoning her frantically. She slid down the rocks into the freezing water, desperate to get out of there. The cold shock brought her to her senses and she turned then, terrified of what she might see, of what had been pursuing her, but, of course, there was nothing.

"Come on mum! Where've you been?" cried Daryl. "We've looked all over for you." She didn't answer him, just continued to clamber over the almost covered rocks until she reached them both. They hauled her up onto a large boulder and she sat, panting heavily, shuddering, her phone still clutched in a death grip.

"What…Where were you?" she asked, grabbing Marcus' arm. "I was looking for you!" She was slowing now, calmer, and behind that calm she could feel a wave of pure anger sharp on it's heels. "Marcus!" She spat his name and his eyes widened.

"I...what? What mam? We went in the cave, you were there, we went exploring a bit, then we said we were heading out because the sea was coming in and you said 'ok'."

"What?" she asked.

"Yeah. And then we came out and you didn't so we sat for a bit and threw rocks into the sea cos you were looking at that thing on the wall and then you still didn't come so then we went to check and you had gone. We thought you had come out already so we looked and then we went back to check the cave again and you were there running like a fuckin'...I don't know. What happened mum?"

"I lost you both!" she snapped. "Last I saw you, you were taking Daryl into the cave-"

"We walked past you mum," said Daryl. "Like literally right past you and said we were going out and... well, it isn't Marcus' fault!"

"He led you down there! I told you both not to go in! You both ignored me!"

"What was in there mum?" asked Marcus again.

"Just... nothing. I don't know Marcus. I just... I think I scared myself. It was dark and I heard something," *mother*, "and I just. I don't know boys. I panicked. I don't remember seeing either of you leave! That thing made me feel a bit funny and the dark and... I don't know."

"You've cut your leg," Marcus pointed out. "Are you ok?"

"I am love. Yes. But please, when I say not to do something, please listen. I can't handle this at the moment Marcus." He nodded slowly and then rooted around in her pack before bringing out her first aid kit. They patched up her knee and ate a sandwich each and shared the tea before the waves started encroaching on their perch and forced them back to the grass. "Right. I'm feeling a bit better now, still want to go up?" It was the last thing she wanted to do, she really wanted to just curl up on the floor and sleep. Or just disappear or something else, just not climb this fucking hill with that fucking cave below them. The alternative however, would be to just walk back to the centre with two dejected teenagers. In their eyes not much had happened, just a wee detour before the main event. They hadn't been scared shitless or almost pissed themselves or fallen onto rocks or....had a panic attack at precisely the wrong moment and began hallucinating or whatever it was she thought had just happened. No, best keep the boys happy and busy and push on up. Nothing bad happened outdoors anyway did it? Already the daylight was purging the memories, making them abstract and causing her to actually doubt herself. Much like her husband used to do, the daylight had a way of saying, *that didn't happen like that did it? You just had a moment? Nothing sinister, just stress Hazel.* Had there really been someone, something, lying in the sleeping back, smiling at her, or was it just the stress of this week coming home to roost? Had there been footsteps? Had the cave grown bigger and bigger? Yet, despite all of her retrospective denial, that voice, that word, was lodged like granite in her mind.

Mother.

She *had* heard it. She had. And the voice that had uttered it was like no human voice and-

"Mum? We going?" She turned, dazed. Marcus had her by the arm and was slowly helping her off the boulder. Daryl had already leapt to the next and was humming something as he went. Her knee throbbed but it was nothing she couldn't handle and the painkillers she had taken would take the edge off.

The wind had dropped now and the blue skies from this morning had now set up residence in the heavens above whilst white clouds skudded across quickly, but the day was turning out to be much warmer and brighter than anticipated. They had retraced their steps, Hazel pointedly ignoring the other tracks in the mud, and had rejoined the main path that led up. After a few hours they had stopped for more tea and a sandwich each. The day was fresh, a stiff breeze coming in from the North but not too unpleasant. They had stopped again halfway up, Hazel handing out more sandwiches and soup. "Can we go to the snout mum?" Daryl had asked. The snout was a ledge that looked out over the northern shore and was a good drop onto the rocks below.

"On the way down hon," she had said and Marcus had then regaled them with more lurid history of Muchach and Daryl had almost ran the second half of the trail, so keen was he to find the spot of the grisly deaths. They had stopped at the summit to gaze up at the tall column and take some pictures before eating their lunch.

The view was nothing short of spectacular. They had been lucky that it had cleared up and was now such a bright, clear day. She had missed this. The fresh air, the effort, the reward. You felt alive standing at the top of a mountain. The sea glittered around them and to the South, Scotland stretched on endlessly, her hills and mountains undulating into the unseeable distance. They had sat at the peak for half an hour or so, discussing other activities to pursue in the days to come, Hazel choosing to keep their early departure tomorrow a secret for now. Right now she was happy and she didn't think she could face another sparring session with Marcus. Daryl was keen to take on the assault course and Marcus was keen to get the kayaks out. They had taken a few more photos and drank in the view before beginning the decent. It had taken them just over four and a half hours to get up and it was past mid-day, the detour to the cave had cost them and, although the day was clear, she knew it would be getting dark quickly.

When they were over halfway down, Hazel took a sharp left at a small column of stones, hand built and weathered from years of Scottish weather. They followed a small broken track which headed in a northern direction. After another good hour of walking they rounded a grassy verge to see a large table of rock sloping down to a ledge that ran out over the northern face of the mountain to a drop onto the rocks of the shoreline below. They approached and she felt her breath catch in her chest. It never failed to unnerve her, this sudden end of stability. This place was what those familiar with the mountain called the Snout and was what gave the mountain it's unique appearance. She had stood here before but, for whatever reason, she was acutely aware of that immediate drop, metres away from her. It would surely mean death if you were unlucky enough to fall from this height, or at least be so broken that you'd spend years in recovery or eating through a straw, stuck in a wheelchair with only the memories of falling, of plummeting to the ground, of smashing onto the brutal boulders that looked up from below. "Don't go to the edge please boys. The winds are unpredictable up here and you could easily lose your balance or something and then you're done for. We have no ropes or pegs so no edge please. Marcus?" she added.

"Yes mum," he replied with all the scorn and contempt for a mother's worry a teenager can summon.

"Marcus. Is this where they pulled out the guts?" asked Daryl. "And where they left people to be eaten by animals and that? And threw them off the edge?"

"Yep," he replied. "We should look for bloodstains!"

"Oh my god yes!" shouted Daryl and immediately began scouring the site. Hazel tutted and turned her face into the gusts that came from the sea. The wind was fiercer up here and on the three compass points, the mountain sloped easily away into scree and short scrubby grass, but that northern ledge held a dread over Hazel that she had never experienced before. It was more than the wind that made her keep her boys back from it. She supposed it was her newly acquired and much more detailed knowledge of the spot that gave her pause. Knowing that so many people had died here, had died *painfully* here; it gave the site a macabre aura that sunshine and fresh air could not dispel. Herself and Ronnie and a few others had visited Auschwitz once and that had had the same aura, and, had she known nothing about the place, she believed she still would have felt the wrongness and absolute evil that had leaked into the stones there, that had bleached the joy and colour from that part of the world. The snout felt like this. She imagined the tears and the agony and-

"Mum!" Daryl was losing patience as his methodical, forensic approach to souvenir hunting proved to bear no fruit. "Mum!" he yelled, "What if we go on our bellies?"

"What do you mean?" she asked him, snapping out of her reverie.

"I want to go see over the ledge, if we all go on our bellies, and hold hands, can we not edge out and have a look over? Its not that high!"

"Oh yes Daryl!" exclaimed Marcus. "Come on!" He grabbed his brother's arm and ran towards the ledge. Her heart stopped.

"Marcus!" Hazel screamed and he turned to her grinning. "It is that bloody high and-"

"Come on Mum!" He ran back towards her and held her arm and she felt herself being pulled slowly down.

"Come on Mum!" shouted Daryl and grabbed her other arm. Despite the pain the cut in her knee gave her and her horror at this place, she couldn't help but grin at their enthusiasm and childish glee as they all ended up sprawled on the floor, still metres from the edge.

"You bloody arseholes!" she groaned as the coldness of the rock began to leach the warmth from her legs and stomach. The cold smell of the ground was in her nostrils and she was able to study the small broken stones and lichen up close. She closed her eyes as the wind rippled across her back. She struggled and quickly threw her backpack off closing her eyes. She breathed in through her nose, taking in the scent of the area, the rock and moss, the salt and enjoyed the sensation of lying prone, accepting the elements around her.

"Right. SAS crawl guys!" yelled Daryl and set off towards the edge.

"Wait!" yelled Hazel, snapping to, and set off after him with Marcus grinning alongside her. This time, Daryl did listen and she caught him quickly. They linked arms and began a slower shuffle towards the edge, boots, legs, stomachs, arms all shuffling them along the stone. Closer and closer they got, slowing when the wind picked up, her stomach flipping with vertigo as inch by inch, the drop got closer. She had been up here several times and done the ears several times but never with her boys, never at this time of year with the wind so lively and never when she was so shaky.

As one, they reached towards the ledge, pulling their heads clear and stared down directly to the shore below. The wind tugged at their hair and clothes and Hazel had another sweeping rush of vertigo and she grabbed the stone, and her boy's hands, as tightly as she could. Below, waves pulsed gently into the granite boulders that littered the shore amid the shingle. The waves would break into blossoms of white as they hit the resolute stone then collapse and retreat, only to try again. It was a hypnotic sight, being so far overhead and watching the same routine nature had enacted out for millions of years, unknowing or uncaring to those who observed. She watched for a while, finding small details, calm pockets of water amongst the chaos, seagulls hopping across the rocks or gliding above the waves. She breathed out slowly. The wind whistled into them, and she breathed deep, again appreciating the smell of the stone and lichen, the smell of the earth, of constancy, of ancient land, the mosses and grasses, the-

"Mum! What's that? Is that a..." Daryl's shrill cry pierced the roar of the wind and her contemplation, and she opened her eyes slowly against the bright daylight. "Is that a foot? Or a head?" The panic in his voice was clear and she looked down to what he could see. She scoured the shore, looking for what he was pointing at.

"What is it Dar?" shouted Marcus.

"In the sea, by those rocks, right below us. There. It's a head. I'm sure it is. A head and an arm or something." Hazel strained to see, terrified that she actually would. "A body! Arm and a head! There. In the rocks! No there!" he yelled again. "The sea is...it might not be...it looks like-" he lowered his head further over the edge, pointing with his spare arm. "I can't. I can't see if it is. It could be rubbish, but it looked like a head mum!"

"I cant see anything," shouted back Marcus across her. "Can see a bit of wood or something. Is that it?"

"Aye," shouted back Daryl. "It might be. But it looked like a head Marc."

"Well, it's not. It's definitely wood. The wood looks like wood, not a head, but I can't see any head or anything else either." Daryl dipped his head in frustration. "Plus the sea is coming in so..." Marcus added.

"No, you're looking at the wrong spot! I can see what youre looking at, and that's wood, but up from there. A head. Its tiny from here!"

"Nah. Don't think so Dar," shouted Marcus. She felt Daryl sag a little in defeat, but also in relief.

"Okay boys, we done here?" she asked, gently pulling both their arms away from the drop. Daryl put up a little resistance, desperate for another glimpse of what he thought he could see.

The boys jumped up quickly despite her protestations and headed back towards the path. As Hazel slung her backpack on, she noticed something red on the palm of her right hand – blood. It looked like blood at least. A dark, dark crimson, almost brown, the way dried blood looks. She checked herself quickly and noticed more of it down the front of her jacket, contrasting against the bright orange of her Rab coat. "What?" she murmured, checking herself again. The only cut she had was from her knee and that had been dealt with hours before. She looked back to the ledge. *No*, she thought to herself, *I haven't just lay in someone's blood!* She wiped hurriedly at her jacket and hands, emptying her water bottle over her hands and jacket scraping and scratching at the red splotches until it paled into a barely noticeable pink. She heard the boys yell for her, but she quietly walked back towards the ledge eyes scanning for blood on the ground. *It was mine, from earlier, its obvious*, but it wasn't it. Because she knew she hadn't got blood on her coat earlier and she knew she hadn't any blood on her hand because she had wiped her hands clean with a wetwipe after she had applied the plaster. *So whose fucking blood was it?* She edged closer still, scouring the ground as the wind picked up, whipping her hair round her head in a frenzy. She heard Marcus roaring for her and turned, he was running back to her. *Enough Haze. Enough. Get off this fucking hill and get them back.* It doesn't matter if there was blood there to be seen or not – the point was that it wasn't her blood so some poor thing, and it could just have been an animal or something, but something, something, had bled up here.

And she thought she had seen the head too.

Bobbing brown hair, one pale arm stretched beyond it, pale ribs swallowed then exposed, swallowed then exposed by the relentless sea.

It had definitely been a head.

Chapter 10

The walk down was quieter. The wind had died now, as had the exuberance of Marcus and Daryl. The look on Hazel's face as she had walked back from the Snout, absently wiping her hands down the front of her jacket, combined with Daryl's insistence on his gruesome sighting had been enough to douse their sparks of enjoyment.

Instead, they disappeared into themselves, eyes on the ground as they wound their way down the mountainside. Hazel kept thinking of how to cheer the boys back up before they reached the centre but was constantly pulled away by the events of the day. Tears leaked from her eyes with no wind to blame it on. It was a nightmare and now Daryl was infected with it as well. Marcus knew something was amiss and seemed to believe Daryl's insistence on what he had seen. She had to change the narrative but couldn't seem to summon the energy to penetrate the boy's sombre auras. The more fundamental reason however, was that she was terrified and didn't trust her own voice not to betray this.

She couldn't stop picking at the day, like a day-old scab; still sore to the touch which you still pick and pull at, knowing you should leave it but continue to worry until it bleeds, until it's painful. She would be thinking of a conversation starter – video games, music, school etc. and then that black, black face and that sickly smile would appear and she would forget what she was thinking and start replaying the moments in the cave, (*Mother!*) and how long had she been in there? How had she lost herself, trying to deduce if it was just her imagination and the stress and the lack of sleep, the sheer exhaustion, or if it had been someone else in there with them? And then she would feel the fear of that possibility and deliberately rouse herself, looking up to the two quiet boys ahead. She would start thinking of a topic for chat then she thought of the blood on her hands, on her jacket, the head and limbs she thought she had glimpsed in the foam. They had been close enough to make it out, and if Daryl also saw it, and there was definitely blood up there on that ledge, and – *enough!* And again, a deliberate refocussing of her thoughts and what her priorities needed to be.

They had to get off this island. She didn't care anymore. The ferry was due in two days, but she was done. They were done. She couldn't handle it. She felt on the brink of complete, catastrophic failure – a full blown mental collapse which she would not be able to hide, and which she probably would not recover from, and which would result in the complete abandonment of her children. Again, a blackhole of negativity called to her and asked her to jump in, to speculate on all the terrible things which could happen if she fucked this all up and collapsed and failed. Would Fraser have the kids? Would she wind up in a nut house somewhere? Raving about caves and eyeless, twitching rabbit heads? The way ahead seemed black and unnavigable and despair grew within her, whispering that they were truly fucked now. That there was no way off and she was only making things worse for Marcus and Daryl.

She thought about that then. Leaving them to it. What if she just did a complete one eighty and headed back on up to the Snout and just pitched herself off the fucking thing? Just head first, straight into those rocks and water. Would she feel it? Would she scream on the way down? What if she didn't die? What if she broke everything, ruptured everything, and was alive to feel it? Lying there, gurgling in the wash as her boys looked down on her from above. Could they-

"Mum!" She looked up, guilty, Marcus was waiting for her.

"What?"

"It's them. Up ahead." And, yep, there they were. A gang of young men waiting for them at the bottom of the path.

Her first instinct was to turn around and take them straight back up the way they had came but what on earth would come from that? It was ridiculous to consider running back up a fucking mountain but the thought of going down there, into that cadre of aggression and testosterone, exposing them to that bastard Sol, looking at him, after what he had done and knowing she was effectively powerless and- "Fuck them," she hissed and began walking down the path, picking up her pace, overtaking the two boys. *Fuck them*, she thought. *Fuck them! Fuck them for coming here. Fuck them for making me feel like he used to, like some powerless, helpless little girl! Fuck them for that! Fuck Sol! Fuck Fraser!* She was sick of these men, these fucking *bullies*, who knew they were physically stronger, who could harness their aggression and power, and expected the world to bend for them because it always had. Who had had her thinking about giving up, of running away. No, fuck them. She powered on, anger driving the car now, not fear. The group were at the foot of the path where it met the road, at least twenty minutes away.

She was down in ten.

The group, *Them*, were waiting for her. Marcus and Daryl had kept pace with her, both asking hesitant questions, if she was okay, what was she going to do and every response had been the same: she didn't know.

As she drew closer, she could see them beginning to mill with anticipation, smiling up at them. She had no idea what she was going to do or, what *they* were going to do for that matter, but she was sick of being scared. No matter what, she would not be scared.

They were metres away now, again, incredibly, some of the gang were topless, shirts tucked into their tracksuits or shorts, others with tops knotted round their waists. They were gathered around a row of boulders that separated the road from the path, directly in their way. "Come on boys," she commanded, an unwritten instruction in the tone of her voice to stick close, and aimed a course through the group ahead.

The one she remembered as Pritchard held his hand up in greeting and approached. "Hazel," he said. "It is Hazel isn't it?" He had a rough burr to his voice which lay at odds with his attempts and politeness and civility. She nodded curtly and pressed on, sidestepping him and weaving a course through the group, head down, not slowing. "Hazel," Pritchard said again but again, she ignored him and pressed on.

"Mum!" shouted Marcus. She turned her head slightly but kept on.

"Come on Marcus! Don't stop please," she called behind her. She was through the bulk of them now and the path towards the Eye lay before her. She stomped on, putting good distance between herself and the group, her blood up and risked a glance back. *Oh for God's sake!*

She was walking alone.

Behind her, Marcus and Daryl were surrounded by the gang, blocking them from her view. One of the gang lurched violently inwards, to what she couldn't see, but she had a horrifying idea. "Boys!" She began jogging back to the group which suddenly opened up. Within, Daryl was smiling, talking to one of the older boys. Where was Marcus? There. There he was, talking to two others.

She drew nearer, a cold lump of fear doing its best to control her but she was still furious and used its heat to push her forward. "Boys. Let's go please!" she barked.

"Mum!" shouted Daryl. "They're okay. This is Tyler," he said gesturing to the lad he had been talking to. Tyler turned to her and grinned. They all did, they were all looking at her. At least her boys weren't hurt. Yet.

"Hazel," tried Pritchard again. He walked slowly towards her. She stopped and fixed her attention on him, his wispy moustache, his pale skin.

"What?" she snapped. "What? What do you want?" She just needed her boys to start walking again.

"We want to apologise actually," Pritch replied.

She blinked. "Pardon?"

"Aye. What Sol did the other day. In the canteen. That was well outta line that and I wanted youse to know that that's not right that, you know? Spittin' in your face? Bang out of order." His voice seemed older than he looked, there was a timbre to it that spoke of a maturity that belied his appearance. Marcus and Daryl looked mystified and she could tell they were desperate for her to fill in the details.

"And," he continued, "Sol here would like to apologise." The group parted and sitting on a boulder, hidden up to this point, was Sol. He smiled at Hazel and for all her years, that smile was the saddest she had ever seen.

"I..." he began but the words seemed to dry up.

"Spit it oot Sol," a bigger lad said, walking closer to the older man.

He looked at her then and she saw tendons in his neck and jaw flexing as he wrestled with something. "I'd just say sorry," he said. "Really unforgivable that. What happened. I... I cant explain it." He held his hands out and stood, making as if they would embrace. "I really hope you can look past this Hazel," he said. "I don't know what got into me." What? He wants forgiveness? And then what? Do the same again? What if I have to speak to him again? But she could feel the group's willingness for her to forgive Sol, for her to build a bridge between the two groups, maybe finish the week positively? Show her boys that forgiveness was the higher road and led to union and understanding and-

Fuck him!

She stepped forward and spat directly in his face.

There was the smallest moment of silence before the group erupted, hysterical laughing and jeering broke out around them. They cheered her boys and her, slapping their legs. Others held their heads in incredulity, shocked at what they had seen. "My god Hazel," laughed Pritchard. "Fuckin' hell man! That's how you do it eh?"

Sol stood there, face ashen and then slowly pulled up his own sleeve to wipe off her spittle.

She didn't feel good. Her boy's faces were etched into her brain, stunned at seeing what their mother had done. The woman who had always taught them that violence solves nothing, that they should never stoop to their level, to be the bigger person, and they had just seen that same woman spit in a complete stranger's face. But, oh, it felt good. At that moment it had felt very, very good, spitting in that prick's face. And then had come the laughing and the cheering and then she had seen Marcus and Daryl and then she had felt shame like she had never felt.

The group were all still chuckling and some of the boys were now talking to Sol who was still looking at her, the expression on his face seemed to be one of confusion and profound sadness. She grabbed hold of Daryl's hand and began leading him from the pack. He pulled back, "Don't pull me." His face was one of anger. "Why did you do that?"

"Not now. Marcus!" she shouted. "Come on!" Marcus made to leave but another lad put his hand on Marcus' arm and spoke softly to him, gesturing to Hazel. She began to walk towards him but was cut off by Pritch.

"Hazel, that was... a shock," he said. "Cant say the old fucker didnae deserve it."

"We're leaving," she replied. She was exhausted. The day had been too much and she just wanted to get back to the cottage. Despite her fatigue, she would get that fucking internet up and running and she would find a way for them to get back to the mainland. "Please Pritch," she said. "I just want to go."

"Aye, no problem Hazel," he said with a grin. "We're heading back as well, we'll walk with you no?"

She sagged in defeat, no argument brimming to the surface, "Fine," she muttered, some of her anger still simmering.

"Lets go boys," he called to the group, and everyone, including Sol, began walking back to the centre.

They didn't stop when they reached the Eye. The food was gone and she had no intention of dragging this experience out any longer than needed. The big lad, Conal, led the way, grubby white hoodie still on. Behind her, she could hear both of her boys talking. Daryl was answering questions about his school and life in Glasgow and she winced at how open he was being, school name, teacher's names, local football team and she desperately wanted to turn around and hiss *What the fuck was that safety project we did all about eh shit for brains? Why not just write down your address and give 'em the fucking key!* But she didn't. She was tired and he was happy and that was enough for now. Further back, she could hear Marcus engaged in a conversation of his own, but what that was about was anyone's guess.

"So Hazel," Pritchard said, interrupting her thoughts, "good day on The Pig?"

"Not really Pritch," she said.

Her refusal to add any detail to this statement became an awkward silence which Pritchard quickly rushed to fill.

"Shame, shame," he replied. Again, despite his thick accent and mannerisms, she still had the impression that he was older than he made out. "We had a great day on the Loch," he added.

"Why are you here then? The loch is the other end of the island," she asked, rather sharply but who cared.

"We finished," he said. "Thought we'd go for a walk." Again, the silence dragged out. "To be honest, I've been hoping to find you and fix what happened the other day aye? Been looking for youse."

"Well, we've been here Pritch. We didn't go anywhere yesterday but you guys haven't been about for a while. Where were you? The cave?"

"Cave?" he asked. "What cave's that? Is there a cave here?" His response seemed genuine and she didn't have the energy to pursue it. But the anger was growing. Just having to walk with him and talk with him and pretend that they weren't here illegally and that they hadn't ruined everything was draining.

"Why are you here Pritch?" she asked, turning to look at him. "I mean really. Gavin and Ronnie didn't invite you cos he would have told me. You were not booked in. You brought bolt cutters. You knew it was empty and you hadn't banked on us being here, had you?"

"Aye. Well. I suppose so. We come here a lot Hazel. An awful lot. More than you'd think. And we know this island and love this island and we normally have it booked but Sol fucked up. The bolt cutters was his idea. I honestly thought he had booked it till we got here and spoke to youse. Then he pulls out those fucking bolt cutters man! Couldnae believe it." He seemed genuine but she didn't care. She just wanted to be gone. "But. Truth? We're glad youse guys are here. Believe me. An I'm tellin' you now, you'll get nae grief fram any o' us. We'll keep an eye out for you Hazel. You'll nae want to leave."

"How many are there of you Pritch? It is Pritch isn't it? Is it short for anything?"

"Well, it's actually Jamie," he answered, ignoring the first question. "Jamie Pritchard, but everyone calls me Pritch."

The centre was visible now, the sky was growing a soft shade of orange in the West and she was bone tired.

"Well? How many? Seems you are thin on numbers," she knew this was a dangerous line to be following considering the things she thought she had seen, but a part of her wanted to push back. Wanted to challenge him and his warm words.

"Well, there's eighteen of us, including Sol. Couple o' the boys are with him still on the loch. We did it in two groups like and we finished first. We set up. They'll tidy it all away."

She nodded, unconvinced.

"Aye so," he continued. "Youse away Thursday aye?" he asked.

"Tomorrow," she replied. "And you'd better be too. I'll be going straight to the police," she instantly regretted the threat but it was out now but Pritch just continued on.

"Aye, you're right to be doing that. If I was with my weans, I'd no like it – a bunch of neds turning up wi' bolt cutters. Not your place and you're looking out for yer pal's place, I get that." He gestured behind him to the group. "These here, these are my pals Hazel, naw…" and he paused. "More than that. They're my brothers like. My family, An' they don't have maws or pas and so Sol has to make do but, as you've seen, Sol isnae perfect and thinks being in charge means showing aff but," and he looked at Hazel now, "seeing how you are with yair two weans. Wi' Marcus an' Daryl, that's good to see Hazel. You're a good maw." She nodded politely, unsure how to answer him. Was he being incredibly patronising or was it a genuine moment from someone who had never known the support and love of a parent? She didn't know and again, an awkward silence appeared between them. The truth was, deep down, she appreciated his words. He was a teenage boy with no frame of reference but to hear any kind of compliment, especially regarding her motherhood, was so good to hear. She had doubted herself for so long. Questioned every decision, lamented every mistake, gnawed away at herself, were the boys ok? Should she have left sooner? What damage had already been done? Should she have stayed with their father? She looked at Pritchard then, he was sincere. She looked back to the path ahead.

"Don't you worry about anything else now Hazel," he said. "We're looking out for youse," and he gestured idly, encompassing both her and Marcus and Daryl. "No one's out to get ye. We'll be looking out for mum no?" and he smiled then. "Hey Conal!" he yelled up to the boy ahead of them. "We looking out for mum now eh?" Conal grinned back, half his face obscured by the hoodie and gave a thumbs up. He yelled it behind him too and more boys voiced their hearty agreement.

Hazel put her head down and tried to walk faster.

Mother.

Back at the cottage Hazel turned the oven on and emptied an entire pack of oven chips and another pack of sausages onto two baking trays and slammed the door shut. Her head was banging and it was hard to believe the sandwich making and bag packing that had occurred here fourteen hours ago was part of the same day, it seemed a lifetime ago. Her feet ached but not unpleasantly unlike her back and neck which just hurt. She decided she would have a bath before packing up their gear.

Outside she could hear Daryl still talking, this time to a boy called Hugh who was telling Daryl all about the different animals that could be found on Muchach. "Daryl!" she snapped. "Get in, get changed, wash for tea and say goodbye."

"In a minute mum," he called back.

Bloody' kid! She was close to crying. She was exhausted. "Now!" she yelled. "Get in. Close the door."

"God's sake!" she heard him moaning, then make his apologies and then softly close the door. She walked past him and locked it. "What's your problem mum?" he demanded. "They're alright! Hugh is decent. Why are you being like this? And why did you spit at that guy? What did he even do?"

"Not now Dar," she said, brushing by him. "Do what I said. Go get changed. Get washed, then we'll have something to eat."

"God!" he hissed as he set off towards his room.

"Same for you Marcus. Go get some comfies on, get washed, we'll all be stinking." She looked down at her nails and imagined the black crud under them was blood, despite having scrubbed her hands raw the moment she had got in. Marcus could sense her mood and calmly followed his brother.

She let out a sigh and switched the kettle on before collapsing onto a kitchen chair. She held her head in her hands and closed her eyes.

Mother.

What was that in the cave?

Thump!

She rubbed her eyes and sat up, the noise of the bellowing kettle giving her an excuse to leave her thoughts at the table.

She made her way to the cupboard and pulled out a mug, giving herself a very generous helping of coffee before opening the oven and giving everything a rattle around. The crackle and smell of the sausages was reassuring, but she knew their time here was done. They were leaving tomorrow. She walked out to the small office and wiggled the mouse of the PC, waking the thing up from Gav's photo montage screensaver, she would check the police and ferry after food. She then retuned to the kitchen and poured her coffee.

She made her way to the sitting room and added more wood to the fire which Marcus had started before adding a splash of Gav's MacCallan, to her coffee. She gently eased herself into the soft armchair and watched the flames lick the sooty glass.

Her coffee was almost finished when Marcus and Daryl came back, both in their pyjamas and slippers, Marcus in black shorts and vest, Daryl in some bright blue Fortnite ones his dad had bought weeks before she had kicked him out. She had finally stood up for herself.

It had been Marcus discussing his options at school after doing well in his Highers that had lit the fuse. He had scored well, all As in fact, and had mentioned following science and maths as he fancied engineering as a career. He knew several of his friend's fathers were engineers with one being very successful, travelling the world and making very good money. As Marcus had been singing this other man's praises Hazel had noticed Fraser's eyes slowly darkening. He had usually saved his poison for her, contradicting her, criticising her, threatening her, ignoring her, gaslighting her, reducing her and she had become used to it. She had medication which dulled the sting of his words and dulled the ache of misery deep inside her and she coped, but the look her husband was giving her son caused a sinewy hand of fear to reach into Hazel and whisper. She recognised that look. It was sheer malevolence and for whatever reason, simple jealousy of another parent or the realization that Marcus would one day surpass Fraser, in success, intelligence, height, sporting prowess or whatever tiny insecurities the man nourished, it meant that her son was now the target.

Before she could speak and dilute Marcus' gushing, Fraser had interrupted. He had spoken softly and quite innocuously, but she knew that Marcus had wandered blithely into very dangerous waters. She knew the rage that boiled beneath the placid nature and small open face of her husband. He didn't look mean. He had beautiful, piercing bright blue eyes and a small mop of blond hair, nestled on top of his tanned face giving him the look of an older, more travelled Tin Tin who had spent too many years investigating. Fraser was unassuming and had been quite charming when Hazel first met him at the Student Union. A ready smile and an infectious laugh, she had fallen for him instantly and even when they dated, his small, controlling habits came across as romantic and the actions of a love struck pup. Insisting she popped in when passing so he could make her something to eat, asking her to come back to his after she had had a night out with the girls, befriending her group of pals and always tagging along, she had been delighted with the attention and level of interest and engagement he had shown. She had never known someone to wait up for her, to ask her about her days and nights, who listened to her stories and opinions and even when he softly corrected her or told her that she might have been wrong, it was lovely, because it showed he cared.

Now, as she saw the innocent questioning begin, she was instantly taken back to her own experiences with the man. The questions that appeared innocent and interested were exercises in information retrieval, not a genuine interest in the speaker's life, but a collecting of ammunition, a stockpiling of tripwires and landmines which he would later use against her: "You said he was a bag of hot air," he would state weeks later when Hazel showed admiration for a colleague. "I thought he was boring?" he would repeat, bringing up comments Hazel had said months prior. Hazel would stutter and backtrack and eventually agree that yes, it probably wasn't such a good idea to meet up with this person or that colleague and that Fraser was, indeed, right and that she, was indeed, an idiot or a liar or both.

It was sickening to see him turn these weapons onto his own son. He had normally gone easy on them in this respect, the odd spiteful comment here or there but nothing on the level that Hazel was used to. Her insides knotted as Fraser probed and poked around Marcus' life plans and gave engaged head nods of encouragement interspersed with the odd contemptuous chuckle. He was so insidious, open encouragement with a snort of derision when Marcus suggested something that inspired him. So subtle, but it was there, she saw it plain as day even if Marcus didn't, this imperceptible undermining of Marcus' confidence. She knew nothing would be said today, nothing too harmful at least, this was just the start. Fraser would spend months now on derailing Marcus, on sucking his self-confidence and motivation away, just like he had done with her. In days or weeks to come there would be more questions, then other questions, questions asking Marcus if he felt he was up the challenge of something like that. If Marcus felt he was actually able to do something like that; how Marcus would cope if something went wrong, if there was a fatal mistake, how would he cope knowing it was his mistake that caused it, how would he feel competing against more able men who had been to better schools and who knew the people in charge, if he remembered how upset he got when something he was making failed, and could he make those kind of mistakes in the real world? She saw it all playing out ahead of them.

And that was that, she had to get them away.

That very night, as he lay sleeping beside her in that creepily silent way he had, after checking that she was fast asleep of course, she had softly gotten up and walked to his bedside table where he had placed her phone. Heart racing she had padded to the toilet, heart racing, closing the door oh so softly and locking it before installing a messaging app on her phone. She used this to send a text to her only friend. She had asked Ronnie for a number of things and the first one was that all communication go through her work e-mail as this was one avenue of communication that Fraser had never checked and, to her knowledge, had never even considered. She sent Ronnie the email address and had then deleted the app, knowing full well that it could be discovered if he chose to look, that all electronic communication was retrievable and hoping that he didn't suspect anything. After pulling the flush and making a good show of washing her hands, Hazel had walked back into the bedroom. It was too quiet in there. She desperately wanted to pee now, the terror that gripped her as she walked so quietly to his bedside to replace her phone. He would be lying there, eyes open, watching her return. He watched and saw everything. She had prepared a flimsy excuse, something about checking the weather for tomorrow but she still knew he would open her phone, check her messages, emails, call log, web searches etc. Maybe not at that moment but that day. But he had not been awake, he lay there still, eyes shut, silent. She grimaced silently, placing the phone down as softly as she could but still hearing a painfully loud *thunk* as it hit the bottom of the drawer.

She hadn't slept the rest of that night and as he sat in his chair the following morning, she realised that she hadn't actually put in any weather searches and that if he had woken and had questioned her and had checked then she would have been trouble. But he hadn't.

A day later, Ronnie had provided Hazel with an escape plan, the names of three solicitors who dealt with divorces, shelters that accepted abused women, hotels if Hazel felt that was too extreme, money put into a different account which they had shared when they had flat shared and which Ronnie had never closed and, of course, an open invitation to the island. Hazel had wept quietly at her office desk when she had opened the message. Of course, it was months before she acted, and in that time, Fraser's behaviour to both her and Marcus not only continued but deteriorated as if he suspected that she was complicit in Marcus' achievements, as if it was a deliberate undermining of Fraser by the pair of them. What made matters worse was that Marcus was not like Hazel, he had his father's anger. Combined with Hazels' intelligence, he very quickly began to push back at Fraser's belittling comments. The threat of violence was tangible in that house with Fraser increasingly angry at his family and even the smallest perceived infractions provoked scathing and vicious comments about people's intelligence, weight, hygiene, looks until one day when Fraser threw a mug at Marcus after he had made a particularly flippant comment about Fraser's status in life. The mug had just missed Marcus head and had scared him badly. That had been enough to get Hazel moving.

And now they were here.

In the middle of nowhere.

Outnumbered.

She thought about her old comfortable, sedated life. Would she trade? Would she choose a week of living with that nasty, manipulative coward or a week on this windswept outpost with God knows what else living in the dark under the hill?

She didn't know. Both were different forms of hell, but she was in no doubt that she would give anything, maybe even going back to him, if she could just get them off this fucking rock.

They were goosed as her mother used to say, and she had no idea how they were going to get back to the mainland but get off they would. She would dig in. She would stay the course. What she did know was that she had changed. She liked this new anger. This anger had made her strong. She hadn't been strong in her marriage; she had been scared. Scared of upsetting him. Scared of his mean comments. Scared for her boys and them seeing what their father was really like. Scared that she was raising two more bullies. Scared that they would turn out like him and destroy their own wives. The anger hadn't been there then. It hadn't been the tool it had been today. Maybe it was the risk to her boys which, despite his many failings as a husband, Fraser had never posed to the boys, at least not physically. She supposed it took years and years of beating and forging that tool before it became useful. It needed extremes to temper it. Well, it had been used today and had served her well. She hadn't collapsed, she hadn't folded, she had dug in. Well, until she pissed herself when that thing had smiled at her.

When she thought about the cave and what she may have seen today, the fear quickly arose. It was still there. But that seemed almost healthy. Who wouldn't be scared of a big black cave with creepy stuff going on?

But her fear of *Them*, of the group, was gone. She was done being afraid of men. If asked now, if she was ashamed of spitting at Sol, in all honesty, she didn't think that she was. She was glad she had done it. She wished her boys hadn't seen, not least because of the obvious explanation they were still demanding from her and also the wild hypocrisy every parent feels when their child sees them doing something they have spent years being told not to do, but her shame from earlier had left with the daylight and now she nursed a righteous justification. She still recalled his smug face as she left the canteen. *Fucking spit at me?* She thought, *I'll spit at you.* That was the law that bullies understood no? The 'stand up for yourself- bullies hate it', mantra pedalled by countless desperate and exasperated grown-ups the world over after rising above it fails?

The boys had been rooting through the remaining DVDs and were just settling onto the couch, "Your food is in the oven boys. Sausage and chips. Make me a plate Marc," she said gently. The whiskey was working its magic and she was warmer and calmer now. Marcus tutted and shoved himself back up to his feet. She leaned over and poured herself another glug of Gav's good stuff into the last inch of her coffee. It was much stronger and she smacked her lips after taking a sip but it was great, the warmth of the liquor heating her from the inside out.

The boys came back with their food, quiet and on edge, not entirely sure of this woman who was sitting with them. This woman who walked headlong into a group of men and spat in their leader's face. Marcus put her food on the coffee table within reach. "Put something on Marc, I don't care what."

"About today Mu-"

"Not tonight love. Please?" she asked. "I'll tell you everything. Everything," she repeated, "Just, not tonight. Tomorrow. I'm done. I just wanna eat my food, have a bath and go to bed. That ok?" They both nodded a quiet agreement before Daryl leapt up and put on one of the Matt Damon spy films Fraser had liked so much. Hazel didn't watch. She slowly ate her chips, watching the flames. Her eyes grew heavy.

Marcus woke her.

"Mum. Bed. The films over and its time to go to bed. Daryl went a while ago." She nodded and allowed Marcus to pull her to her feet. She ached but she was warm. The two of them walked to their rooms, Hazel not noticing the Google logo glowing brightly on the PC monitor.

Hazel now next door to the boys in Room 9 after what had happened the previous night, hugged them both and went straight to bed. Her sleeping bag and all that it contained was under three layers of binbag and in the outdoor bin. Her bed, made up that morning from spare duvets lifted from the cupboard, was soft and inviting and she sat down heavily, eager to be in. She swore softly as she knocked several of the beach stones onto the carpet as she plugged her phone in, they had made the transition to the new room also. She had meant to give them to the boys but for now, they were still littering her room.

She yawned and rubbed again at her eyes; she couldn't remember being so tired. Kicking off her shoes and jeans, she shrugged off her fleece and got into bed and was gently snoring within seconds.

Thump.

She awoke sharply to that by now familiar noise.

She lay there for long minutes, but there was nothing except sleep softly calling her back, her breathing slowing, eyes closing.

A giggle. Was that a giggle?

She stayed silent. The room was silent. There was another sound. What was it? This one, a whisper.

No way.

Was it her boys? No. She knew them well enough to know the shape of their voices.

It was *Them*. They were inside again!

They were inside?

How?

She listened again.

Nothing.

She strained her ears, desperate for silence, for that fake reassurance that everything was ok- that she had imagined it – that she could go back to sleep; but she knew that was bullshit. She had definitely been woken by a noise. A noise that sounded very much like a stifled giggle, like a rushed whisper.

She quietly pulled back her cover and reached over and switched on the lamp.

Something creaked. Outside her door, the floor had creaked.

Her heart lurched.

She was sick of this. Sick of these fucking turds and their bullshit.

Unless it was Sol.

That stopped her. That gave her reason to fear. The giggle though. Was it the boys just messing about? Sol? Giggling? Doubtful. Was it a giggle though? She was still exhausted, and her mind was not the most reliable at the moment. She looked at her phone: 4:12am – Who plays pranks at four in the morning?

What if it wasn't a prank? What if it was something more serious? Something sinister. Something that a woman and two boys couldn't stop from happening? She moaned softly as her mind played out horror after horror. Pritchard had said not to worry but so what? Who was he? Some upright, trustworthy pillar of the community? She didn't know them and what she had seen of them was that they were violent and vandals and trespassers.

There had been no more noises, of that she was certain but there was no way she was going back to sleep. Adrenaline was doing its job, and she was wide eyed and alert, if not scared and wanting to panic.

This feeling of terror, of fear. She was done with it.

She took several slowing breaths and looked around the room, spotting the collection of rocks on the bed side table. She peeled off one of her socks and stuffed a couple of the heavier looking stones into it, one of them being Daryl's baseball stone. The sock was thick and the weight was good – it was better than nothing. She remembered reading a book by Stephen King where the hero carried around a weapon like this, she thought it was a sack of pennies though, a happy slapper he called it and another film where it was pool balls in a sock. She prayed she didn't have to use it as she had never swung a loaded sock at anyone before in her life. She almost laughed – *loaded sock!* Her humour almost gave way to anguish as a wave of terror and desperation grabbed her. She was so tired of this constant feeling.

She sat silently again, but again, there was nothing.

Softly, she rose from her bed, anger, fear, caution, concern all jostling for position. She crept silently towards the door, one bare foot, one socked, easing forward, one by one. She put her ear softly to the door and waited. Nothing.

She held her breath and, ever so slowly, began to turn the handle to her room, making the faintest clicks as it unlocked. These doors had a mechanism for easy access in case of emergency and the door opened silently. The corridor light was on, but maybe she hadn't turned them off, she honestly couldn't remember. She had been so tired that it was quite possible she or the boys just hadn't switched them off.

Cautiously she edged out of the doorway, looking left and right, but the corridor was empty. She crept out, heart thumping. It seemed safe, in a way that you know a room is empty, even in the dark, but she had definitely heard something. She was sure of it.

She walked softly to the boy's room and, as quietly as possible, punched in the code to their door and turned the handle. It was pitch black inside with only the slim sliver of light from the corridor behind her to see by.

The boy's room consisted of several bunkbeds, with Daryl taking the lowest bunk, nearest the door. The light from behind her showed his angelic face, one dark forelock of hair across his face, he breathed softly and evenly, fast asleep.

She pushed open the door a little further frowning, something wasn't right.

As the rectangle of light revealed more, she saw a white, muscular arm draped over her son, holding him in an embrace. She dropped the sock to the floor with a clatter. A feeling of absolute horror stole through her then, her skin broke out in goosebumps and a wave of pure disgust engulfed her. "No," she hissed. "No."

It wasn't Marcus' arm, it was too big, and too white, it must...had to be... It was the large albino, cuddled in tightly to Daryl, sweet, trusting Daryl. One eye shone brightly, looking directly at her. He smiled. "NO!" she screamed and lunged forward from the door, grabbing Daryl, sleeping bag and all, and yanking him with all her might from his bed. He awoke with a start, as did the albino, his white hair frizzy from sleep blinking rapidly in surprise. Daryl landed with a crash on the floor and starting yelling in fear at what had woken him: the unholy terror that was his mother's rage. "Noooo!" She continued to pull Daryl across the room as the larger boy scrambled back on the bed, eyes wide in shock now, holding his hands up in defence and, what seemed to her, terror. She had a brief image of what she must look like from his point of view, and this infuriated her even more. Why was he even here? The rage welled up and she leapt forward, slapping and kicking him to move, to get the fuck out of her son's bed, their room! She was possessed – the sacrilege, the profane sacrilege of this thing, this foul beast, in bed with her child, she felt sick. She felt actual horror and was almost overwhelmed by the pure rage she felt.

"Kenny!" shouted Daryl. "Mum! Leave him," he was struggling to free himself from his bag. "Kenny," he yelled. "Kenny, Kenny!" Behind her she dimly heard Marcus shouting as well but the rage was in control now and she continued to slap and kick.

The tall boy wailed and began to scramble for the door, opening it partially. She pushed him savagely forward with her heel of her foot and he fell face first into the edge of the door. He gave a cry of pain and fell forward out into the corridor holding his face. She saw blood, bright red against his pale skin beginning to seep through his hands that he held to his face. She paused then, the anger leaving her as quickly as it had arrived, leaving a nausea in its place. "I..." she stepped out into the corridor; Daryl close behind her.

Suddenly a door opened further down the corridor, then another. Pairs of young men stepped out into the corridor, all clearly awakened by the noise. Pritch stood in a pair of boxer shorts looking at her.

She looked up at them in stunned silence.

"My god Mum. What have you done?" It was Marcus. Still in his sensible pyjamas and bare footed.

"I..." she said. She could feel the eyes on her and the only sound was the snivelling of the boy on the floor at her feet.

"Kenny!" shouted Daryl and pushed past her to his knee, putting his hands on the boy. More of the gang were appearing and Sol, Pritchard and a few others rushed to the two boys on the floor.

"What happened?" asked Sol, reaching Kenny before the others. He looked up at Hazel, then down to the blood-stained boy. "Oh, Hazel," he said. "My God."

"Kenny? Kenny?" spoke Pritch quickly, Kenny was sitting with his back to the wall, resting heavily on Daryl who was getting blood on him as he held Kenny's arm. There was something obscene about this she felt, yet somehow she felt as if she was now the villain of the piece *Why the fuck was he in bed with my son?* Kenny moved his head slowly towards the new voices. "Let's lie him down Daryl aye? You move yasel back there wee man and let Kenny lie down."

"He's a child mum!" shouted Marcus. "A bloody child. He has the mental age of a seven year old! What the hell!"

She was numb. She just stood and watched as they lay the big lad gently onto his back as he moaned softly.

Pritch pulled Kenny's hands gently away and winced at the amount of blood down Kenny's face. A deep scarlet gash could be seen in his forehead, sliced cleanly open by the door, the wicked white of pale skull could be seen.

"I..." she was still in a daze. Was this all her fault? Emotions threatened to suffocate her. She didn't know how she was supposed to feel and she searched for her new tool. The accusatory stares were almost physical and she felt the anger returning.

"Back to bed lads," called Sol, but none of them moved.

"Bed," ordered Conal and this time they started to disperse back to the bedrooms.

Their bedrooms?

"I... Why are they here? Why are they here Marcus? Why was he here? In bed with him. What's going on?" She pointed to Kenny who now had his head tilted back, one bright pale eye looking directly at her. It widened when she moved and he held up an arm in terror, his body jerking painfully. Red hand marks and a couple of scratches could be seen against his bone white skin from where she had caught him and there was something funny in that she thought but, maybe not funny right now.

"Shhh Kenny pal," soothed Pritch. Behind him, Daryl sat with his back to the wall, head in his hands giving her a baleful look. Blood continued to pour down the front of his face, pooling in the folds of his stomach before continuing downwards, dark burgundy coin sized droplets staining the floor – we'll have to clean that first before leaving she thought in a daze. Daryl looked up at her, his eyes brimming with tears.

"What?" she snapped. "Why are they here? Marcus? Daryl? Hmm? What on earth is going on?" Kenny cried out in pain as Conal attempted to clear some of the blood from around the wound.

"I'm...My god," she said. "I didn't mean for that to happen. I just wanted him away from you Daryl." That face. Her eyes were beginning to sting, and her own tears were very close. "Marcus?" she said. "I don't understand. Why are they here?"

Marcus sighed. "We let them in."

"What?" she asked. She felt sick. "Why?" What was happening? "How?"

"The other night," he answered. "When it was lashing down. You were asleep and we had spoken to Pritch in the drying room, well he asked, cos they were wet and cold, and we knew you'd say no, so we said we'd let them in later and that they had to be pure quiet. And they were-"

"'Cos Heaven forbid you let some young lads stay in a warm bed in a fucking storm!" hissed Sol. He gestured to Kenny's face. "What were you thinking Hazel? Look at him."

"You shouldn't be here!" she snapped back, glad he was being a dick, lighting her fuse and giving her an output for her feelings.

"Anyway, there's another way in, so we said okay because it was wet and cold and I think normally you would have said yes. If Ronnie was here like. So, we said we wouldn't tell you." He trailed off into awkward silence. She was still reeling. She felt sick to her stomach. Sick at what she had done and sick at her sons' betrayal. They hadn't told her. *They had chosen Them!* "Why on earth was he in Daryl's bed?"

A boy with dark skin had pushed gently past them, offering a small towel to Pritchard. "Cheers Craft," he said. He began to dab softly at the wound. Kenny repeatedly flinched and tried to push Pritch away, but he murmured softly and the albino slowly relented.

"He's my pal mum," wept Daryl. "I was showing him my Switch games and that, and I must have fallen asleep."

"Kenny is low ability Hazel," offered Pritchard. "He's a big kid. I know he doesna look it, but he's the softest thing. He wouldn't have hurt Daryl. He wouldnae hurt a fly."

"How the bloody hell am I supposed to know that?" she snapped. "I come into your room and see a man, and he is a man by the way, in the same bed as you! What was I supposed to think?" Daryl buried his face in his arms and stayed silent.

"But jeezo mum," said Marcus.

"Jeezo nothing Marcus! I had no idea what was happening. I thought it was this lot breaking in and Sol wanting to get me back or something. My god. I had no idea. Why didn't you say? It's not our place!"

He looked guilty then and looked away. She slowly knelt down next to Kenny, arm extended placatingly. Kenny whimpered. Conal knelt next to her holding some wet flannels and towels he had returned with and gave some to herself, Sol and Pritch and together they all slowly began to clean him, wiping away much of the blood from his face and torso.

"Kenny's special," murmured Pritchard, gently dabbing at his neck and chest. "He is innocent and wouldn't have hurt your boy." Kenny whimpered as Hazel began to wipe gently at his face. She made soothing sounds and placed her hand on his chest. "He looks like a mean fucker, but you'll no find a kinder wee soul on the planet." He shook his head as Kenny whimpered, "He didnae deserve…." He let the accusation hang there.

"He shouldn't have been in there," she answered back. Damned if she was going to apologise.

As the blood disappeared, she could see in greater detail the slice on his forehead, A neat but angry looking diagonal slice. His left eye was also swollen but he could see from it, now that the blood was wiped away. "You ok in there Kenny?" asked Conal, squeezing his friend's arm. "You ok bro?"

Kenny nodded weekly and tried a smile which made him whimper as his jaw moved. "Can you move Kenny?" asked Hazel. "Shall we try and get him up?" her eyes searched the group but everyone avoided her gaze. "Pritch, Conal? Help him up. I have a first aid kit which we can use."

Her resolve to not apologise was tested as they slowly lifted Kenny up from the floor. The blood spatter was excessive and was on the wall as well as the floor. The dry blood was already turning from burgundy to a darker hue and had dried in the creases of his pale skin. He whimpered softly as he was helped to his feet, Conal applying pressure to his head wound. "Lets get him back into a bed," they all nodded and took him to Room 2, opposite hers. They got him comfortable and pulled a duvet from the cupboard, draping it over him. "Ill go get my stuff and some pain killers. Marcus, go make a hot cup of tea for Kenny, plenty of sugar."

"Make a few big man," added Conal.

Marcus nodded silently and slipped out of the room. "Go help him Daryl. And bring some biscuits, chocolate and stuff as well?" Daryl followed, as mute as his brother.

She rose and went to her room. She planned to go straight to her pack and lift the first aid kit but the first thing she saw were the rocks, scattered about on her bed side table and the floor surrounding it – what could she have done if she hadn't had dropped the sock rock? Nausea squeezed her stomach tight, and she barely made it to the toilet where she dry heaved for several moments, eyes bulging, neck straining. Thin tendrils of spit hung down and, when she had finally finished retching, she sat back on her haunches and reached for a towel, wiping at her mouth with shaking hands. Slowly she bunched the towel and then slowly put it to her mouth and then bit into it as hard as she could. Tears began to fall, and the sobs came soon after. Experience had taught her how to do this silently, lest anyone should know she was falling apart and, despite everything she had promised herself, here she was again, screaming silently. Her teeth ached with the pressure, her jaw burned, her chest wracked and it was nothing – nothing compared to what she had done to that poor boy. That young man who was moaning in agony, head sliced open, because of her. And why? Because her children didn't trust her, didn't think they could tell her about their compassion – compassion she herself hadn't come close to showing. What was fucking wrong with her? She hadn't doubted her choices up to this point, but this? This changed everything. Was she just a paranoid wreck who couldn't be spoken with or reasoned with? Why hadn't they spoken to her, told her?

No!

Fuck this, no! They were in the wrong. It wasn't their place! They weren't invited, they weren't welcome, had forced their way in, had broken in – well, no, been invited in by her two moron boys – and one had been in bed with Daryl; no matter how you dressed it up, that was so, so wrong. She breathed deep and shuddered, more in acceptance of her choices, rather than the shame and guilt which had threatened to derail her. She stood by what she had done. She had been ambushed.

She forced herself to stand and made her way to her pack, taking what she needed and then made her way across to Room 2, holding onto the wavering flame of indignation that she had fostered, aggrieved at the feelings they were putting her through, the trial her and her boys were enduring.

They sat in silence, surrounding him, all save Pritchard who was sitting on the bed with him, gently asking him questions which Kenny tried to nod to. He was trembling. "He tried to fall asleep a couple of times but we wouldn't let him, would we Kenny?"

She offered him the first aid kit but he looked baffled and gestured for her to do it. "I havnae got a clue Hazel." He gently made way for her.

"Sol? She offered.

"No Hazel," said Pritch. "You've to do it. Isn't that right Ken?" Kenny nodded softly, his unsettling eyes locked on her. She wondered at Pritch's sudden authority and looked questioningly as Sol, who looked away, an unreadable look on his craggy face. She grimaced as she drew closer to the cut and began dabbing with the anti-septic wipes.

"We'll need to get him to a hospital," she said. "We have my car." She took another calming breath. "The ferry is coming today. Boys? We're leaving today. Sol, Pritchard, so are you. I have booked tickets for all of you. I'll take Kenny to a hospital and I will also be contacting the police." She felt Marcus' eyes boring into her but she pressed on. "I can butterfly stitch but he needs a doctor so he doesn't end up looking like Harry Potter." The silence and blank looks that met that told her they weren't in the mood for jokes.

"Good luck with that," said Sol, breaking the silence, "there's never a signal."

"It's already done. Booked yesterday. Have the code and everything. It's happening. Best get yourselves packed."

"Aye, we will Hazel," said Pritch.

She spent twenty minutes with Kenny, dressing his wound and administering the painkillers with the tea that Marcus had brought and, later, some soup. He was no longer fearful of her, which seemed incredibly bizarre to her. She was painfully conscious of one of his sinewy arms lying on her leg but she couldn't embarrass him and remove it. One by one, the room had emptied, leaving just herself, Daryl, Sol, Marcus and Pritch as the others made their way back to their rooms. At one point she had made to leave, thinking Kenny asleep, and he had grabbed her with surprising strength and shook his head. "Its alright Kenny pal," Pritch had said. "She's no going nowhere pal."

"Yeah Kenny," said Daryl softly. He was lying on another bed. "I'll be here Kenny. She won't hurt you again," Hazel looked at her son in hurt wonder. "I'm gonna go get my sleeping bag mum," he said, oblivious to her expression and trotted out.

"Are yeese alright Hazel?" asked Pritch. He pronounced her name *Hazer*, and she nodded, smiling politely.

"I'm really sorry I hurt him," she said, and she knew it was true. Despite her righteousness, he did seem like a sweet boy, and she wished again that either of them had just spoken to her. Was she that distant, so unapproachable? She was still in shock at the night's events, about the fact that *They* were now all tucked away in beds thanks to the deceit of her two children, the two people closest to her. She was also shocked at how badly she had hurt Kenny, accident or not, she had kicked him in a burst of rage and, it could have been worse. To rub salt in the wound was that he did seem to be an innocent, wide trusting eyes and small smiles and shrugs.

"He'll be alright, eh Kenny? Tough island man aint ya?"

"Aye," Kenny nodded happily. It was the first time she had heard him speak. He had a deep voice, but soft, and she smiled as his childlike grin. She felt a stab of guilt again at the plaster that covered his forehead.

"Lucky he is though," muttered Sol. "Could have been worse. And for what? Us needing a warm bed?"

"Aye, you've made your point Sol," answered Pritch.

"I have. And she split Kenny's head open Pritchard," returned Sol, anger flaring. He stood and approached Hazel but she stood her ground, her dislike of him adding to the resentment she felt and, she realised, mainly at him. He was the 'leader' of the group, he had cut the chains, he had spat at her.

He opened his mouth to speak but Hazel beat him to it, "I'm going to bed." She turned away from him, looking at Kenny, "Are you alright Kenny?" He nodded as Daryl walked in and set up his sleeping bag on the bed opposite Kenny. "You sure you're ok sleeping here Daryl?" she asked.

She was not okay with him sleeping with this strange boy, but she knew that any protestations would not only fall on deaf ears but likely stir up a hornet's nest of anger and animosity and this was not a hill worth dying on tonight. She left the room and Marcus followed, outside the room she said, "Will you please get your gear and sleep in the room with them Marcus?"

"Oh for fuck's sake," replied Marcus. "What for? They're fine mum!"

"I know. But it's still a stranger. And Daryl is only twelve! Please!"

"My god!" he hissed and stormed into his room. A moment later he stormed out, pushing past her into Room 2.

"Don't forget to pack as well. We're leaving. Marcus, I'm sor-" but the door slammed loudly behind her and she lowered her head and turned into her own room as her son's angry voice muttered from behind the closed door. It was freezing in her room.

The windows were wide open.

She closed each one and locked it.

A feeling of abject misery enveloped her as she climbed into her cold bed, the lights were off but the grey light outside was creeping in and she could hear rain softly pattering against the glass, she prayed that the weather would be calm enough for the crossing to happen. Normally she would not have bothered trying to sleep but she was exhausted. Later that day she would be getting them off the island and getting to a police station. She lay there, scrolling through her phone and the pictures and videos she had accrued. She was wired now though and eventually gave up, there was no getting back to sleep. She may as well start packing she thought. They were getting off that island that day. She forced herself up and began stuffing her meagre belongings into her pack, together with the first aid kit she had brought back with her. She then went into the boy's room and did the same there, there were bits and bobs lying about the cottage including devices and chargers but they could get them later. She struggled to lift all three bags but managed to drag them into the corridor. She paused for a second, listening. Behind Room 2's door she could here low voices; definitely Sol and maybe Marcus? She couldn't tell. She didn't care. They were leaving that day, either by boat or kayak or ferry, or bloody swimming, but they were leaving.

She got the luggage to the cottage and began sweeping up their belongings and arranging them on the table as the kettle boiled. The ferry was booked for 10am which was six hours away but it was better to be ready than rushed.

As she was thrusting the various wires and cable dotted around the cottage into the bag, the glare of the PC from the office caught her eye, the photo montage that Gavin had set as a screensaver. She walked into the tiny room and wiggled the mouse, instantly removing the image of Gav and Ronnie, both wrapped up in waterproofs with Gavin wearing an orange paper crown, grinning into a camera at the top of Ben Lomond as they celebrated a Christmas from years past. The much longed for Google logo greeted her and she hissed in triumph, thankful for something positive.

She instantly opened her email account to see if she had had any replies and sighed heavily at the automated response from Police Scotland. She scanned downwards and saw there had been a reply from the ferry company confirming the collection for 10am today.

She then resent her email to the police, this time adding further details and informing the police of their imminent departure. She also used one of the cables to hook her phone up to the computer and added several photos to document her experiences. She was aware that her boys would not approve of her actions and that several of the group weren't that bad, especially poor Kenny, but the truth was that they had broken into the site and had used items which would need cleaning and which would cost money. Ronnie was her best friend and she felt responsible for what had happened. If, by collecting evidence and documenting the group's actions Gav could claim some money back then she would do it. She hit send as a particularly loud splat of rain hit off the kitchen windows. She pressed the send button and the blue 'thinking' circle spun on it's eternal loop as she checked her phone to see if her network was running, but all the evidence she had forwarded to Ronnie was still showing as not received, *but that's what happens when you're living on an island trying to contact someone who lives on a boat.*

Hazel glanced behind her at the clock, it was creeping up on 6am. She had spent longer than planned on the computer but was glad she had got the messages sent. She would give the boys half hour more, then she would wake them quietly and head out to the ferry point, it didn't matter how wet it was outside, they would wait, she just wanted away from this place, and she also needed to get the police involved – she was planning on driving to the nearest police station and explaining everything. She wasn't sure if she should take Kenny with them or if the police would take care of him when they got here. The wound was not life threatening, but it did need stitches and she had not been lying about the ragged scar that would result if not treated properly. Would she be in trouble? GBH? She was sure the circumstances would get her off the hook but they would definitely want to speak to her but they could speak to her at home. She scooted back from the desk with renewed vigour and made her way back to the kitchen and gathered up the bags.

She would need to get their coats and boots beforehand, she thought – better way to get out quietly. She slowly opened the door to the sleeping dorms and closed it softly behind, pausing for the sound of voices, she didn't want to have to explain herself right now but she had decided to bring Kenny with them, they had the room, it had been her loss of control which could mean he was scarred for life and if she could make restorations in some way, then she would.

But.

There was something wrong.

She knew instantly that the place was empty. Some deeper, subconscious part of her knew that every room was already empty; it was that still silence, uninhabited and dead.

Chapter 11

Hazel punched the code into the room and sighed as her stomach flipped at the sight of the empty beds. She ran to the next room and did the same, with the same result. Blankets, sleeping bags, pillows all folded neatly at the foot of each bed.

No boys.

Where were they? Where had they gone? Had they taken Daryl and Marcus or had they both gone willingly.

Thunk.

That fucking noise! What was it? Instantly dismissing it she ran down the corridor and burst into the drying room, Daryl's boots were gone – Marcus' too. Their jackets hung from the hooks though, meaning they had headed out into that freezing rain without their jackets.

She sat and pulled her walking boots on as quickly as she could, before throwing her jacket on and zipping it up.

Thunk.

That was louder and seemed to come from directly above her. She looked up and saw a small hatch in the drying room ceiling. Hazel had never noticed it before, it seemed to be half a metre across and positioned in the corner.

She didn't have time to waste investigating that noise, yet she felt the answer was right above her. And, could the boys be up there? She cast about and saw that a bench could be dragged underneath the hatch and give her access, the bench had a wall of steel mesh built as a back to the bench and a wooden plank of hooks that ran along the top and that would give her the necessary footholds to-

"Shit," she murmured. Scrape marks on the floor showed the bench had been dragged to that position several times. Pale lines arced across the concrete and dirt of the drying room floor, made from where the bench had been slid back and forth to help *Them* access the room.

"Bastards!" she hissed. Had Marcus been helping them? Was this how they had got in? How they had accessed the canteen that night? The dorm? The rack wasn't flush to the wall either, it looked skewed.

She glanced at the door to the outside but already knew she was going to pull on this thread because, if this was how they had done it, how they had got in, it was vital for Ronnie and Gav to know about it and she needed to seal it off but, more importantly, her boys may be up there

right now. She pulled her phone and checked the battery, she would probably need the torch function. She took photos of the hatch and scrapes in the floor before zipping it safely away in her fleece.

Breathing slower but with a cold pit of fear gnawing away at her, she pulled at the heavy iron bench, grunting as it slid stubbornly across the floor. When she felt it was directly beneath the hatch, she climbed up, putting both feet on the narrow slats of the bench before climbing higher onto the steel mesh. She leaned slowly over the wooden plank that ran along the top of the bench, leaning against the wall. She slowly looked up and, gripping the top plank tightly, reached up with her left hand, tentatively pushing against the white wooden panel above her. It moved so easily she almost lost her balance and had to grab the plank with both hands.

She tried again and pushed up, the hatch lid was surprisingly light and she was able to move it easily to one side, beyond it was perfect blackness. She noticed scuffs and smudges of dirt on the wall where she was planning to put her feet, left by previous entrants although, how old these marks were, she couldn't tell.

She had a wave of doubt wash over her. This was a stupid idea. Her breathing was quickening, it was black up there! Why would they have pushed the bench back? What if it was a trap and they were waiting for her or- "Go!" she told herself and she reached higher, grabbing the lip of the now open hatch, she swung her other hand up and then scrabbled against the wall with her feet, finding purchase as she pushed herself up. The bench was heavy and allowed her to push hard with her legs, startled at how quickly she found herself rising up into the gloom. She was able to support her own weight for a moment and squirmed herself up onto the lip of the hatch. She sat there then, legs dangling in the light, the rest of her in darkness, and tried to calm her breathing.

She was terrified.

Her boys were God knew where and she was about to go scrambling around a loft space with no idea of what was up here. Yet, she was compelled. The idea of climbing back down was absurd. What was up here felt like part of the puzzle and, although she doubted it, there was a chance her boys were up here also.

The air was damp, smelling of old, cold stone and ancient dust and something else, something foul. She was facing the exterior wall, large grey bricks, lit from below from the light of the drying room which faded quickly to black. Ever so slowly, she turned herself around, twisting at the hip and bringing her legs up fully, convinced at any moment that some giant unseen thing would reach out and snatch her. "Hello," she said, but her voice wasn't strong, and her words were swallowed up. She felt exposed with her back to the darkness and, tapping the floor around her, she slowly rose to her feet, vertigo feathering her as she balanced next to the pool of light to her left. The floorboards creaked softly, a noise that carried out into the gloom.

Carefully she brought out her phone and thumbed it to life, swiping down for her torch. The light it offered struggled against the darkness and offered her no depth, merely illuminating the area immediately in front of her but that was enough. She could easily see the footprints left in the attic's layer of dust that coated the floor. She bent closer, examining the myriad footprints before her; a range of shoe treads and bare feet, some surprisingly small, almost child size – Daryl?

But some seemed smaller than Daryl's
Children?

Or was it some other bare footed creature that lurked in the rafters of the old building? Fear was with her now, grabbing at her and whispering to her, convincing her to turn back. She imagined a Lord of the Rings, Golumn-like goblin hobbling out of one of the shadows towards her, naked save for a ragged loin cloth, feral hunger in its eyes, saliva spooling from the several teeth it had left- "Stop!" she hissed again to herself but not before she raised the torch to check. There was nothing.

Hazel felt a cold tremble travel up her back and she let out a ragged sigh and lowered the torch to the floor once again, slowly following the trail of footprints *why are there children here?* as they headed forwards into the blackness. There were so many, *it's just Sol's boys coming and going, that's all. Stop scaring yourself.* She continued to move forward and realised she must now be above the dorm room corridor now. How long was it? If there were ten rooms down each side-

A sound. A chuckle.

She froze. That laugh, and it was a laugh this time, a high pitched, childlike snigger, the type a child would make when laughing at something they shouldn't, stifled and quiet but out before they can suppress it. A laugh she had heard before. A laugh that she had heard just outside her bedroom door. A laugh made in the darkness.

And a laugh far too high for any of the people she had met on this island to make. Higher even than Daryl's voice.

She thought to turn back and looked back towards the narrowing trapezium of light that offered her the sanctuary of the drying room. *Yeah, this is how they get in,* she told herself. *So bloody what? There's no one here. This is terrifying and I'm up here wasting time when the boys are out and exposed to the elements and up to God knows what and what the bloody hell am I doing up here?* She was furious with herself. What on earth had possessed her? Her heart was racing, and she could feel her breathing quickening. It was clear that the loft was empty, for now at least, save that fucking freaky laugh, but her boys were not here, so she didn't need to be either. *Let's go,* she told herself. *Let's go find my boys.*

The light in the drying room went out.

The darkness was absolute. She hadn't realised how much light the hatch had been providing till it was gone.

A small gasp of fear escaped her and she felt her legs go weak. She clutched her phone with both hands and screwed her eyes shut as her breathing sped up.

A rational part of Hazel's mind was stating, *It's the motion sensor, the motion sensor. It's switched the light off, that's all. The motion sensor! Nothing more.*

Yet, it didn't feel like nothing more. It didn't feel like a rational explanation. It felt deliberate. Whatever was here was doing this. Another attack on Hazel's crumbling defences.

Her eyes ached they were squeezed together so hard and- she was back in the cave now, she could hear the drip of ancient water landing in the puddles at her feet, the cloying, claggy smell of the seaweed, the chill of the rocks, leaching what little warmth she had. She could hear the sea lapping at the slimy stones, the water dark and cold. She couldn't open her eyes. If she did, she knew absolutely that she would see the thing under the hill, that black figure with too bright eyes, too old those eyes as well. Ancient, with yellow stain edging and the too wide smile standing there before her, centimetres from her face. She thought she could hear it breathing now, on her, a low sound but unclean somehow. Fetid air dredged from within. She moaned again and felt the chill whisp of the sea breeze on her face, the-

Thunk

It was in here. Whatever was making that noise was so close and yet, still seemed so distant. *So bloody what, she thought. Who cares? Get out Hazel!*

But getting out meant opening her eyes and, for all her desire to move, she couldn't bring herself to open her eyes. She still knew with one hundred percent certainty that when she did, she would see something she could never unsee and which could probably bring down the last wall of reason, hurling her to pure insanity. She was in a loft in an old barn and

119

a motion sensor had turned a light off but right now she knew she was in a different place, someplace terribly old, and somewhere she felt she did not belong and was not welcome. She sensed others around her now. More than one being, for that is what it was, what it felt like. Nothing human. Her legs were turning to rubber and she slowly lowered herself down, hand groping the floor, eyes still closed, breathing ragged.

  Her knee touched the floor, she reached forward with her fingertips, the floor was cold, too cold, like stone, wet stone. She breathed deliberately and calmly, eyes squeezed tight. Something breathed close to her, too close to her, deep, guttural cancerous breaths, but she focussed on her own, her breaths coming in thin, whistling blasts through her nose. She turned what she assumed was a half turn, one hand feeling her way, the other clutching her phone tightly and began crawling back the way she had come. It hadn't been that far. Hazel knew that at some point she would need to open her eyes again lest she fell down out of the hatch and really did some damage. Yes, she would have to open her eyes but for now, just keep moving, keep breathing. Her chest was rising and falling more slowly, and her small and methodical movement, left knee, right hand, right knee, left hand distracted her from what she couldn't see. She brought to mind her boys. Their faces, Marcus and Daryl, smiling, laughing, wind tousling Daryl's blond hair on the ferry, Marcus sweeping her up in a huge hug, and kept moving. After what she deemed a reasonable amount of time and distance she stopped. Her breathing was calmer, she knew that it was a carefully constructed façade and that at any point hysteria and panic could join the party but, right now, she had this.

  Her feeling of another presence in there with her now had also diminished, chased away by her self control and measured approach and she was almost smug about how she was coping. She hadn't dissolved. More and more it was beginning to feel like an over reaction to something that had a relatively easy solution.

  She could remember a time when Marcus was only a few months old and she would take him out on daily walks in his pram, constantly checking to see if he had dropped off to sleep. A walk in the pram was one of the failsafe methods she had for getting him to sleep and she also loved this walk around her neighbourhood. That feeling that she was a mother now, a member of the oldest gang in the world and it felt great. It really did. Yes she was exhausted but nothing could rival that feeling of holding a tiny, fragile little hand, touching those impossibly small fingernails and feeling that hand grab yours and knowing that you were their entire world, and they yours. That you had made this perfect little being and that you would do anything for them, and she had looked down at him then and he hadn't been breathing. The eye that she could see was locked and glassy, looking directly at the wall of the pram an inch from his face. A fear more profound than any she had ever experienced seized her and her panic only made it worse. She shook Marcus then, firmly, but he hadn't moved, not even a blink. She had run then, ran because she didn't know what to do and her husband might. Running back up her much sought after, tree lined street, screaming for Fraser who had actually stayed on the doorstep of their house watching them leave. Her panic and alarm as she had ran infected him also and he came running out, holding his head, fearing the worst. "He's not breathing Fraser!" she had screamed. "He's not breathing!" And she had looked down into the pram and had seen two bright blue eyes twinkling back at her, a smile on her baby's face at seeing his mother.

"What?" yelled Fraser, normally the coolest of cats, "He's fine! He's fine! What are you on about?"

And as she had sat in the hospital later that day, alone, explaining to the doctor what had happened and as she endured the pitying smile and condescension and patronising explanation to the tired young mother who had 'had a moment' she had been slowly convinced that it had just been an overreaction – a trick of the light, an exhausted mind, whatever – it was just Hazel over reacting. But she knew, *she knew,* that something had happened to her boy. Something had passed over him or through him, and then decided to move on. She hadn't imagined it and she would never forget that pale, unblinking stare of his and that frozen hand that had squeezed her heart so cruelly.   Nevertheless, as she had returned home, the logic had taken over and by the time she had reached home and her husband's contempt, she had almost convinced herself that it had indeed been an imagined incident. Almost.

And Hazel felt like this now.

After the blind terror of the darkness, she was now able to rationalise and deconstruct what had led to her panic, it was helping to slow her breathing and it would help get her out of there, but, deep deep down, she knew she had been right to be scared. That there was something here, something really old, and she really didn't want to see it.

She held her phone closer to her face and opened one eye, the brightness of the torch was her buffer, so bright in that dark place that it was all that she could see. She rose unsteadily to her feet and began to walk, one eye fixed to the floor, following the trail of footprints. They were orientated in both directions, both coming and going, and to her mind it seemed there were much more than she remembered. No matter, just get out. She kept walking and, as she did, an uneasy feeling in her stomach began to grow – *I should be at the hatch by now, I have easily covered the distance I made coming in – where is the hatch?* She stopped and looked down at the floor closer, the path of footprints was there but as she scanned her torch's weak beam forwards, it seemed the trail went on and on, she couldn't have passed it, or could she? No. There was a wall. Where was the wall? But, she hadn't walked that far, she hadn't counted her paces out but this wasn't making sense. She turned around and retraced her steps, counting her paces, working out the distances in her head, where would the drying room start, the dorms? She walked further and further each time, back and forth, the pale white light her only beacon of sanity. Her breathing was becoming ragged again, her phony sense of control sliding rapidly towards the abyss as each step increasingly defied the logic she had relied upon her entire life. The footprint trail seemed even wider now, too wide, hundreds of footprints metres across, most of them now barefoot, fading into the gloom on either side of her light, most of them barefoot, the five toed prints of children mixed in with men and women's prints, and all barefoot. No trainers or boot prints, just naked feet and toes. And blood. There seemed to be blood here too. Old blood, dark with age.

Then she saw it, a small rectangle of pure black in the darkness.

She let out a little sob of joy. She was almost out. She edged closer, beam focussed on the hole in front of her, it still seemed too far but it was getting closer with every step. As she drew nearer to her escape, the light of the Drying Room came on and in that instant she saw a shape in the gloom standing next to the hatch.

Perfectly still it stood, a dark figure, only just visible.

"No," she whispered, terror seizing her anew.

She looked back at the glowing hatch but could still see the edge of a leg and maybe a hand, standing there, still and mute as a rock.

Her stomach twisted in fear and she gritted her teeth against a sweeping tide of panic. Part of her wanted to just shut down. Just collapse and sleep and switch off. This was the last straw. The figure, this person, this was too much for her to cope with and it would be so much easier to just stop. Curl up and stop existing, but primeval Hazel knew that that was a false solution and would not save her, would just make her an easier target. Her boys still needed her and she couldn't just give up on them, no matter how scared she was.

She edged closer, almost crouching, squeezing her bowels tight. The urge to pee was staggering but she still had too much awareness to lose control like that. *Just get closer to the hole* she told herself. *Just get closer and fucking jump. Just get out of here. But what if it grabs me? Just get out of here Hazel. Just get out of here. Just get out of here.* She repeated the mantra over and over, edging closer and closer as silently as she could. The figure was stock still, unmoving, standing right next to the hatch.

It was tantalisingly close, so close she fancied she could sprint the last metre or so and slide down and she began to steel herself to do just that, she adjusted her body, readying for the most terrifying sprint of her life when the beam of her light caught the foot of the figure. It was a walking boot. A black and yellow Berghaus walking boot.

She shone the light over the figure. It stood there, rigid, clad in jeans and a purple fleece and as she raised the torch, she saw the tendons on the figure's neck, stretched taut, head held far back, looking up.

She saw a figure to the right of the first, taller, brown boots, she knew they were Timberlands, a brown, tan jacket, also head back, neck stretched impossibly far back.

"No," she murmured, shaking her head, "no, no, no." Her bladder loosened and felt the warmth of urine spreading out as ice covered her as she realised what she was actually seeing.

She shone the light towards the body of Ronnie, her brown ringlets were coated in dust, as were the rest of her clothes and as she crawled nearer, her bile began to rise. In the weak light, she could make out a bundle of sticks protruding upwards out of her friends mouth. In her mind's eye she could see the bundles that would be protruding from her eye sockets, and Gavin's. "No, no, no," she pleaded. "No. Ron," she sobbed.

Ronnie's head slowly began to move forward, moving slowly down to look at Hazel who stood crouched shaking her head in unfathomable anguish. The horror she felt when she saw that the sightless eyes did indeed contain a bundle of sticks forced into each, but, unlike the rabbit, there was some blood around the sockets and the mouth where they had been forced in. Hazel looked into those sightless eyes as whatever the thing was lifted its left leg and brought it down heavily on the wooden boards - *Thunk!*

Hazel screamed with everything she had, with pure terror and lunged towards the light, foot stepping into nothingness, as she fell, she felt her head smack off the lip of the hatch and a crunching pain in her ribs as she hit the bench then thudded to the hard, concrete floor. As she passed out of consciousness, she moaned as the hatch above her slowly closed.

Chapter 12

She awoke with a lurching gasp, taking a huge lungful of air and convulsing into a sitting position. She immediately wailed and bent over foetal, cradling her side, panting. Her head was throbbing and she moved her hand to the back of her head where she had knocked it on the way down. It was tender and something had congealed and crusted in her hair. Her hands came back with the brown smear of dry blood and a wave of nausea swept through her. Her trousers clung tightly to her thighs, soaked through. She felt her old friend panic making his familiar entrance and could feel the rising heart rate, the tightening of her hands, the rapid breathing: today's panic attack was going to be one for the books, "No," Hazel snarled. "No," and she slowly twisted herself around so she could reach the bench. "No," and she was reaching for the bench with one hand, pushing herself up with the other. Her breathing was fast, her heart was fast. "No," she said, and stood, just enough to get herself on the bench, the pain in her ribs a damn against the rising tide of terror. She focussed on the pain, head between her legs, eyes shut, she focussed on her breathing. "Marcus," she exhaled. Breathed in again, "Daryl," breathed in again, "Marcus...Daryl..." She continued this as her breathing slowed and her heart rate fell, falling back on her breathing exercises which had saved her so many times. She had to get out there and find her boys. Despite what had happened in that room above her, a part of her was still angry with herself about going up. She didn't deserve the panic attack as it had been her poor judgement that had led to whatever had happened.

An image of Ronnie's face, sticks protruding from her face, flashed for an instant. Had that been real? Impossible. How did she- it, stamp? How was it moving? Why was it just standing there? Had it been there this entire time, waiting to be discovered? She knew it was an easy process to just go up and check but there was no way on God's green earth that she was going back up there again. Not whilst her boys were out and not while she was in this state. More likely, what she had seen was a hallucination brought on by extreme stress and fatigue.

If not, they murdered my best friend and her husband.

This thought threatened to overwhelm her but also, a colder thought surfaced: *My boys are out there with murderers* which was closely followed with, *Did they help?* The idea was ridiculous, and she forced it from her mind even though the boys were much closer to the group than Hazel could believe. She went back to her room, removing her wet clothes and slinging them into the bathroom before towelling herself and putting dry knickers and thick, insulated leggings on. In the kitchen she upturned her bag, removing everything she didn't need and keeping the essentials – a torch, first aid kit with foil blankets, water and energy bars. She gingerly pulled on her jacket, wincing at the pain in her side and shoulder and slung her bag over her back before zipping it up and jamming her hat on tight. Rain lashed and railed against the window, and she decided to get her proper gear on; waterproofs, gaiters, gloves and her pack. By the time she was ready, the clock on the wall read half past seven, how long had she been in that attic?

She took a deep breath and prepared to leave- The ferry. The ferry was at ten. Two and a half hours from now. She moaned in frustration – she needed to find them but listening to the drumming rain and howling wind, she doubted it would even be running. But what if it was? What if this was her chance to escape and get help? She stood stock still, one hand on the door handle, frozen in indecision. If she jumped in the car now, she could make the ferry, but what if it was cancelled? If she left, alone, she could return with the police. They would help end this nightmare, save her boys, get them all home. However, what if something happened to her boys whilst she was waiting in her car at the ferry port or on the mainland? Could she ever live with the knowledge that she left them here alone?

Alternatively, if she didn't take it, if she just set out after her boys, would they ever get another chance to make it off? She had no idea what was happening to them, no idea where her boys were now. The wind howled beyond the door and she noticed that their jackets were still on the hooks. Her boys being out there convinced her. She ran back and shuggled the mouse, waiting for the log in screen, she typed the password out twice before she realised, she had hit the caps lock, swearing softly she logged in again – no internet. She opened her email which she had left open and composed a message to the ferry company, cancelling today and asking for a 12pm ferry for tomorrow. She hit send and saw the no internet message appear. She hit send again, hoping it would send as soon as it came back online. She winced as she stood, her side aching, and headed for the door.

The door was almost ripped from her hands as she opened it into the black morning, freezing rain and howling winds greeting her in a brutal embrace. She turned her head as the raindrops stung her exposed face and closed the door behind her, then flicked on the high beam torch and set off across the site. She had considered a bike but the conditions and visibility would make progress slow. She had to lower her head against the biting wind, each rain drop feeling like a pin prick, raising her head every few seconds to make sure she was on the right track, the wobbly beam of light picking out the broken path that headed out across the island towards the Eye and then up to Muchach, raindrops highlighted silver in the strong beam.

The cold was insistent, the areas where her skin was exposed were already numb and tingling and her hands were ice, despite the thick gloves she had on. The rain seemed to be hitting her from every direction and even though she had the hood of her high-quality jacket pulled tightly, her hat sat heavy, the front laden with freezing water, slowly inching its way down her forehead and Hazel had to keep pushing it up so she could see. After two unforgiving hours she could make out the black monoliths that made up the Eye. She felt soaked, through rain or sweat or both she couldn't tell but she was very aware of her temperature and the tremble that was beginning in her hands and legs. Her teeth were beginning to chatter, and she was aware that she would need to find shelter soon. Her face burnt from the stinging torrent, and she swallowed a sob of misery. Hazel trudged on and would have missed the body, strung up between two of the rocks is she hadn't stumbled, the torch swinging off its course and highlighting a white arm, bright in the torchlight, stark against the black night behind.

Stumbling forward, the beam of light picked out the torso of one of the gang, white and naked, arms and legs wide open, rope coiled tightly around his wrists and ankles, biting into his skin, hands and feet blue, secured against two huge rectangular slabs that towered either side of the wretch. It was one of the boys. His skin was chalk white and his eyes were wide open, looking directly at her.

Then she saw the plaster on his forehead.

Kenny!

Her hand came to her mouth as the torch light picked out a symbol carved into the left-hand side of his body, along his rib cage. Blood ran down his white skin, mixing with the rain. It was not the same as the other symbols she had seen, the one left outside the car on the beach or the one in the cave – this one was different. His eyes darted back and forth as she approached, manic and she wondered how the hell he was still alive in this weather.

She began to pull at one of the ropes with one hand, shining the torch with the other, she could see the rope had bitten deeply into his skin all but stopping his circulation, his hands dark and swollen. She searched frantically for a knot. The wind and rain howled still, deafening, but as she pulled, the boy began to shake his head violently. "No!" he yelled at her. His voice was almost drowned out by the wind as it slammed into her hooded head, amplifying itself, but she could see his lips in the torchlight and could just about make out his insistence. "No, no, no," he kept repeating. She was struggling to make any progress, using one hand whilst the other held the torch was not going to work and she cast about looking for somewhere to place the light so she could use both hands. She placed it down between her feet, the light shining upwards, illuminating the rain and his frantic face creating lurid shadows as he howled at her. "No, No, No!"

The tremor in her hands was worse now and the adrenalin that had coursed through her on finding this boy was wearing off quickly. Her bulky gloves struggled to find any purchase on the knots and his convulsing and thrashing made it even trickier, yanking the rope from her hands again and again. She wailed in frustration and ripped her gloves from her hands, "Keep still you idiot!" she yelled through the torrent, grabbing at the knots and desperately trying to find some give, some play in them which would help her work them lose but they were so tight. The cold bit into her hands and she groaned in pain. Freezing rain poured down her face making it ache. In desperation she moved to the other arm, moving the torch with her feet, but it was the same story. Her teeth were chattering violently, and she wished fervently that she had put another layer on before leaving. A jumper or t shirt or anything. She was not a big lady, not big at all, and the cold was beginning to have an effect. She was struggling to close her hands now and every time she was able to grab the knot, the boy would jerk so violently that it was snatched from her hands. "I can't," she sobbed. "I can't."

She looked across to his face, his manic, grinning face, "Leave me mother!" he screamed at her. "Please leave me!" Water poured down his face, drops spraying from his mouth and she wailed in anguish again, her hand to her mouth. If she had a knife or anything with her she could saw the ropes but she had nothing.

"I'm sorry," she shouted through chattering teeth, "I have to go!" She backed away, her heart bursting as the wind buffeted his lank body, as it pulled him this way and that, as the rain lashed and whipped him, the ropes holding fast as he was pulled against them. She knew he would die out here. As sure as the sun was rising, so too would this boy be dead by the time it came. "I'm so sorry," she stammered again as she thrust her torch under her arm and pulled on her gloves. "I have to go," although she was too quiet and too far, the storm too loud for him to hear her. She had no choice. The knots were too strong. She was far too weak. "My boys," she murmured, "I have to get my boys." She staggered backwards and then turned away. She was numb now, numb through cold, numb through exposure, numb through exhaustion, yet her body propelled her onwards. Torch light bobbing she staggered in the dark, occasionally stumbling over a rock but never falling, sensing the looming presence of the mountain. She knew where she was heading as well, knew that the only place she could go if she was to be of any use to her boys was the cave. She had to get out of this weather and it was also the only place that they could be as well. Nothing could last for long out here, well, nothing apart from a naked boy tied up between some rocks. Her tears mixed with the rain as she hunkered down and pressed on.

Her teeth were chattering uncontrollably as she made her way down the slope towards the cave entrance. She fell several times, twice painfully, cracking her elbow on a rock and once hurting her ribs which were already in bad shape after her fall in the drying room. The slope was treacherous and slick rocks and other obstacles all looked to trip her. Her torch made out the entrance to the cave and she made the final yards sliding on her bottom, grateful she had put waterproof trousers on before leaving.

Her feet splashed down into sea water, fully enveloping them but such was her cold that she barely registered the shock. She stumbled on, one arms out in front for balance, the other holding an increasingly shaky torchlight and as she entered the cave, the wind died almost instantly. She breathed out in shuddering relief and took several breaths but she was not safe yet. The risk of hypothermia was very real and she needed to get warm again.

The sea was mostly out, the floor a mass of bobbing black seaweed and slick rocks looking oily in the torchlight and she came crashing down several more times as her feet slipped or something tripped her. She was exhausted but pushed on, pushed on towards the back, to where it was dry. To where there was once a fire. To where there was a sleeping bag.

The darkness was absolute and she clutched her torch desperately afraid of losing it's guiding light. She clambered upwards now, on dry stone, past the symbol on the wall, a symbol that seemed to change every time her white light hit but she had no time for that now, she needed to be dry, she needed to be warm. She could not recall ever being as cold as she was now or had been and she was dimly aware that the fact she felt nothing now was her body actually beginning to shut down, its way of saving energy and focussing on her internal organs and she also knew this was a pretty bad sign. Up ahead the torchlight picked out the small bundle of sticks, some blackened and charred and others new and untouched sitting in a small cone, waiting to be lit, waiting for Hazel to come light it.

  She dropped to her knees and wrenched her pack off, moaning at the pain in her ribs, her shoulder, her knee, her hands and she vaguely wondered how badly she had hurt herself tonight. However, she was also organised and she knew exactly what she was after and where to find it. She yanked open a side pocket and pulled out a small plastic bag which contained a wad of cotton wool and an old orange zippo lighter, a relic from her university days. Before leaving for this place she had refilled the zippo and also thrown the lighter fluid into the bag for good measure. Hands barely able to grab the cotton wool, she placed it between the wood and then tried desperately to strike the zippo. Her hands were so numb. She brought them to her mouth and blew on them, begging them to respond, to do her bidding like they had always done. She could barely hold the zippo now, her hands were shaking violently but she tried again and suddenly there was fire; a bright, solid flame, wavering before her face. She lowered it towards the wool, both hands clutching the lighter tightly and eventually the flame touched the wool and it took, and it burned, and the wood above begun to curl and catch and then there was a fire, and heat, and she put her hands out towards the flames and she smiled at the feeling, at how she may have been down, but she wasn't out. Not yet.

  Her hands tingled as the warmth of the fire began to undo the storm's work. She was still shivering violently but she was out of the wind and the rain. Her teeth chattered painfully and as the fire grew, she could make out piles of driftwood all along the cave's wall, as if put there. She shone the torch back to where she now sat, looking for the sleeping bag she had seen on her last visit.

  There it was, off to the left, several metres away, just as she remembered it, but with no figure in it this time. A dirty red in the torchlight. She looked away, scared, remembering the figure that she thought she had seen it in.

  That I did see.

  She added more wood, the light of the fire growing, showing her even more of the cave. As feeling returned, she pulled off her gaiters, boots, jacket, hat, spreading them out around her then shuffling closer to the crackling blaze. Small tendrils of steam curled and eddied up from her damp leggings and top and she was mindful not to get to close. The numbing properties of cold could very easily allow her to sit too close to the flames, burning her without her even knowing.

She span on her bottom, allowing the heat of the fire to caress her back and neck. She shone the torch towards the back of the cave, to where darkness met the orange glow of the fire, to who knew where. This torch was more than up to the task, slicing through the murk with ease. She was sure that her boys, and the rest of them, were back there also, deeper under the mountain. Where else would or could they be? Yet there was no sign of them, no sound of them, and she had no doubt that sound carried very well in this echo chamber, the crackling of the fire ricocheting easily off the walls being the only sound. She blew into each hand, alternating between the torch, shining the beam down towards the darkness. She winced as the heat on her back grew and moved again, facing the fire, opening her legs to trap as much heat as she could. She still shivered, she was still bitterly cold. She cast the torchlight again, this time seeing a new symbol, painted in white on the opposite wall. Had it always been there? It was a new symbol again. A series of circles, linked one over the other with jagged lines crisscrossing. It meant nothing to her, but it did remind her of the symbols that had been carved into Kenny's side. The boy she had left out there to die.

Her mind refused to allow her to dwell on what she had seen out there. She pictured his bulging eyes and chattering teeth, his black hands, how he had sounded. She remembered the rope well enough, and the symbols carved into his skin. The symbol had been sliced into him, rough, jagged lines, and she wondered if the elements had done enough to numb him from the pain he would have felt. Why did he say no? Why didn't he want saved? Why had he called her mother?

She looked back to the symbol on the cave wall, frowning now, had it changed? It seemed like it had but obviously it hadn't. There seemed to be new shapes added now. She ignored it, even if it had changed, what could she hope to do? She was somewhere else now. And pretty fucking helpless to do anything. Her friends were dead, murdered, and so was that boy. She couldn't focus on this. She had one job, find her boys and get them off Muchach. That was it. She could process everything later, dwell on the details and jump two footed into as many panic attacks as she wanted but, right now, she needed this Hazel. The Hazel who jumped out of attic doors, who spat in men's faces, who could light fires when most needed.

She hugged herself again, embracing the warmth, pushing it against her freezing skin. She added some larger branches, eyes gazing upwards, watching the orange sparks drift upwards to the roof of the cave then returning to watch the flames lick at the new wood, sniffing out its new prey, taking hold and blackening what had once been alive. The shadows moved and swelled in the firelight. She was drowsy and she knew it was dangerous to sleep in this state but she wasn't too bad she reasoned. I was pretty cold but not dangerously cold, I think I'd wake up if I slept.

It's the morning though. The boys are out there somewhere, *in here* somewhere, and you don't have time to sleep. She turned again, rearranging her damp clothing and then sitting with her back to the fire again. She picked up the torch and shone it into the recesses of the cave, the beam still unable to pierce the darkness.

She looked over to the sleeping bag, frowning, it lay next to her, within reaching distance, the top side open and pulled back invitingly. *Was it like that earlier?* The deep red of the material shone in the fire light. There was a pillow also, she didn't remember the pillow being there either but it was so tempting.

If I just lay on it, she reasoned. *Just a nap. I need it.*

The fire once again began to burn her back and she spun once more, this time gasping at the symbol on the wall, three times as big as earlier easily and this time definitely different. Her eyes roved the lines, the imperfect symmetry, the shapes and as she looked, she derived meaning. It meant something to her this time. Although, the lines were moving this time, the symbol was moving, changing, before her eyes, changing. The shadows around her seemed to be moving in around her but she was fixated on the evolving symbol before her. What did it mean? It was old. Very old. As old as this hill she was under maybe. Derived when the very land was still forming Next to her she was aware of a black shape slowly moving out of the shadows, moving closer to her but panic was a distant relative now, someone she barely knew, she was transfixed by the undulating lines before her, moving together and breaking like water and she had no way of pulling her eyes from it. The figure to her left grew closer, the breathing, that guttural breathing, growing closer. In her periphery she could see the shape of its head, a white eye, coming closer. The smell of the fire was gone now, the light of the fire was gone now, it was dark, and cold, so very cold, and yet, she was unperturbed.

"Mother," it said.

Chapter 13

And she's awake, and it is daytime. Bright and crisp and warm, blue skies overhead and the sun, the sun is hot on her back.

There was music too. Drums and a whistle and singing. She turns her head and she is not alone. There are hundreds and hundreds of people around her, all walking with her, some smiling, others less so and some with grave expressions but all walking, walking with her. Are they following her? It feels like they're following her.

Who is she?

She wears a simple white gown and nothing more, it is thin and delicate but it is a warm day and she is comfortable.

She reaches for her name; her identity, but it alludes her, like the remnants of a vivid dream, on the tip of her tongue, but when she reaches for it, tries to speak it and thereby conjure up the memory, it fades, diminishes, yet she does not feel despair at this, does not weep at her loss of self for she has a purpose. She knows this. She has a purpose and that is why they follow her, to see her purpose enacted. For them.

A cool breeze blows through her hair and she can feel her gown lift and sigh on this brightest of days, she reaches outwards and feels hands clasp hers, children's hands, trusting and pure and full of love. She looks down at their faces and smiles and then winces as she stands on a small stone, hidden in the grass, but even this is a gift. A sign for her, that there is no escaping pain, that life has hidden surprises but that they can not stop your journey, nor should they, and her next step onto the cool, soft grass is the most beautiful step she has ever taken, the sensation heightened by the pain of the step before.

The music swells and they approach the circle, smoke billows and eddies and she can see the   a' tabhann awaiting them, clad in robes of blue. The crowd envelope them, stroking their hair, hugging them tight, tears of joy stream down many faces. The smoke envelopes them for a moment and she senses the intoxication that this smoke holds. Yet the a' tabhann's reactions vary. Some are still in the grip of the herbs and mushrooms they have ingested over the last several days, some writhe on the floor, lost in communion with the soil, other gibber and speak the language of the root, some lie with each other, naked and fertile and so very alive, others smile at the approaching crowd, standing to greet and be greeted, to be loved and seen and thanked for what they do. Other a' *tabhann* are quiet, and do not smile as the crowd swarms them, yet they do not turn away, and they do not resist the hands and the touching, and their stillness, to her, seems the most profound for she knows they have not partaken of the earth's gifts, they want to experience the *Ceangal* for what it is, have no senses dulled, have no sensation denied them. She holds them in her hands, she whispers in their ears, she holds them close as some sob at what awaits, and she stills their fear and stills their pounding hearts and thanks them for what they choose and they in turn thank her and she feels the import of all that they do here and she breathes in the fumes from a nearby fire and delights as the smoke billows in colours she has never experienced, feeling her feet come away from the soil and becoming part of the air and floating high above, high above it all.

She can look down on the thousands that flock around the *altharr,* the crowd billowing and flowing like the water that surrounds them, like the air and smoke that they breathe, like the grass that moves with it all and she weeps with joy and turns, as if in answer, to the Lorrsayeth, the Dhia, the earth itself, and it raises it's mighty head, so vast that the crowd below are cast into shadow, so fast that waves 100 spans high race away from the shore to the endless skies and as the people scream in terror and awe and love and humility Muchach opens its eye, brighter than the sun herself, blinding her and bids them come for it is time.

She lies on her back. She is panting. Her legs splayed wide. The days have been long and warm and her body aches, for food, for water, for shelter. She notices the children first, she always has. Some cry, others are curled up in groups against the fingers of the *altharr*, whilst others still run and play despite the long days. Waste is strewn amongst them, the smell of their dung offensive in this place yet, what can they do? People still sing and dance, others sit in groups and discuss what people have always discussed, other sit in commune with the *a' tabhann* or with the soil itself, they have partaken of the root, their eyes are black and they are in commune with *Lorrsayeth* itself. Some sleep, huddled together, others love as we have always done but when she stands, brushing her white gown down, the place fall to a deathly hush for the first time. She doesn't speak, just turns, and begins to walk towards *Lorrsayeth* and the path it has provided.

A great sound arises from behind her, a thrilling sound from the thousands who have gathered here, rapture and terror and excitement in one sound and her stomach twists at the anticipation and macabre dread of what is to come. The great healing.

And once again she is walking, crowd at her back. It isn't as warm now. She feels the toll the past days of celebration have had on her, the ache in her bones, the chill of the wind, the lack of sleep, but it all leads to this moment and now she steps onto broken stones and rock and this time there is no relief in the next step. This is a path they all walk, one they all need to walk, one that reminds them that life will always provide difficult but necessary paths to deliverance. Some cry out, but not many, and she is mindful not to wince or hobble like those around her do. She is mindful that, although she feels the rocks beneath her, just as the others do, she is their mother, and she is the way to *Lorrsayeth* and its wisdom and the healing and that pain is fleeting. She is aware of the power she holds and although unasked for, it is hers alone and her bidding to show others the way to light.

On she walks, for hours and hours, and though she doesn't look down once, she knows her feet are in bloody tatters, ribbons of skin cut and peeled and torn from her feet, and she knows many will have similar and she knows that all are still with her. It is a quiet procession, yet you cannot hide the of thousands of feet and again she smiles as the sun shines out bright as she crests the last peak and sees the *Snuadh* ahead.

Standing there waiting is the *Dalyn Goffri*, just as she knew he would be, just as he has been for every healing, his appearance unchanged, his face exactly the same as it had been when she first saw him when she barely old enough to walk, a gnarled stick clutched in his left hand. He is motionless and even the high breeze seems to leave his long hair and garments alone.

She joins him at the ledge, turns and greets those who limp and hobble behind her. No tiredness or pain does she show, just warmth and love. The *a' tabhann* arrive and make their way to the front, the crowd parting, singing the Song of the Stones as a lone bonepipe plays. Some of the *a' tabhann* accept the herbs and mushrooms proffered them, this will bring them closer to the soil and closer to Lorrsayeth and others shake their heads, many with tears rolling down their dirty, loved faces. One younger has soiled himself, the reality of his position loosening his bowels. He lowers his gaze and backs away shaking his head, choosing to not partake in The Healing. She approaches him and softly asks if he is sure. He says he is. She kisses his cheek and allows him to leave, the crowd swallowing him up. There is no shame here. No consequence. All *a' tabhann* are willing, have offered themselves, some are children, some are elders, some know their time is limited and have existing ills but all are willing, all want to experience the love of Muchach, of *Lorrsayeth*, and all want to heal this land for their families and love of the earth.

Another song begins, this one a twisted and lonely song, started by the *Dalyn Goffri*, the ancient druid to her left. He is from distant lands; far, far, far from the south, his words and rhythm so different from what she knows, his beard twisted and matted with the bones and sinew of small animals entwined within. The song is a rattling, archaic dirge that she has always hated, ever since she first heard it herself as a young girl at this same spot. The language he uses is older than her own and it offends her deeply, yet she couldn't say why. He hasn't changed, this man, his skin brown and leathery, faded black and blue marks covering his skin apart from where his light grey hair sprouts. Yet, for every Healing she has been to, and this is her seventh, her third as Mother, this song has always been sung. This song that so upsets her, that causes her skin to itch and her hairs stand on end. She never sees this man other than at these moments, and she has often searched for him, to know his name or how he alone knows this song, yet she has never seen him beyond these moments on the *Snuadh*, but, amongst the *a' tabhann*, there is a moment when the healing can begin, and it begins when his song starts.

At the terrible harmony, a young a' tabhann, no older than eleven winters, walks calmly to the cliff edge and steps off.

There is no sound from the crowd, no movement, only an awed reverence and the old man's lonely song.

As if preordained, an older woman now steps forward and stands at the edge of the cliff top. Her long brown hair lifts and falls in the warm breeze. She holds out a hand and another woman from the crowd, one of the *crach*, her head wrapped in linen dyed a deep red, places a sharpened stone into it before returning to her place. The red haired woman doesn't turn. Her back to the crowd, she breathes deeply several times before they see her arm start sawing back and forth and then a torrent of blood and viscera spill from her, hitting the stone floor in a series of wet slaps. The woman lets out a moan and falls to her knees, blood pooling around her. She crawls forward, her entrails dragging out behind her and turns onto her back, propping herself up against a boulder, cradling her insides like a new-born. She smiles, her eyes glazed and nods. The murmur of awe that the crowd make is genuine. This woman has chosen *freth grethalc*, the Sacrifice of Days. She will remain at this boulder until Muchach deems fit, feeding the beasts and birds, the crawling and buzzing life that live on it feeding off her destroyed body. The pain will be exquisite, the Mother knows. She has heard the screams from the mountain on previous occasions which can last for days and she feels a profound love for this woman who offers so much for them. The *crach* will leave water for her if she desires to prolong her days further.

The healing continues for hours. One man, a similar age to her, sunken eyes looking out of dark sockets has each bone broken in turn before being cast over the side, two *crach,* one man, one woman, methodically lifting and smashing rocks down onto his limbs and torso the dull thumps and soft whimpers barely audible over the song of the *Dalyn Goffri*, before hurling him over the ledge onto the brutal rocks and foaming see that waits below. Another has his limbs removed by saw, another his head, their screams, if they do scream, are stifled by their adoration of the *Lorrsayeth*, others stifled by the connection the mushrooms and herbs have provided. One young *a' tabhann* has his back broken by a rock and is then hung by his feet upside down from the *Snuadh*, another long, drawn out *freth grethalc* and again she marvels at their selflessness, their fortitude, their love. Another, deep in communion with the root, eyes black with connection, peels his arm before burning himself, all with a serene smile on his lips, only when the flames really begin to bite and his hair and beard start to burn does he scream. All the while the crowd are silent, the druid sings his song as the sun moves across the sky and the shadows begin to lengthen.

Not many remain now, and each has been more painful and excruciating than the last, each designed to bring the person closer to Muchach, to know it's ways, to honour the earth and bring forth life. Blood covers the stone, trickling and pooling amongst them. No one moves their feet to avoid the red tide that flows among them, the feeling of the oily liquid brings them all closer to those who save them. She had considered being *a' tabhann* not long after her moons had started, but she had never followed this notion, and, having seen them, she knew she lacked the conviction and depth of courage these people have. She knew her path lay elsewhere, in guidance and direction, in nurture and compassion, in helping those *a' tabhann* on their path, identifying those who could one day be their saviours. She envies them, for now their suffering is over, they are now one with the earth, one with *Lorrsayeth*, they are in the soil and the root, the water and the clay and they will be remembered, in song and in verse for evermore for they had saved their people from starvation.

The last to go is an elder, easily over 40 winters and stooped low, hobbling on bloody feet though whether the blood is hers or *a' tabhann* is unknown. Her long hair is streaked with silver. She starts with her eyelids -

Hazel awoke with a scream, looking directly into the black face, wide yellowed eyes staring down at her and she screamed again, lashing out in panic and terror and then she was alone in the black. The darkness was absolute, as was the silence. Her heart slammed against her chest, as she writhed in an ecstasy of horror and panic. She gripped the sides of her head and screamed and screamed and screamed. The screams echoed back to her and shot around the cave, reverberating and looping against the fresh ones that ripped from her. Her throat was raw and slowly her screams subsided into a low mewling, she pushed her head along the floor, bunching the sleeping bag material and her legs pushed out behind her, try as she might the images of the mutilation, the pain and suffering she had just seen *for what seemed like hours* refused to leave her head.

She lay in that position for several long minutes, head on the ground, butt pointed upwards, knees aching against the stone floor, breathing slowly, desperately calling for blankness, something to null the images that had seared their way into her mind. She willed the blackness, embraced the silence and just controlled her breathing. The low funk of the sleeping bag was the first sensation she was aware of as she slowly came to. The foul odour creeping into her nose and dragging her back to full consciousness. A deep, coastal smell of decay and corruption. It brought to mind the stench of the seaweed piles she would walk past when on holiday as a girl, the warm, overpowering stench of tonnes of seaweed, cleared into huge mounds which would sit out in the sun for days, reeking. She opened her eyes but needn't have bothered at she was surrounded by a darkness so absolute that not a single thing could be seen. She slowly pushed herself up so she was on her hands and knees and turned her head slowly, searching for the dull embers of the fire but there was nothing. Slowly she carefully began to grope around, patting her immediate area hoping to land on the reassuring chunkiness of her torch. She widened her arc each time, rotating and searching all around her but she found nothing. She put her hands into the remains of the fire, feeling the charred, crumbling remains of the wood – it was cold. How long had she lain here?

Panic returned with a smile, brushing it's cold, electric fingers up her back and she whimpered. Here she was again. Terrified. The urge to curl up small and close her eyes was strong and she succumbed, lowering herself painfully down, her rib agony as she folded inwards, wrapping her arms around her legs. The pit of cold fear in her stomach was gnawing again. She was cold. She was hungry. Her clothes felt dry but the cave was far from warm and the brief respite the fire had provided was long gone. She ached and took her time moving, again she had the sense that she wasn't alone in that cave.

Slowly she pushed herself up, the dark so pure that she had a moment of vertigo and almost fell as a dizzy spell pulled at her. She began to move her feet out slowly, hoping to brush the torch with one foot but there was nothing. Then she remembered her lighter, the zippo she had used to light the fire with. She checked her coat pockets and found it straight away. Hazel flicked it open and struck the wheel twice before it caught. The light was blinding at first, such had been the dark, and she had to squint painfully, but as her eyes adjusted her heart stopped as hundreds of faces were illuminated by the tiny flame.

She shrieked and clasped the lighter closed with a loud snap that rang out softly in the chamber. She stood there panting, head down, trying to regain control of her heart.

She counted silently in her head. *It's not real. You're stressed. You're hallucinating. Calm yourself. It's not real. You're stressed. You're hallucinating. Calm Yourself.*

She restruck the lighter and slowly opened her eyes.

The first thing she saw were feet. All caked in old blood and mud, scarred and mutilated. She brought her hand to her mouth and gazed out at the sea of faces. They all looked at her in mute indifference. She could see some with physical wounds; missing eyes, broken limbs, head trauma all staring at her with pale, lifeless eyes. All in blue gowns, many mutilated beyond comprehension, many more drenched in the dark crimson of their blood. She sensed no threat from them though, no malice, but their very presence was causing her to breathe too quickly and her heart was still racing.

"Hello?" she said quietly to them but there was no reply. She held the lighter tight to her chest, turning her entire upper body to look round, she was surrounded and the press seemed to stretch out in all directions.

Suddenly there was an audible shifting, the shuffling of feet on stone and the group began to move. As one they parted, offering her a path. It was narrow and although she had no idea of her bearings, she had no doubt it took her deeper under the mountain. A deeper part of her knew these were the *a' tabhann* she had witnessed when she had been the other woman – the Mother. How many were there? Hundreds? Thousands? All that pain! All that suffering. For what end? What was it for? When she had been the other woman, there had been the belief that the suffering was for a cause. And what had Gav said? That it renewed the land? The sea of mutilation before her was a testament to that deeply held belief but the sheer horror of it was beyond anything she could have ever imagined.

Hazel stepped forward and breathed slowly, calming her mind once again, then took another step. Her foot kicked something heavy and she bent quickly, grasping the torch tightly. A small victory. Switching it on she gasped at the brightness and the bright white faces it exposed. Many of the bodies were adult but smaller shapes also looked up at her in mute neutrality. She struggled to see over the surrounding heads but she felt that the cave was full with these pale folk. She gasped as a woman with both ears missing grinned dumbly at her from a toothless, blood stained mouth, dried blood caked in her hair and naked shoulders. She shone the torch forwards down the beckoning path and started walking, head down.

She was calmer now and focussed on the floor before her as the figures either side of her continued to watch her but with an ambivalence that gave her the courage to keep moving. It wasn't long before the path of bodies began to veer slightly, and she surmised she must be well under the mountain now. The path was also sloping downwards, and she wondered where it would eventually take her. She tried to avoid the ghastly sites that surrounded her but occasionally she would see a bone protruding from flesh or a sightless, gouged socket and remember where she was and what was happening but she also felt slightly detached from it, as she was certain that she should be on all fours screaming and pleading for the nightmare to end yet she continued to put one foot in front of the other and acknowledged that she was in some way curious to see where she was heading. It wasn't long before she found out.

As if there was any doubt, the black figure awaited her.

It was the smell that told her of its presence. The foul, rotten odour that had accompanied its every visit. The path tapered away and Hazel felt she was in a much larger chamber now. Again, her torch struggled to illuminate the darkness and then that stink was in her nostrils and she brought the torch down ahead of her.

Sitting in a small pool was the figure. Hazel moaned softly, in fear or disgust or hatred and she saw the figure's mouth turn up into a broken smile. Small broken teeth and white eyes the only indicator of a face. Its black oily hair hung matted to its head and it lolled back, supported by its arms, legs splayed in a vaguely obscene manner. Another wave of repulsion washed over her but the figure kept smiling and gestured for Hazel to enter the pool also. Her light showed the pool to be filled with an inky black liquid which didn't look very much like water. She hesitated and looked around, the figures stood dotted around her and she looked to see if she could figure out the way she had come; she had a vague idea but she doubted she would make it very far. The option to leave wasn't on the table at all.

She moved closer to the pool and the figure hissed at her. It gestured at her in anger and Hazel stopped in her tracks. My clothes. I need to take off my clothes. She quickly unzipped her jacket, shrugging it off before removing the rest of her gear. She wasn't cold and strangely, she didn't feel self-conscious. There was no leering from the figure and Hazel realised she hadn't assigned a sex to the black thing that was looking at her. As she peeled off her sock, she looked closer, slowly realising that it was indeed feminine. Its skin was covered in a black, oily tar which slowly oozed across its body. Yet, beneath that, the small swell of breasts could be made out, the splayed legs were now obviously female; slender and long. She was naked now, warm, standing before this creature with no shame or self-consciousness. The woman's hair was long and matted, and her smile was one of invitation.

Her eyes are wide and Hazel cannot shake the feeling of déjà vu which now washes over her – she has been here before – she is certain of it. Calmly she steps into the pool and the tingle of pleasure at the liquid's warmth is almost erotic. The deep heat coming from the pool spreads through her and she shudder again as she lowers herself in, hands then buttocks breaking the surface of the oil. Deeper and deeper she sinks into the oil, for that is what it is, an oil so black it's almost blue, and no fetid, chemical stench of crude oil made for machines; this oil is a warm embrace, the rotten seaweed smells fading, changing, turning into the smell of life, of vibrancy, energy and light and growth and love and all the while Hazel's eyes are locked on the figure's and as the oil rises over Hazel's hips she realises there is nothing to fear here. Deeper she sinks as the woman sits above and the pool is now impossibly big. She is happy now, so warm, and secure. Dimly she is aware that the other woman still seems to recline on top of the oil whilst Hazel sinks deeper and deeper, eye level to her open legs Hazel breathes out and allows the oil to cover her head.

Chapter 14

A fire snaps and crackles as an orange twilight bathes the world in warmth and shadow. A slight breeze dances softly around her, bringing a chill. A rough blanket is wrapped around her tightly and she is grateful for the warm fur wrapping her feet and legs. The heat of the fire is welcome and in her hand she clasps a stone bowl containing a piping hot stew of some kind. The smell is intoxicating and she sips it gently, grateful to have this sustenance provided for her.

Across the fire sits a woman; *the woman.* Her deep brown eyes peer at Hazel from across the dancing flames. She wears a similar blanket and holds a similar bowl of steaming broth. She has a long, dark, handsome face and the freckles that dust her nose only accentuate her beauty. "Hello Hazel," she says. Her voice is calm and strong although her accent is untraceable.

"Hello," she replies and sips again. She doesn't feel worried here but there is a deep pit of questions inside her. "Who are you?" she asks. "Where are my boys?"

"They're here, with us," the woman answers smiling. "I am Aila, you are Hazel, and you are very welcome here."

Hazel sipped her broth. It was delicious. "Could you please tell me where I am and tell me what's happening?" Her calm and sense of security wobbled as her emotions struggled to engage with what she was seeing and she closed her eyes tightly, squeezing the warm bowl, feeling the heat seep into her hands. "I just...I don't......I cant....stand...what is happening. I can't handle this. Aila. What is happening here? What is going on?" Again, a small heartbeat of terror bloomed inside her before the warmth stilled it.

"It's just your time, you are becoming the mother and you must leave the boys to themselves. They will be fine. It is you who needs time and care." Aila sipped her bowl and smiled. "Lorrsayeth," and she gestured around her, "This place, this land, these people – need a mother." Hazel felt a small droplet of ice-cold fear begin to trickle down her spine.

"Bu-"

"I have been mother for too long now. I ache. I am so very hungry and so very, very tired and need to move on."

"What do you mean?" asked Hazel. "What on earth do you mean? Mother? I am a mother? To two boys and we just want to leave. We want to go home."

Aila smiled a warm smile, a smile filled with sympathy and yet vaguely patronising, a smile that pities a small child who hasn't yet grasped a simple concept. Hazel hated that smile, noticing the lines that bunched around Aila's eyes and mouth, and neck, when she fucking smiled like that. "You are home Hazel," she said in her odd dialect, a voice that seemed so old now. So very, very old.

"No Aila," Hazel replied patiently. "I live in the town of Kilmarriton, and we need to go home. Please help us? As a woman. If you've ever been a mother. Why can't we go home?"

"There is no home now. There is no *there*," and her voice changed a wee bit. Rougher. There was contempt in that voice. Hazel decided she didn't like it. Didn't like her accent and didn't like this woman. She noticed darker strands in Aila's pale brown hair and her freckles stood out angrier now. "This is your home. I am away to sleep and dream on Muchach," and the guttural, spittal filled pronouncement of that word filled Hazel with a deep disgust, "I have been Mother for far too long. This is why the land dies, this is why it all fails. I can no longer summon the *a' tabhann* for who would flock to this? You will bring them Mother, you will guide them and love them. You will teach them to sing with *Lorrsayeth* and allow it the chance to soar up, to bless the lands, to bless the earth and waters; the very air." She took another swig from her bowl, spilling some of the dark liquid on her chin but if she noticed, she didn't care as her voice rose. "This very place is soiled. The waters are empty and poisonous, the land grows weaker, the life it provides almost gone. As a mother, you guide, you help renew, you encourage." At this last word she let out a small hacking burp, "You cannot go Hazel. You must guide more to Muchach. Bring them. In their thousands, help them give. Help them love. Love them, as you love your children, help your children." A small, black column of liquid was running from Aila's mouth. Hazel could hear the desperation below Aila's words. It seemed like a plea from a beggar rather than the command of a jailer.

"I'm sorry Aila, but you've got the wrong person. I'm getting off Muchach. I'm getting my boys and we're going home."

The woman opposite her groaned and smiled. "Where would you go? Where does one run to when all is gone? If there are no safe bays or shelters of provision, why move your feet at all? There is sickness, and you see it and if you run, you run to naught." Hazel could see slow tendrils of black oil slowly running through Aila's hair, one began to pour slowly down her forehead, between her eyes, following the curves of her brow and nose as another began to roll down the side of her face. Her voice became more guttural as she spoke. Hazel began to feel cold now. In fact, she was freezing. She clutched her blanket tighter but it was gone, everything was gone, she sat huddled and naked. "I have been mother for far too long. Isolated and alone with scant children to care for. I am spent and cannot renew. It must be you, for there is no one else. There never was anyone else, I have been waiting for so very long. It must be you." Black, oozing oil began to flow freely down from her head now, running over her eyes and lips and she smiled. "It must be you."

Hazel's eyes opened and she almost fell backwards. She was sat in a foot of freezing water. Her torch sat to one side, illuminating her pile of clothes. She leapt from the pool quickly and scrambled to her clothing, thrusting them on, praying for warmth. She was cold down to the bone and her hands trembled as she tried to grab buttons but they could barely close, all strength and power gone. Of the horde that had accompanied her to the pool, there was no sign. Pulling her damp hat down onto her damp hair, she thought about her next course of action. Her teeth chattered loudly as she drew her fleece top round her. She had no idea where she was but the pool gave her a rough idea and so she pushed on further into the darkness.

She had no idea how long she had been there, under the mountain. No idea how long the pool had held her for or how long she had been speaking to Aila. She was exhausted, but she carried on, stumbling forward in the darkness, deliberately ignoring the fact that the torch light was dimming perceptibly and that her field of vision was shrinking quickly. She was mumbling softly to herself, extolling herself to keep going, to keep putting one foot in front of the other, but she knew that she could only keep going for so long. It felt like she had been walking for hours. Everything ached, she was rubbed raw in places where wet fabric had chafed and she had developed a couple of blisters.

On she went.

She would occasionally quell a rising panic that insisted she was doomed, that she was lost down here and that she would never be found again; that the torch of her battery would die quicker than her and that she would soon be stumbling around in the pitch black, dehydrated and disorientated before spraining an ankle and falling to the floor. Hurting, blind and lost, she would drag herself onwards, calling for her boys, increasingly desperate and increasingly faint, until she couldn't anymore.

Until her energy left her and she stopped moving for a bit, stopped for a rest maybe, slept for a spell. And woke up weaker, and colder, and hungrier until she died, wherein she would stay there and rot, fall apart piece by piece, still clad in her hi-tech outdoor gear, her empty sockets staring into the blackness, flies landing and planting their eggs, her eyes being the first to be eaten by whatever lived in the depths, worms-

No. Shut Up. That's Old Hazel. Keep going. Find them.

So she did, she kept walking and eventually she realised that the torch had died, that she was walking completely blind. She banged it several times but nothing happened so she threw it away. She kept walking, slower now, one foot in front of the other. She switched off, just arms out before her, feet gingerly testing the ground ahead. Occasionally she would stumble or trip, she would whimper or gasp, she would fight the urge to stop, to collapse. She was so tense. Everything ached. Once she walked into the cold dampness of the cave wall but then that became her guide, one arm always touching the wall, the other held out in front. And then, suddenly, she thought she could see the ridges of the wall. The ceiling was discernible without the torch, and soon the walls and floor too. It wasn't light she knew, it was just less dark and up ahead a large opening was clear against the grey sky. She sobbed in relief and picked up her pace, a slight limp to her gait due to the painful blisters but nothing worth stopping for.

The sound of waves could be heard and she wondered where on the island she was. She emerged to a cold but much calmer and dryer Muchach, an icy breeze slapping her to full alertness. She breathed deeply of the sharp sea air and ran her eyes over the terrain. Large, black rocks rolled down to meet the blue ocean which broke in white plumes upon them. She was grateful to be out of the darkness, but any relief was smothered by her realisation of how cold it was and her desperation to locate Daryl and Marcus. It was bitter and the unforgiving wind was quickly exploiting her damp clothing, leaching the meagre warmth she had managed to generate. She briefly considered heading back into the cave to get another fire started but there was no neatly stacked piles of wood to be seen and she couldn't afford the time. She looked around in a vain attempt to find any kind of path away from the cave mouth but knew it was a hopeless gesture – when had the island made any part of this easy? Of course, there was no path. She began to pick her way slowly Northwards, clambering over the large, uneven boulders.

Again, passage was painfully slow. Her heels were agony where the blisters had now been rubbed raw, she shook with cold and exhaustion and she could barely see ahead of her. She had spent much of the day inside the mountain, her watch reading 3:39pm. Several times she had caught herself before slipping, a foot sliding on slippery algae or a rock moving under her weight. On occasion she had been forced to sit down, lowering herself down gingerly onto the next plateau. Her legs trembled, from tiredness or shock she couldn't say but the tremor was building. Her blind walk through the cave and now this, the state of tension she was in, her neck and back still ached fiercely, her feet were sharp bites of pain, her breathing was becoming more ragged, and, despite her efforts, she could not warm up, the merciless coast wind exploiting any gap in her clothing.

It was exhausting, up and down, over and over, banging her shins and scraping her hands despite the gloves she wore. Eventually she came to a stop, hands on hips taking deep lungful's of brutally cold air before squirreling herself backwards into a crevice, away from the wind's grasping fingers. She clutched her knees to herself and lowered her head, rocking softly, willing herself to warm up. Her teeth chattered and she could imagine what she must look like, wet hair escaping her soggy beanie, plastered to her face like dark tentacles, blue lips thin and peeled back against chattering teeth. Her strength was gone and she knew she couldn't last much longer.

She sat like that for some time, rocking slowly, breathing, trembling, tears running silently down her cold skin. She was so deeply miserable it felt like a physical pain. The cold had her and was not letting go. She had failed. The boys could be anywhere, on the other side of the fucking island or in bloody France for all she knew. They could be on the other side of the giant boulder she now sat at and she doubted she could find the strength to clamber over it. The trials she had been through, the steel she had recently found within her, the sheer defiance of life and the shit it continued to throw at her, it all meant nothing. She was done.

She rolled softly onto her side, curling up tighter, the cover she had found still not completely protecting her from the incessant gusts that rose and dipped above and around her, the rock she lay on gleefully pulling more heat from her.

There was no panic now though. No mounting hysteria or mind scouring anxiety attack that would leave her spent. She wondered if that was because she had conquered that part of her mind, that aspect that couldn't deal with her daily life, that allowed her to become swamped and flicked the panic switch or if her body just knew it didn't have the resources for such fireworks anymore. If subconsciously, some internal management had just said we just cant afford that today.

Little matter, she was done. But done was not finished however, there was a difference. She knew she was going to crank back up to her feet at some point. She knew she would keep clambering over those bastard rocks until she couldn't anymore, but she also knew that it wouldn't amount to anything, that her boys were far from here, probably back in the centre with their new pals, oblivious to their mother's plight, uncaring and maybe even glad. Delighted perhaps, delighted at their new freedom and autonomy and at this moment, she hated them.

Hated them for their lack of loyalty, the betrayal, the abandonment, of not needing her. She had given them everything, she had put her very being into raising them, of shielding them from the monster that had helped create them, and they, in return, had saved her; had given her a reason to keep on, day after day.

And yet, had they not also been the anchor with which she had remained tethered to her misery? Had they not been the reason she could not escape? What mother would leave her children to live with evil whilst she fled? They had prevented her from escaping, hadn't they?

And now, because of them, she was here; freezing, lost, alone on an isolated island off the coast of Scotland with no chance of being found, no chance of being rescued and brought to safety, no chance of the three of them snuggling up on the couch with the fire on, watching TV. The tears continued to roll gently, hot for a scant second, before the island turned them cold.

Did she deserve this? Had she been a bad mother to them? Neglectful? Why had they left her? She had saved them! Got them away from that madman, that cold, spiteful man who used words as well as any butcher with his knife, carefully dissecting and reducing his family with an ease and callousness that could be breathtakingly spiteful.

It had been his slow redirection of his bile towards the children that had finally prompted her to get out of that marriage. To gather the remaining strands of who she had once been and push with all her might against his control, to get herself, and her children out of that poisonous atmosphere before they too became like her, a ghost, functioning and alive but not really there, not really anywhere, just an apparition that people noticed out of the corner of their eye, who sailed through their days, undistinguished and unremarked upon, day after day. Beaten down and dismissed by that which is supposed to love and value you the most until you yourself fail to see your worth.

It had been a Saturday. She and the boys had been to Daryl's football where his team had won 6-4. Daryl was goalkeeper and had had a good match. She had had her bags of shopping and was considering making an early start on the food. He had been in his armchair watching a Netflix documentary and something in her had just splintered, like cheap plaster. It was the lie she was telling herself, even as she walked past him into the kitchen, the lie she repeated just lost all meaning. She hated him. She was miserable. She wanted a divorce. There was no lightbulb, no revelation, just a cold certainty that her life was a joke. Everything she had dreamt of was gone. She had no dreams now, harboured no ambition, just a daily, fervent desire to stay on his good side.

She had walked back into the living room. She had begun to talk and he had held his hand up, and she had stopped, waiting for him to watch whatever it was until he was ready. Finally, he had paused the television and looked to her.

"I want a divorce," she had said.

"No," he had replied, and pressed play.

"I want you out of this house. Today. I have a lawyer. I have the police on speed dial. I have friends who can help me. If you say no, I'll phone the police right now." Her heart had been trip hammering in her chest. Her voice had wobbled ridiculously, and she had felt the urge to pee as he had looked directly at her. She had wanted to rewind to a minute before. She wished she hadn't said anything and was right now chopping potatoes and slugging on an overly generous glass of wine.

He had risen slowly, never taking his eyes off her. *It's now* she thought. *This is where he hits me, or beats me, or kills me* and it had taken every ounce of power to not whimper as he moved closer. She held up a shaking hand, the number of the police clear on the screen, her thumb above the call button.

"I'll go Hazel. For now. I'll go. You're having a moment. That's clear to see. I'll go to mum and dad's. I'll be back tomorrow and we'll have a chat, when you're more rational." He had taken his coat from the stand and slipped his shoes on and turned and said, "But this is my house. Not yours. And if you think I'll just walk away from everything we have then you're more fucking stupid than I thought. I'll burn this place to the fucking ground, with all of us in it, rather than have you think you can just kick me out. You absolute fucking idiot. I'll burn you in your fucking bed." And he had left. And she had walked calmly to the bathroom, locked the door, ran the taps and curled up on the floor, towel forced as deeply into her mouth as she could, lips aching, and screamed and cried and sobbed and shook and finally, when it was done, she had sat up slowly, and smiled.

Then the abuse had begun. The phone calls, the visits, the social media rants. But she had stayed the course. She had dug in. She had had the locks changed. She had had the police out on several occasions, twice when he had been drunk, standing outside the house and three times when she was sure he had been outside the house but couldn't see him. She had had to repair her car and windows more than once, but she had stayed the course.

And now she was here. Freezing to death and alone in the bleak and she was so angry. This wasn't the way it should have gone, her life that is, not the holiday, although it had also gone pretty pear shaped. Just, she had had such potential, such spark, and it had all crumbled to nothing. She had let this man just squeeze and crush her down and done nothing about it. Why had she done nothing for so long? Why had she just allowed the cruelty and undermining? It didn't make sense to her now, lying there on the stone, she couldn't understand how he had done so much damage without her even knowing.

Well, it was done now. And even if it was the end for her, she was not going out lying down, defeated. She had done that for too long. She would dig in.

She got back up to her feet realising that even if she died here, she was proud of herself.

Chapter 15

It was dark and cold but Hazel had somehow managed to flick a switch in her head lessening its bite, that or her body was beginning to shut down again. It didn't matter. On she went and as she did the sky grew dimmer and dimmer. Rocks were barely discernible now and she couldn't see the coastline. However, the boulders were less, scattered between smaller stones, and Hazel was able to plod from rock to rock with greater ease, feeling with her hands and feet as went. She wasn't exactly nimble, not in her condition, but her pace was quicker, and she began to cover ground.

At a certain point she rounded a bluff, the island cutting back in. Waves crashed upon the black rocks ahead and, looking up, she realised she recognised this place. The snout was way above her to her right and across the rolling waves, Hazel felt she could spot the place where her, Marcus and Daryl had eaten their picnic. Up ahead would be the spot where the three of them had lain on their tummies looking down onto these rocks.

Where she and Daryl had seen a corpse, floating in the waves.

Another one.

How many was that now? How many bodies? There had been the boy in the surf maybe, plus Ronnie and Gav, plus the boy tied up in The Eye and the one her and Daryl had seen. She wasn't sure if any of them counted. Such was her state of mind and the vagueness or sheer hallucinatory nature of this week, she would not have been surprised if it turned out that no one had been killed here this week. She pushed on, aware of the looming shelf high above her, black against the greying sky. As she progressed, she realised she was subconsciously scanning for the body her and Daryl thought they had seen. Her blisters were sore, cutting through the fog of exhaustion and she stumbled on, foot over foot, wondering if-

She slipped and her ankle twisted; a white-hot pain lanced up her leg, blocking all else. She screamed in pain and frustration and rage and fell sideways, banging a hip painfully on a rock, her broken rib electrifying in its pain, taking her breath away. She lay there gasping, clutching at her ankle. The pain was sickening, and nausea rolled within her and she tasted bile, her ankle already throbbing against her tight, damp boots. She moaned in agony, unsure what to do. She had fallen into a small pool and freezing water soaked most of her lower body and was making inroads under her jacket, which was somehow colder than her already icy skin. She screamed again and tried to adjust her position; but the slightest movement sent fresh jolts of agony up her leg and every time it did, it seemed to collate in her stomach and make her want to vomit, spit flooding her mouth.

She sobbed once and then tried to control her breathing. There was a detachment to what was happening, a cool rationalism that accepted that this was probably it now. No more walking blindly. No more walking. Just a long, long wait on the shore till she-

Nope. And she heaved herself upright. The pain was horrendous yet less than what she imagined it would be. Okay. And shaking hard, she heaved again and managed to lift herself out of the water, bringing herself to sitting upright. "Okay Purp," she said through chattering teeth. "Not over yet." She sat like that as a fierce trembling took over her. Her teeth rattled together painfully and her whole body was in freefall, shivering and sweating. "This....might........b..b..be the ..e..end..." she murmured to herself and that's when the hand clasped her shoulder and she screamed.

"Mum!" It was Marcus. "You okay?" he asked her, crouching round her.

"Oh Marcus," she said quietly and sobbed quietly into his arm. He held her for a while and she felt herself drifting away

She came to what seemed hours later. Wood smoke filled her nose and she struggled to open her eyes. The first thing she realised was that she was warm. Very warm. And dry. Comfortable would be pushing it. Her hip throbbed, her ankle was also waking up, angry and already sending a sickening throb up her leg but for now, warm and dry was a hell of an improvement.

She listened and heard the low crackle of a fire and the murmur of voices, whispered but also amiable and conversational. She listened harder and there it was: Daryl's high voice, talking.

She opened her eyes and tried to turn her head, her body wailed in protest, everything ached, and she wondered how much damage she had done to herself in the recent days. Her ankle, her head, her ribs, her hip, her knee..

"Mum?" It was Marcus. Definitely.

"Yes love," she replied but her voice was a cracked, raspy thing and she barely heard it herself. She tried to move herself up to a sitting position, but her ankle sent an electric warning and she gasped in pain.

"Woah Mum," came Marcus' voice again. "Don't try and get up."

"Can I get a drink please love?" she croaked. She still couldn't see anything. Her eyes looked upwards to dark sky, masked by swirling smoke, lit orange by the flames. The occasional star could be seen high above, shining brightly.

Cool, crisp water trickled into her mouth and she felt it course down her dry throat and bloom beautifully within her. Awakening further she tried to move again, steeling herself against the inevitable pain and, when it came, she grimaced and turned herself so that she was facing the fire and the source of the voices.

It came as no surprise that it was the entire group sitting round a very large fire, much larger than she had first assumed. Pale faces, many with concern etched across their features, gazed back at her. Marcus crouched close by, water bottle still in hand. "What time is it?" she asked Marcus quietly.

"About six o clock," he replied. It was a still night with barely a breeze.

"You've slept all night and all day mum," came a familiar voice. Daryl crawled over to her and she felt hot tears well up quickly.

"Boys," she said, reaching towards them. They both knelt closer to her, leaning on her softly as she grasped them into the best embrace she could manage. Daryl's head rested painfully against her cheekbone, and Marcus was aggravating her painful hip but she didn't care. She breathed them in deeply, relief and joy and love given free reign as she held them tight. And yes, there was a slight tinge of anger and resentment that she was lying here in pain, surrounded by the group but, right now, it couldn't outweigh her joy. She had found them, and they were safe and that was more than enough. For now. There would be words later. She had a lot of questions, but they could wait.

They finally eased off her and she grimaced again, trying to get comfortable.

"Good to see you Hazel," a familiar voice said.

"Hello Pritch," she replied. She saw him across the fire from her, smiling.

"You're pretty banged up there," he stated. "Was it your ankle?," he said, wincing dramatically, "not too sure what youse hae done there but we heard you scream."

She nodded in soft agreement. "It feels nasty Pritchard," she said. "It's throbbing and I can't move it."

"It needs looked at," another voice cut in. She groaned inwardly. Sol.

"Hello Sol," she said, craning her neck to see him. He sat far to her right so she could only just see him at a stretch. She sighed and sagged back with the effort, looking down her body towards her raised foot. It was so painful and even the joy at seeing her children was being eroded by the constant throb. It was still clad in her boot, and she sighed miserably at the situation. She could see multiple sleeping bags covering her and she knew she was wrapped tightly in one, her damaged leg poking out the bottom. She felt lighter now though and could feel the fabric of the bags directly on her skin. It felt that she was wearing her bra and nothing else on her top half. Her jeans were still on though and slightly damp still. She wondered who had stripped her and where her clothes might be. She pulled the bag tighter to her chin.

"It's gonna need strapping at the very least," said Sol. A few other voices added their agreement.

"Yes. Well. Maybe," she answered. *Like fuck*, she thought to herself. *What do they know?*

As if reading her thoughts Sol said, "I'm first aid trained Hazel. I know what I'm doing." His voice was soft, but she detected an edge to it even now. Had her contempt for the man been that obvious? He was subdued and she wondered if he was angry with her, for the incident at the Eye. "But the boot needs to come off."

"Where have you been?" she asked, ignoring him, directing her question to her two sons. "Have you any idea how worried I was? What were you thinking? You just left me!"

"I knew she'd be angry," said Daryl to his brother, instantly breaking off from whatever conversation he was having, as if he had been waiting for her disapproval.

"This is why I'm on my back with a swollen ankle you know?"

"I know Mum, sorry," answered Marcus. "It's... Well. It was the right thing to do. You'll see. Won't she Pritch?"

"Aye," nodded the older boy. "These lads needed to come wi' us and you needed to be on yer own Hazel." He paused for a moment. "It's what she wanted."

"What on earth do you mean?" but she knew exactly what he meant and who *she* was.

"Aye. Ye know," he smiled, again that feeling off having her mind read.

"But..." she started. She wanted out of this nightmare. "No Pritch." She looked around at the faces, all watching her. "I'm not...." She trailed off, unable to articulate what she was experiencing. What the fuck was this? What did they want from her? What did this island want? *Lorseyeth* or whatever it was called, what was she expected to do? "What?" she demanded. "What do you want? You lot? Eh? What? I just want my lads and off this island. You lot are welcome to it. You can stay here as long as

153

you want. Have the place! I. Do. Not. Care. You can throw my phone in the bloody sea for all I care! No police. I promise. No reprisals. Have the bloody place. It's yours. Just let us go home. Can we just do that? Please."

Pritchard shook his head gently, the small smile still playing on his lips. "You can't Hazel. No."

She sagged and looked at Marcus. The fear and hopelessness of the last few days curling up tight inside her. The hateful, almost monotonous threat of tears stung at her eyes as that hopeless, useless panic made its presence felt. "Marcus. What's going on? Why are you with them? Why are you helping them?"

"They're helping you mum. And then, in turn, you'll be helping them, and then everyone. Don't you see it yet?" She shifted uncomfortably again and let out a small moan as her ankle sent a fresh wave of pain up her leg and she was almost grateful for a moment as it snapped her out of her fear. She tried to shift her weight. They had raised her leg so it rested on a rock but the pressure on her sore hip was becoming unbearable. She tried to focus on her position rather than dwell on the nonsense these boys were spouting but she was finding that nothing alleviated the pain.

"This will help," said Sol and from behind a rough hand passed a half finished joint towards her, its acrid smell clearly discernible beneath the wood smoke. "It will take the edge off."

"No thanks," she said as she continued to fidget. She was much warmer now. The heat of the fire and the sleeping bags and the pain all adding their own temperature; sweat was beginning to bead on her forehead and neck. It was a still evening for once and she shook a bare arm free to cool down, aware that she was exposing herself before these adolescents but just too hot to care. The cool air landed on her exposed skin pleasantly. The offer of weed was retracted, and she shoved herself onto her right hip more and let out a yell as that bruised part of her, and the ankle sent more pain racing through her.

"Try this instead," said Pritchard and he stood up and dumped a carrier bag of what looked like dry leaves and small white roots onto the roaring fire. A huge crackle went up and a plume of white and yellow smoke erupted from the fire. The smoke washed over her, and the smell was unlike any smoke she had ever known. She was instantly dizzy, head spinning and she felt herself clutching the ground as the world began to tip her off. She panicked as she became disoriented, the ground tilting treacherously, surely rolling her towards the inferno to her right.

Laughter and a buzz of appreciation went up as the smoke did its job. "What was...?"

"Shhh Hazel. It's alright," and she saw Pritchard loom closer to her, casually throwing the empty bag onto the hungry flames. "Let's have a look at that ankle, shall we?" She dug her fingers into the ground as the world lurched sickeningly. Her stomach roiled and she closed her eyes, desperate for the spinning to end. Her whole body was buzzing and she swallowed, conscious that the need to throw up was approaching. She curled her body as much as her leg would allow, which wasn't much, more like a slight kink to one side but it helped.

She lay like that for a while, eyes closed, breathing deep and controlled, trying to ride the spin. It was slowing now but she was still so warm, uncomfortably so and then she heard footsteps crunch towards her. She tried to raise her head as he approached. "No," she slurred but if whoever it was heard her, he made no sign of listening as he squatted down next to her. She felt very lightheaded now, almost as if she were melting, melting softly into the ground. She looked down to her left hand, watching the firelight play across the skin, illuminating her arm hairs into a small golden army that marched across her skin, the raised veins creating shadows that moved and shimmied in the dancing light. Far, far away, somebody had picked up her leg and she turned slowly, lifting her head to see but it was so far away. She let herself lie back down; head beautifully cushioned by clouds as her hair floated softly around her.

Shapes and bodies stood around her and she was sure she could see Marcus nearby. She smiled at him, at the thought of him. Of how amazing it was to have a Marcus, with his broad back and shaggy dark hair and how more people in the world should have a Marcus as then they would know what real love meant. And a Daryl she thought, and tears brimmed as she experienced an all-encompassing love for that boy, his rosy cheeks and beautiful pale hair and wide smile and she almost screamed at how lucky she was, instead choosing to ram her fist into her mouth to stifle the laughter. Her leg was higher now and she saw Pritchard and Sol, bandanas on around their mouths, sawing away at her laces with a very large looking knife. She was dimly aware that they may be attempting to saw her foot off and the thought sent a fresh wave of hilarity through her, forcing a high pitched giggle from her. She would have dissolved into laughter but noticed something. Around the fire, someone had put some music on, some throbbing, repetitive track that ordinarily she would have hated, but, right now, was the best song she had ever heard. She raised one hand in appreciation and approval, lips pushed forward into a ridiculous pout as the music began to fill her up. She could feel the vibration in her arms and back and neck as she breathed the sweet-smelling smoke down to the very depths of her.

A couple of miles away, two men were working at pulling her boot off. There was pain there, somewhere, she knew she didn't like it, but it was as if she had been sent an email telling her she was in pain. She dutifully sent a reply, stating that she didn't like the pain but the music was fucking banging so she would focus on that.

In that far off country, her leg was also pretty fucking cold and she could feel cold metal slicing its way up her shin, shearing the fabric of her jeans away but that was boring news and she looked back out at the young men who were all dancing away and talking. Some had drinks in their hands, others had discarded their tops; Marcus was talking to a small group, gesturing wildly, a huge grin plastered all over his face, mirroring hers. Past the flames, Daryl was rolling on the floor, laughing into the night, a giant boy sat next to him, grinning. How lucky she was, Hazel marvelled. To be surrounded by all these lovely people. How lucky.

Another young boy approached Hazel and crouched before her. His face was moving all over the place and she struggled to look at him. He had dark hair that hung down in front of his face and seemed to move of its own accord, like the woman with the snakes on her head and she partially stifled a guffaw. "Hazel," he seems to say. "I'm Petey. I've to give you this," but did he actually speak? His mouth was moving at a much different speed and was closed now and from a bag he pulled a handful of thin, straggly mushrooms.

"No thank you," is what she meant to say but instead she just gurgled some happy sounds. She wished Petey would 'do one' as the youngsters like to say, do one and let her listen to the music but he moved the mushrooms closer to her mouth and deep down she was aware that she shouldn't be taking mushrooms and that she doesn't want to eat these mushrooms and that her boys were here somewhere and that in another country her ankle is hurting very much but they kept coming closer. She moved her hand up to stop them but her hand decided to move much slower than she intended. She felt like she had maybe had enough smoke for now and wanted to say something but then she felt cold matter being put delicately but quite forcibly into her mouth.

"Eat these up Hazel," she hears. She wants to spit them out and dimly she hears another voice, "are ye sure?" and then more mushrooms are being forced into her mouth. "Try and chew them Hazel." And now there is a slight panic growing inside her. She doesn't want these mushrooms. She knows this. Yet there are mushrooms in her mouth. And the music is too loud now and the world is tilting again and she digs her fingers into the ground to stop her rolling off, rolling into the fire. "She manages to let out a roar of defiance and attempts to spit the mushrooms out but there so many in her mouth.

And then Marcus is there, next to her, stroking her hair. "Shh mum," he whispers. "Eat the mushrooms, they're really good for you," and she sees he means it and so she tries to. She bites down into the tasteless mulch again and again. She gags slightly and her eldest son offers her some water which she sips and which helps. He offers her more mushrooms and she opens her mouth and he pops them in and after a while she is done. He is smiling down at her and she is smiling up at him and the bitter mushroom taste is fading and she is happy again and the music is great and she is so, so warm, still too warm, and so she thrashes at the stuff that covers her and bats it away so that her skin is open to the perfect cool air and he pushes the hair out of her face because loving sons do that for their mothers and she smiles at him again and she tells him he is lovely and he looks at her puzzled and then she asks him to keep an eye on his brother and again he looks puzzled but she is confident in him so she drifts back to the music and starts humming to the track which she has never heard before in her life but which is by far the greatest song she has ever heard in her life.

She is breathing cool night air again and the boys are mostly sitting and talking although some are still dancing, the planet is still trying to tip her up, but not so violently now, just gently, and as long as she remembers to hold on, she can stay anchored and not roll away so she digs her hands deeper into the ground, clutching the grass tightly, then releasing it, then clutching it again, then releasing it. This plan pleases her and she smiles inwardly, smug at her own problem solving skills. As she breathes calmy, the feeling of perfect happiness slowly lessens. She feels sleepy now but there is something wrong. Her senses have returned although her foot is still pleasantly disconnected, aching somewhere but not anywhere close to be important. She raises her head again to see Sol and Pritchard, masks off, kneeling over that foot. She wriggles her toes and they both look to her and smile, she smiles warmly back and allows her head to fall back again into whatever her head is resting on.

And then a thought hits her. Was Sol's head ever so slightly wrong? She lifts her head again and sees Sol and Pritchard in the same position. She wriggles her toes again, slightly worried this time. And they both turn, exactly the same as last time, and both smile at her, exactly the same as last time, but are their smiles too wide this time? Like too big for their faces? She puts her head back quickly, unsure if they know that she has seen through their disguise, that she now sees them for what they are.

Or does she?

Maybe she is a bit tired and didn't see properly.

She lifts her head again, wriggles her toes again, they turn again, but now their eyes and mouths and gaping wide. Eyes open so wide, mouths that stretch into rictus grins and she gasps and puts her head back down, heart racing. She can feel their strong hands on her leg and foot, it feels slimy, like slugs, like they're rubbing slugs into her foot, but she doesn't want to look down there again, to that far place and see those demon faces grinning back. So she looks towards the fire and looks to see if anyone else saw what she saw. She was made to eat mushrooms, that's what that is, just hallucinating, its just LSD or whatever was in those mushrooms. She feels slugs on her legs, making their way up her body, up onto her stomach. She can feel everyone's eyes on her, and she turns her head quickly to see who is actually looking at her but no one is looking at her, they are all engaged in private conversations, but every time she looks away, she feels their heads turn and the staring start but when she looks back, they are turned away, lost in chat.

She closes her eyes. Disorientated and upset. Where has Marcus and Daryl gone? Why aren't they with her, reassuring her? She feels alone and she feels that she is being looked at and laughed at. She wants to cry but knows now that she probably couldn't, even if she wanted to. But this isn't nice anymore. She rests and breathes, eyes closed.

Hazel is aware of her hands still grasping at the soil to either side of her. One hand holds tufts of grass loosely. The other pushes into soft earth. *This is better* she thinks. *This is honest.*

She can feel the soft thrum of the music in her fingertips. She breathes deeper and opens her eyes. She blinks a few times. Above, the stars move slowly. She watches them for a time, aware that the stars are dancing to the music. She marvels at how they are able to hear this little speaker from lightyears away, yet they do. A little pulse of joy returns, and she realises that the beauty of the universe is in the unexplainable, not the logic of an answer, just the *is*ness of a thing. The *is*ness. "Isness," she repeats out loud, stunned at this profound realisation. "Isness," she says again and slowly repeats this perfect word over and over, rolling it around so that it loses its meaning for a second and then that awareness prompts a second wave of *isness* appreciation and she is happy again. All the while she watches the stars moving, some faster and more energetic (they must be closer she reasons) until she becomes aware of a much deeper and much more profound sensation. Beneath the hum of the music is a deeper vibration, a longer and older and wiser thrumming and she gasps as she realises her fingertips are connected to the island and it is the island's pulse.

Muchach is alive she realises, alive and aware of her, aware of her lying on it! She pushes her fingers harder into the ground and feels the connection strengthen. She arches her back as she feels the ancient stone, impossibly old, millions of years old, formed from violence and heat and thunder and electricity and left to cool and hiss and steam and the frozen seas that washed over it and the very earth as it squeezed it and shaped it and pushed *Lorrsayeth* from the ground where *She* was created. *How?* She asks nobody? *Why?* And she knows the answer. *The isness.* There is no answer. No reason why. *Lorrsayeth* was created from rock and fire and lightning and love and space and now *is*. She can feel every living thing that grows and feeds on Muchach and that has ever lived and has ever fed and which died and became one with the island again and which fed those that came after, the slugs and the mice and the worms and the eagles and she feels the surrounding seas lick and smash and lap and caress *Lorrsayeth* and she weeps at the beauty of this sensation and smiles as humans find her, so many years later and make their homes here and then the child who first spoke with *Lorrsayeth*, the child who became the first mother and she arches her back in a near ecstasy as these revelations sweep through her.

She opens her eyes and she is far, far, far above the fire. She looks down onto the small group and she can see the fire and the group of men surrounding the fire and yes, there she is, spread eagled, half naked, writhing gently in the orange glow. She can faintly hear the music and make out The Eye, barely illuminated by the tiny flames which looked so big when viewed up close.

Her heart stops and a rush of fear and exhilaration surges through her and she knows Lorrsayeth is behind her, awake, and she turns, skin breaking out in goosebumps and as she set her eyes upon the God, her bladder loosens and a sob of pure horror and awe escapes her as she struggles to take in the sight before her.

Vaster than any mountain, older than the earth and possessing a knowledge and experience that threatens to destroy Hazel's mind, it's eye alone is like looking into the sun. She is a flea, standing before a titan in comparison, a dot. Her heart races but, for the briefest moment, she understands everything; she understands the sickness and emptiness that lives on the land now and understands the import of what she needs to do and what all mothers do; the nurture and love and sacrifice that makes a mother and she opens her mind and heart to the blinding light that seems to burn through every part of her and then she is-

Panting and lying on her sleeping bag, the music continues to pound and around her, a mass of legs and arms stamp and jump around her in time to the beat. She is dripping in sweat, now lying in naught but her white knickers. The sky is lighter and she quickly pulls the scattered sleeping bags over herself and shivers at how cold they are. Her ankle is also very painful again and she props herself up to see a swollen yellow and purple mess which used to be her left foot. She tries to move it and it obeys slightly but it is incredibly painful.

She adjusts the sleeping bags, draping them over her, trapping them under her, and curls up. She closes her eyes again, tired but mind racing with all she has experienced.

Like a dream, the memories of the last few hours are elusive, the truths and concepts just out of reach, slipping between her fingers as she grasps to hold onto what she saw.

That she thinks she saw.

That she dreamt.

Who knows?

She is exhausted though and as the music plays and the feet continue to jump and tramp around her, she feels a small body nestle in closely and snuggle into her. She lifts up a cover and allows the small boy in which she assumes is her youngest. Another body comes in on her other side and again, she offers a welcoming arm as a larger body settles next to her. Marcus.

She closes her eyes and this time she sleeps with no dreaming.

She awoke to a bright sky, she turned her head slightly, eyes squeezed tight. Instantly, her ankle began to pulse nauseating waves up her body. Her mouth was devoid of any spit, a desert, dry tongue raking across a dry mouth. A cold wind was blowing, scouring her face and lips of moisture and her thoughts were slow and disjointed. She struggled to work out where she was. She was warm, well, her body was warm. Her exposed leg was very cold and her face felt cold but she was cocooned in heat. The air was chilly and there was a snap to the gusts of wind that would sporadically whistle through their camp, the coloured sleeping backs ruffling and snapping in the sporadic wind. Bodies seemed to be pressed in around her, a small sea of backs and arms could be seen surrounding her. One of her arms was pinned down and had gone numb, under Daryl she supposed. She tried to pull her arm free without waking him. The weight was considerable, and, despite her efforts, her arm remained firmly stuck. She sighed and instead pulled him in closer, his hair within kissing distance, which she did, sniffing his scent – it wasn't Daryl.

She had no idea who this head belonged to but it was neither of her sons. This time she jerked and yanked her arm free, not caring about the throb in her leg and not caring who she was disturbing. She sighed loudly, torn between outrage or resignation. "Daryl?" she croaked, feeling the tug of war between outrage and despair start its now too familiar game within her but what good would losing her temper do her here on this fucking island surrounded by this mob? Who would listen to her complaints and accusations and nod understandingly? Who would sympathise with her plight and help her up, finding her transport and a way home? No one. Not even her fucking sons apparently. Was she just going to drag her sorry arse to the ferry from this spot, waved on by grinning idiots and slither on, yelling a thankyou through gritted teeth? Yet what was the alternative? Giving up? Going back to sleep, just letting whatever was happening happen? She adjusted her position, trying to get a better impression of who was with her.

It seemed to be the whole gang, about 20 bodies lay scattered around, a few were awake, hugging their knees and looking intently into the small flames that some wiser souls had tended to and which were now fighting bravely against the Scottish morning.

Her ankle throbbed miserably; she looked down at the swollen mess. It was twice its normal size, her jeans lie in tatters next to her, removed whilst she had been flying above the island, sailing through Cloud Cuckoo Land or wherever she had been last night.

Her eyes jolted open as fragments of the dream...vision...experience from last night crash back into her. She moaned at what was expected of her. She moaned at how wrecked on mushrooms she had been.

Her mouth had a nasty, acidic tang to it and she glanced around hopefully, desperate to see a bottle of water within easy reach. She groaned softly, a wave of nausea softly growing within her. She could vaguely remember something about mushrooms and having a mouth stuffed full of them, her stomach roiled at the memory and her gorge rose, her mouth filled with saliva and she quickly turned to one side less she vomit all over herself, but nothing came. She leant awkwardly on one elbow which pushed painfully into the cold stone beneath her.

Mist hung low and damp across the land like a cold wet towel, leaching the heat from them. She lay back defeated. What were her options? It seemed to her she had several and all of them shit.

Option one was to lie there, brood over how everything had turned to shite and just go with the flow. What had that woman, that *apparition, Aila* said to her yesterday? *You are the mother now?* What the fuck? I mean, was all of this just a series of hallucinations? The boys were real enough but the cave stuff? Those horrible visions, the meeting with the woman in that pool of oil, was all of that just her mind caving in, crumbling at all she had been through? She genuinely hoped to God it was just her mind playing tricks. Visions and poor mental health Hazel reasoned, was much more preferable than becoming the Earth Mother to a remote Island God that was immortal and that needed the blood and suffering of others to sustain it and thus heal the land. Yes , I'll take the poor mental health please. So just tough it out, wait for whatever was happening to blow itself out, get to the ferry at some point and leave, but do it calmly, accepting that it would happen but that it wouldn't be happening today.

The alternative to this, that this was *all* real, could also not be discounted anymore. Even if was a complete mental collapse and not some giant, ancient god from the cosmos, if she embraced it, the God or the mental collapse, then what would that require of her? If she bought into it? That she stay on the island forever? Believing herself to be some kind of earth mother and a magnet for those willing to come to Muchach and be nurtured by her until it was time for them to flay themselves? Real or not, it terrified her. She wanted to be home now. She was desperate. Everything seemed to be leading her further and further away from what she had worked so hard to achieve.

The third option was to get the fuck up. Grab her boys, get in the car, get to the ferry terminal and get the fuck off that Island. This option was much more to Hazel's liking. She could get them back to the cottage and check the emails and arrange a time. She would sit there, hunker down as it were, drinking tea and eating sandwiches, ignoring whatever else was going on, ignoring whatever the fuck it was she saw in the loft, just sit at the table, drink her tea, chat with her boys, until it was time to leave. Or hide! Squirrel away somewhere till it was time. The problem with this option was that the internet was unreliable and a ferry was dependent on getting hold of the company and then hoping the weather and availability was in their favour; she could be waiting days or even weeks, which did not appeal and brought her back to option one – wait it out.

She lay back, smacking her dry mouth occasionally, desperate for a drink and wracking her brain for another way back to the mainland when a thought occurred to her. Getting back to the mainland was all dependant on the fucking ferry, which was actually all dependent on contacting the ferry and the weather – too many variables but, what if they didn't have to wait for the ferry? They could use the small rib in the storage shed, the one with the outboard motor attached and just get to the other side. This made the weather the only problem and one which she hoped she could overcome. It was only five miles across. This would leave them without a car once they crossed however, but at least they would be away from whatever madness was happening here. She could contact the police and give all the details to Ron and Gav and- tears leaked quickly as the image of her two friends up in the loft, sticks jutting from their face burst into her mind and she bit her lower lip and stifled a sob of pure anguish. She prayed that it was just a hallucination, that all of it was just an hallucination. She brought her focus back to their predicament and possible solution. The longer she lay there, the more she preferred this admittedly more desperate option. There were hurdles to overcome: getting the boat to the shore, getting the boys to help, getting to civilisation without a car and a swollen ankle once they had crossed, but the thought of getting off the island today was so incredibly tempting that she was angry she hadn't considered it earlier. She pushed herself up into a sitting position, sounds were muted by the all encompassing fog but it also meant that the wind was calmer than previous days and this meant the sea was probably navigable.

She croaked out for her boys. She felt she sounded like an old sea bird on a nature documentary, squawking for her young: "Marcus," she rasped. "Daryl?" A few boys turned their heads to her, smiling warmly, with what looked like gratitude and friendliness.

She sat up straighter, clutching a sleeping bag tight around her. Why the fuck were they all just outside on the floor, it was bloody freezing! They had gone to the trouble of breaking in to the centre, why not bloody use it? She slowly pushed herself to her good foot, gingerly unpicking herself from the myriad sleeping bags that clung and wrapped themselves around her torso like snakes. She saw Pritchard further away and hobbled over to him, her ankle agony. "Hello Pritchard," she croaked. "Do you please have any water and do you know where Marcus and Daryl are?"

"Can help youse with the first thing Hazel," he replied in his gravelly Glasgow accent, looking at her with an expectant smile which put her on edge instantly. He wore grey tracksuit bottoms and a white vest, his sinewed, corded arms extended a used juice bottle towards her, three quarters full. She took the water from him, unscrewing the plastic lid and drinking deeply. The water was almost warm which was welcome on such a chilly morning. She felt the water course down her parched throat and only noticed the odd flavour on her last swallow.

"What is this?" she asked.

"Just water," he replied.

"It tastes weird," she said, smacking her lips together repeatedly.

"Aye?" he enquired.

"Yeah," she replied, still grateful to have that painful thirst quenched.

He shrugged. "It's no mine, was just lying about so I took it." She nodded at him as she took another mouthful. "Not sure about your boys though," he continued. "Saw them last night so I did, dancing like fiends weren't they?" he looked directly at her, "Good night that eh Hazel?"

She hugged herself tightly, looking straight back into his deep grey eyes. "Not sure I remember that much of it to be honest Pritchard," she said. "Not a massive fan of drugs and that but, it really helped with the pain, so thanks for sorting me out. For strapping my ankle up." He shrugged modestly, as if strapping up middle aged women's ankles whilst she was high as kite was an everyday occurrence. She stood there awkwardly for a long moment, he turned his gaze back to the fire. "So," she prompted, "any idea where they may have gone?" She felt warmer now and the ankle was already easing off, noticeably so, the pain receding quite quickly. She opened the bottle and sniffed it. There was an odd fragrance to the water, but she couldn't determine if that was from the residue of what had been in the bottle originally or if something had been added to what she had just necked back and, considering the dulling of pain in her ankle, she assumed the latter. "What's in this?" she asked.

Again he shrugged, "Is it no water? I didnae make it Hazel sorry. Just found it." She was feeling warmer now, much warmer. She stood there for several moments, wondering if she had been spiked or if she was just waking up properly. "We're leaving," she said. Why had she said that? Why tell him their plans. That was stupid. But there was something very unassuming about Pritchard. He had been nothing but polite and helpful towards her, despite the situation, and she felt glad that he had been so affable and reasonable. She swayed slightly, her ankle almost forgotten. Poor boy, she thought, rocking softly next to the fire. No parents. Just an orphanage to grow up in. Did they have orphanages now? Or was it a care home? A home for boys? Growing up without hugs and love and support apart from people who are paid to care for you. She felt her eyes fill with tears and she looked at his shaven hair, his strong arms. Poor lad. The lot of them. No one to care for them. At least her boys had her, at least their childhood had been mostly positive. Holidays abroad, Santa Lists fulfilled, uniform, trainers, food, warmth, security, trust. Love. These boys had never had that she reasoned. Maybe in stops and starts. A favourite carer who suddenly gets another job elsewhere or no one to wish you a happy birthday and mean it. A tear ran down her grimy face. She brushed it away, surprised she had any tears left and surprised that it was for these boys.

He looked up at her and shook his head before returning his gaze to the fire and prodding it with a long stick. She offered him the water back but he held his hand up in refusal, "You keep it," he said. She drank deeply again, nodded her thanks and set off limping around the camp, looking for her children. Her head was swimming but her ankle was profoundly less painful. She could feel the world was different again, whatever was in that water was strong but it was useful. She doubted she could have walked very far on this foot without it, so she focussed on her plan. Get the boys, get them back to the centre, get the boat, get off the island. She could do that whilst stoned. If it came to it, Marcus could drive the boat, it wasn't that hard.

She found them curled up together. Marcus had spooned around Daryl, both wrapped tightly in sleeping bags and she felt a smile touch her lips before she spotted a trail of bright yellow vomit trailing from Marcus' mouth. She limped closer and reached down, relieved when both boys necks were found to be soft and warm. She could see that Marcus had been sick though, and it pooled in between himself and his younger brother. The stink was breathtaking and she shook them both awake quickly, keen to get them away from this place. Guilt opined that it was her fault that Marcus had been ill, that had she not been in such a state last night then she could have looked after him and prevented him taking whatever he had taken. But she hadn't stuffed those mushrooms into her mouth, she hadn't smoked that shit on purpose. Too late now she thought, pushing the thought away and marvelling as she did so. Previously, that kind of self-recrimination and judgement would have occupied most of her day but New Hazel didn't have time for self-recrimination. New Hazel was a doer, and this doer was getting her family out of this place.

She quickly roused them, yanking the bags off them, rolling one boy into the other in a chorus of muffled, foggy protest. "Come on boys," she said. "Up, up, up."

"Why?" mum moaned Daryl, "please no. It's too cold." But it was too late, and she gave a final yank, bringing the bright yellow sleeping bag up to her arms. Marcus was slowly unfolding and standing up, his head lowered against the wind, a deep frown carved across his face. He folded his arms tightly in a similar manner to how his mother had done minutes earlier, his face was ashen, his eyes were bloodshot, squinting against the bright white light from above.

"Let's get back to the cottage," she said, an air of confidence and certainty in her voice that brooked no denial and, unbelievably, they both followed mutely – be it through fatigue, habit or necessity, she couldn't say.

Chapter 16

They saw the body a good way off. White and red and limp, stark against the grey stone. Despite all she had seen this week, Hazel's hand reflexively went to her mouth. He hung there quite still, hands raised high, directly above the bowed head, hands skewed in odd directions, legs bent and buckled beneath him. They continued forward, more unwanted details revealing themselves; blood had pooled beneath the body, seeping into the hard dirt below, meandering between the blades of grass. His spindly legs were bent into an S shape, taking no weight and his feet had now swollen grotesquely. Down one side was a river of dried blood which the wind and rain had failed to remove completely, a deep dark red crust that ran down the side of his pale body. It was clear, even from this distance, that he was dead. The body moved slightly, buffeted by the sporadic gusts. The path took them through the Eye where the boy had been strung up. His hands were a dark purple, the blue rope still biting deeply into the wrists. "Oh Jesus," she said. Daryl ran forward towards it, pointing in excitement. Her ankle had eased off somewhat but she was in no condition to run. "Daryl," she shouted. "Stay away from him," but her voice was a tiny thing. Guilt enveloped her.

She had left him.

She had forgotten about him.

And now here he was. Dead. This death seemed to cut her deeper. Ronnie and Gav were still on their yacht and were sipping drinks in Cannes or Montecarlo or somewhere, whatever she had seen in the attic she had subconsciously attributed to extreme stress. It already felt like a bad dream, quickly reasoned and compartmentalised – *I had a nightmare but its probably due to the stress of the house move or my job or Christmas or whatever* and, as she approached the corpse, for that is what it was now, she realised that that is what she had done, rationalised the stamping corpses. The other things she thought she had seen things were unconfirmed, no evidence, no discussion by the group and so unsubstantiated imaginings. A boy in the sea, a body in the rocks, gone a second later; fleeting. Not real. Even the rabbit head – the twitching, spasming rabbit head – had been pushed down – burnt and forgotten - it had all been stressed out hallucinations, like a lot of whatever else was happening here.

She wasn't sure she believed that, that it was all hallucinatory, but she *needed* to believe that; the alternative was far too disturbing to even think about. *I'll take the poor mental health please.*

But this?

If this was real, this dead body, here and now, then there was a strong chance the other deaths were real too.

That was a human body, the body of a young man, strung up between two ancient stones. As real as the stones that held him. If she wanted to, she could touch him, lift his head up, look into his lifeless eyes. He had been sliced open down the side of his body and had died from that or exposure to the storm. And she had left him there.

And he had called you mother!

She walked numbly closer to the body, knowing she had to check to see if he was alive, knowing he wasn't. Marcus had now reached the corpse and just stood there, almost admiring it, one hand on his hip, taking it in. Daryl was much more animated. Worryingly he didn't seem to be in the slightest bit concerned or afraid of the macabre scene. "Daryl," she said, then stopped mid-sentence.

She could see sticks. The boy's head was lowered, his hair was cropped short and beyond the curve of the pallid blue skin, Hazel could see the bundles of sticks jutting from the sockets and mouth, just like –

He hadn't been like this last night she knew. His eyes had been open, wild, desperate. Someone had done this too him later. Someone, or some people, had come to this spot with theirs bundles of sticks and forced them into his eyes, his mouth. She couldn't take another step.

She reached out to pull Marcus and Daryl away but saw that they were both smiling. Daryl was grinning from ear to ear whilst Marcus had a slight smirk of approval, nodding his head at what he saw. "Boys?" she asked and deliberately took another slug of the drink. This nightmare was destroying her from the inside out. *Why were they smiling?* She felt the burst of warmth from the drink, the tangy acidic aftertaste and reached out for Daryl, pulling him away. "What's wrong with you?" she asked quietly, afraid that the hanging obscenity might hear her or see the delight in the children's eyes. "Why are you both smiling?"

"What? Oh. Just. Its impressive mum. *A' tabhann!* That must have been so painful, and he still did it. He wanted to do it." She still had his arm and was moving away from the scene, towards their goal.

"What did you just say Daryl?" she snapped. *A' tabhann?*

"You know why he did it," added Marcus. "You know why mum."

168

She shook her head and turned her back on them, "Let's go boys. We're leaving."

"It was for you mum. For the island."

She spun on her good ankle, furious. "Shut up!" she snapped. "Just shut up! You have no idea what you're talking about!" But, she suspected they did. She suspected they probably knew more than her. She could scream. These boys! Just caught up in all this terrible, horrible bullshit.

Marcus held up his hands to placate her, still unused to this temper and this new version of his mother. "They're dead boys! Dead! And that's okay is it? That's all fine?" She stabbed her finger in the direction of the body. "He's been murdered. He died in pain! He didn't tie himself to those rocks! He didn't slice his body open! And even if he fucking did, that's okay with you two? That's fine? My god, I raised you better than that didn't I? Where's your empathy? Where's the horror? He bled to death in a storm. He's had bloody sticks shoved into his bloody eyes and neither of you think that's a bad thing! My God lads." Her chest was heaving and she wanted to vomit and cry and scream and tear out the sky and rip up the rocks and set fire to this awful place. She wanted to wake up in her bed with her grey brushed cotton sheets on her warm, goose down duvet. She wanted to see Fraser asleep next to her. Right now, she would trade. If there was a magic lamp or a djinn or a leprechaun or a fucking fairy and it said, *"Hazel, you can stay here now or go back to your old life,"* she knew what she would choose. In a New York minute she knew what she would choose. This absolute nightmare was robbing her of her sanity, of her children, her will to go on. You could argue Fraser did exactly the same, but at least there were no other kids involved. Kids! With their stomachs open, exposed to the elements, with their bodies desecrated, with her own children seemingly complicit, no she knew what she would choose, and it was the tears that won out, her anger finally depleted. Raging against everything that had happened had brought her hear, to this spot and no further. She wasn't home, they weren't safe, and she was exhausted. A huge sob erupted from her. She covered her face with her hands, shaking her head from side to side as she slowly lowered herself onto one of the fallen stones. She sat there, fighting the urge to vomit as well, crying softly – no panicked breathing or hyper ventilating in sight however – when she felt a small hand on her shoulder. Another arm snuck round from the other side and she felt herself being embraced by both of her sons.

"Shhh, Mum, it's okay," said Daryl.

"It's good mum," echoed Marcus, his lower voice barely audible. "We'll be fine, I promise. It's all good." They held her tight and rocked her gently and still the tears came. She was afraid to lift her head and uncover her face, to open her eyes, so convinced was she that the hanging boy would be looking at her as well, sightless eyes looking softly upon her, mouth stretched in a painfully sincere grin, wrapped around the bundle of sticks that had been forced into his mouth, down his throat-

"Let's go," she said, standing quickly. She swayed and stumbled, her balance off. The rocks seemed to glow as she rubbed at her eyes, the sky bright after having them closed. She blinked, clearing her vision and in the corner of her eye, the hanging boy's head was up and was looking at her and was smiling and she knew if she did turn, if she did look at that terrible thing, blood running from its eyes, that that would be the end of her, that her mind would simply break, then and there, so she didn't look, she turned away, and started walking. The boys walked alongside. Her ankle was aching slightly, so she sipped at her drink, wondering if it was a good idea but so grateful for the numbing properties it seemed to bestow.

They made steady progress; it was usually a couple of hour's walk to the centre from The Eye on a good day and this was far from a good day so maybe double the time. Despite the numbing of her drink, her ankle still ached painfully beneath the blanket of fog she was wrapped in, but the drink also allowed her to read the heavens. She shuffled slowly, head tilted skywards watching the clouds high above. They seemed to be moving and changing shape before her very eyes. She could see animals and vehicles, white against a pale blue sky, but the animals seemed to move, to turn, to evolve from one to another, it was difficult to keep track of just one as they constantly merged and separated, a kaleidoscope of whites, backlit by a golden light and honestly, truly beautiful. The corpse already nothing but a floating memory, like a dandelion seed on the breeze being carried further and further away. She hummed softly to herself.

Occasionally she would reach across to one of the boys, rubbing their arm, holding their soft, warm hands, squeezing the nape of their neck, cherishing the connection, marvelling at how something as simple as touch, one person to another, could create such feelings of joy and love in her. She would squeeze their hands, feeling their bones through their flesh, the tendons and veins that she had made, that she had nurtured and now got to hold and take strength from as she limped across this barren place. She was happy she realised, this was all she ever wanted, just herself, her kids, nature, fresh air, a challenge, this was her – this was

Hazel. Not New Hazel, the newly invented woman, formed from desperate necessity who was getting them out of this but Original Hazel, the Hazel she had always been, even as a child. The Hazel who loved a challenge, the Hazel who loved exploring and being outdoors, loved her family – and now it seemed that Original Hazel was back and rather happy right now. She hadn't seen her for years. Dimly she was aware that if she thought about the hanging boy or Ronnie and Gav or any number of things she had seen this week, real or imagined, then her fantasy would collapse, would rot like an apple left hanging on the tree, turning brown, eaten by parasites and dripping in its own ultimate corruption- So she drank more of the happy juice and hummed and revelled in the present – the *isness* of right now.

Eventually they reached the centre and she smiled at the northern gate left open, moving slightly in the wind. "Come on boys," she said. "Let's get warm." They headed inside. It felt as if she hadn't been back in years. It seemed smaller and darker, and she instantly craved the fresh air. It was stifling. It seemed untouched, no one had been here since her frantic departure the night before but so much had happened since then. Her scattered belongings still adorned the kitchen table. She wanted to lie down but knew she had to do something first. Something important. Yes! She went to the PC in the back office and logged in. It took a while, during which Hazel polished off the last of the bottle, but it eventually connected. She went straight to her emails. It was difficult to make out the blue text on the white screen. The white was far too bright and Hazel was having to squint to read the words.

Police Scotland had replied and had asked some cursory questions but had wanted to speak to Hazel personally to verify her story and check on her. There had been a follow up email to their original reply, both sent by a Sgt. Stephen Forsyth who said he had phoned several times and that he would continue to ring as well as alerting the nearest station to send out a car to the island. The weather was too poor for a helicopter he has stated, but more information was needed: were they in immediate danger or was it more of a case of squatter's rights being exercised? He had left a number to ring and Hazel wrote it down neatly, adding a small flower to the 8 in the number, before folding the small square and sliding it into her breast pocket.

The ferry company had also replied via a Mrs. L. Worton and that she was being charged two hundred pounds for missing the ferry which had made the crossing yesterday in poor conditions and which had sustained damage which meant it was getting fixed today.

If she needed the ferry now, the soonest it could be would be Monday, three days from now and which would need to be paid for in advance and which would also be her final chance for transport off the island. If she failed to make her next scheduled ferry, they would assume it was a hoax request and not reply to any further requests for transport from the island under her name. Hazel giggled into her knuckles – the woman seemed quite annoyed. Did she know that it was a dangerous job and that their operators had lives of their own? The tone of the email was very serious she felt. She was annoyed that she had missed the ferry but it wasn't as if she had a choice. What would Mrs. Worton have done in that situation she wondered. Left her kids and just got on the ferry. She doubted it, but underneath the fog a small voice whispered that *yes, that is exactly what you should have done. If you wanted to leave this island, ever, that was your chance and now its gone and now you're stuck here for-* She hummed softly, forcing the voice down as she looked at the keyboard and typed what she felt was quite a witty reply, she grinned as she misspelt Harper and left the mistake in. It took longer than normal as the keys seemed to be dancing between themselves, switching positions deliberately and it took quite a while for Hazel to jab at each mischievous key, typing her reply out letter by letter but she got it sent and then followed the link and placed the request, paying for the ferry with her online payment system which, by some absurd cosmic luck, the password she remembered straight away.

The glowing screen was slowly pulsing brighter and it was almost painful to look. Some of the light from the monitor seemed to be leaking out of the front, bright columns of light running down the front of the unit and pooling on the table before her. She frowned and wiped it away, but it just smeared like oil, soft and slippery and she got some of the light on her fingers.

Marcus found her huddled on the floor staring intently at her fingers, twirling them this way and that, clear drool spindling from her lower lip. He turned her head towards him, "Mum," he said softly. Her pupils were almost black. "Come on mum," he said, and he lifted her gently.

He lead her to the sofa and lay her down, propping her bandaged ankle up onto some cushions. He lit a fire then pulled a throw from off the back of the sofa and lay it gently over her. Her eyes were wide and panicked, "Shhhh," he said. She did calm, eyes trying to lock onto him.

"Marc?" she managed, her lips glistened, she had too much spit in her mouth and couldn't see him clearly. A black figure stood behind him though, that black figure she could see clearly, staring down at her, yellow eyes old and mean, grinning. "I....I don't want to Marc," she said. "I don't think... I really don't want to stay here."

"You have to mum. There's no choice," he said gently.

She woke hours later, her ankle throbbing and she hissed as she tried to move into a better position. The reprieve from the weather seemed to be over as she heard the wind howling again. She was cold and it was dark, the fire black and cold. It was dark and there were no sounds to be heard beyond the screaming banshee outside.

She hobbled painfully to the fire, throwing a firelighter into the grate before throwing some wood on top, closing the doors and slamming the vents wide open. The fire grew quickly, aided by the rush of wind from outside that howled down the chimney. She picked herself up and made it to the closest arm chair. She wrapped the throw tight around her and sat looking at the fire. Her mind was blank. She was exhausted, drained of energy and impetus and it was all she could do at that moment to keep her eyes open.

The warmth of the fire began to make its presence felt, seeping through her cold trousers. She rubbed her hands and blew into them. She felt awful. Her stomach was churning and her mouth tasted foul. She sat there for several moments until she felt she could move again, making her way to the kitchen area and putting the kettle on to boil. The clock read 11:17pm, confirming her suspicion that she had slept through the day. She ran the tap and drank deeply of the freezing water, only stopping at the pain in her teeth the cold water created. She sipped it as she waited for the kettle to boil. Her thoughts finally turned to her boys. She had no idea where they were. She assumed they were sleeping in their bed but it was a weak assumption, closer to a hope. She had lost them to The Pig. They were doing what they wanted now, and she held no sway over them. *They came back with you* her mind replied. *But where were they now?* she answered back. She sighed softly in defeat and poured herself a strong coffee. She was ravenous and pulled two hard bread rolls from the bread bin. Hot coffee sloshed over the sides of her mug as she limped back to her seat by the fire.

She had a vague, vague recollection of sitting at the PC, looking at emails – answering, booking but the details were absent. She knew she would have to move to the office and remind herself of what she had booked. More solid in her thoughts was that she was in the middle of Option 2, leaving the island by dinghy.

She sighed as she considered the timescale and everything she needed to do. Locate the boys and get them ready to move, locate the dinghy and hitch it to the car or the jeep, drive to the jetty, the centre's jetty was the closest but the ferry launch was the closest to the mainland and that meant less time in the dinghy so that was what she would go. Make the crossing and begin the walk to the nearest village. She chewed mindlessly on the stale bread. What she needed to think about was when. Should she leave now? Find the boys now and get going, waste no time at all, navigate the sea in the dark? She didn't think that was a good idea and judging by the sound of the wind outside, would be a very dangerous idea. What she could do is find the boys and get them ready so, come morning light, they could slip out quickly. The final option as she saw it, was to get some more sleep then find the boys in the morning and get going then. She ripped another hunk of bread with her teeth, gazing at the fire as her mind began to tick.

Her thoughts turned to the morning and if Pritchard had known what was in that bottle. Had she been spiked or had she drank it willingly? She knew it had tasted funny and she knew it had numbed the pain but she hadn't known what it was and yet had drank every last drop. She felt hungover. She was lethargic, she was lacking energy and her ankle was very painful and even her short foray into the kitchen had left her breathing heavier. A night's sleep wouldn't change much but it was far more appealing than limping about the place right now. She realised she was putting off finding the boys. Her ankle and ribs were painful but even worse, she feared the pain of their response. Their declining of her plan, their refusal to leave. She feared their defiance. She hoped they would agree to her plan and help her get the dinghy hitched but she wasn't an idiot and she knew that it may take some convincing to get them moving. She was putting it off.

She sat and chewed, sipping at her coffee, gazing at the fire, going through the plan in her mind. She sighed and pushed herself back to her feet, hobbled to the kitchen and flicked the kettle on again. She then made her way to the office and slapped the space bar, waking the PC. No internet. She clicked the outlook icon but it refused to load. She banged the mouse down hard onto the desk several times in frustration but conceded defeat and made her way back to the kitchen. She remembered there were painkillers in the drawer beneath the kettle and raked through the organised tupperware Ronnie used to store her medicines, plasters and medical gear. She found some paracetamol and ibuprofen and swallowed two of each – one for the bastard of a headache which was brewing and one for the ankle which hurt like a bastard.

She nursed her second coffee at the kitchen table, still unsure of how best to proceed. She knew what had to done, she was just exhausted and scared.

She needed to change. She was cold and her left leg was still quite exposed. If they were heading out onto the open sea in a tiny boat, she would need warmer gear on, they all would. She would leave the dressing on her ankle for now until she could get it checked out properly, but she was going to have to put some thick trousers on, which would be fun. She would get herself changed and get the boys gear ready to go. She would then find them, if they were in the centre at least, and get them ready. She would bring them back here and they would sit by the fire and wait for the morning and at soon as the light permitted, they would hitch the boat and set off for the ferry launch. That was the plan.

They were leaving.

She made to leave for the dorms and stopped. Keys. Where were the keys? Both her Honda and Gav's Land Rover were fitted with towing bars but she would prefer to use the Land Rover over her smaller Honda. She limped to the key hanger by the office door and saw both sets of keys hanging. She grabbed them and then, on a whim, decided to go check the dinghy out. She wrapped the throw around her tighter and left the cottage.

The wind was brutal, freezing and so powerful, pushing her forwards. She yelled as she came down heavy on her left foot, her hair whipped around her head in a furious dance. The Land Rover Discovery was parked further down the cottage, under the covered area where she had unloaded the kayaks and was also where the jet skis were also stored. Jet skis? She considered how fortunate it was that there were three but instantly discounted the idea. They lay in storage, covered in tarps. They would need to be lifted onto the trailer where the dinghy now sat and she had no idea if they were fuelled or if the boys could even handle one. Plan Z.

She made her way to the Land Rover and pressed the unlock icon, it responded instantly and she clambered in. She turned it on, and the engine coughed into life with a reassuring diesel powered growl, the knocking engine giving her such reassurance that it almost made her cry. This was real. This was the start of her way out. In the passenger footwell was Ronnie's insulated down jacket – she smiled at the luck she was experiencing. She decided to try and hitch the boat trailer there and then, one less job to do in the morning.

Switching on the lights, she eased it forward and then began to reverse it up close to the Rib which sat on the trailer. She scowled as she left the stillness of the car back into the gale and managed, after several tries, hobbling back and forth to the car, to hitch the trailer onto the tow bar of the Land Rover. She then pulled the jeep forward and parked it right outside the front door of the cottage. The fuel sat at just over half. She switched it all off, checking all lights were off and that there was nothing that would drain the battery and give her a nasty surprise in the morning. She was cold, very cold, her hands were numb, but she felt good. This was a big part of the plan and it had gone smoothly. She hung her jacket up; her undershirt and performance tracksuit top would be fine until she got Ronnie's jacket on.

Hazel sighed, time for the next part. She made her way towards the dorms, the painkillers she had taken earlier had taken the edge off her pain and she moved slightly easier, purpose fuelling her. She made her way out of the cottage through the security doors and headed down the corridor towards the visitor area of the building. The moment she pushed through the second set of double doors she knew something was terribly, terribly wrong.

There was a smell, a metallic, iron smell, and smoke? She recognised that smoke. And there was noise. And she recognised that noise. The cheering, raucous laughter of young men and she knew that they were there. They were all there, her boys included. All of them.

In the canteen.

And she didn't want to go.

Her legs slowed. Her purpose dissolved. New Hazel disappeared. All that was left was scared, broken, traumatised Hazel.

She knew what was there, beyond those blue doors twenty yards away. She knew.

And she didn't want to see it.

Yet she kept walking, ever so slowly.

Why? Just get your gear, get the fuck off this island. Leave the boys. They've made their choice. They want to stay here? Fine. You don't. Get going Hazel! There she was! There was New Hazel, speaking sense, being pragmatic, being realistic, but the blue doors kept getting closer, and New Hazel's power wasn't as strong or as unstoppable as she once though because she kept drawing inexorably closer, even when she saw the dark red blood pooling beneath the doors, even as she saw the yellow and red fire light behind the cracks in the door, she kept walking.

She needed her boys, she wanted to save her boys. It was her job. A mother's job, and she was going to save them.

She reached out one thin, trembling hand and pushed at the blue door. It opened easily.

And Hazel screamed.

A scream she had never produced before. A scream so full of terror and revulsion and heartbreak and misery and panic, dredged from the very depths of her. It shredded her throat and shredded her soul and it was only luck that saved her. A black, macabre luck, a luck that reeked and laughed as she slid in the blood that covered the floor of the canteen and which had flowed out as the door opened and had made her twist her ankle and send clean, purifying pain through her body. A pain that snapped her out of the insane horror that had swept over her. It was enough for her to wake up, to turn away from the heat in that room, to spin round and start running, if you could call it running, this wild, lurching, desperate lunging away from that room and those sights.

Had he been holding a leg?

She sobbed in terror. She was going. She didn't care now. What she had just seen. Her boys were not her boys anymore. She was leaving now.

Where was his skin?

Her last strand of sanity was in charge now, her last gasp of surviving this place propelled her, made her run on her broken ankle.

Was the roof gone?

She fell through the doors and fell again into the cottage and fell out into the dark where the wind tore at her, she didn't have her jacket, but there was one in the car, but she knew there wasn't, knew it wouldn't be there, knew someone had taken it or that it had never been there at all and the wind and the cold played with her, raced up her exposed leg where the shredded jean flapped and bit deeply through the thin layers she wore, made her hands shake and tremble but she dug in and found the keys and opened the Land Rover and clambered in.

Was the roof missing?

Images of what she had seen in the canteen kept threatening to overwhelm her but she closed her eyes against it. *No, move,* insisted New Hazel. And she did, the engine roared and she floored it, it was an old and heavy car and although she almost took a chunk out of the wall, she kept it straight and she was driving, driving up the gravelled path which quickly became tarmac, driving out of the wide open gates and the sightless ghoul that had greeted her days before on the MUCACH OUTDOOR ACTIVITY AND MARINE STUDY CENTRE sign and tilting onto the road that looped the island and driving for the launch.

She kept her eyes on the road, her breathing was quick, and she knew she was one step away from a meltdown, a toys out the pram, crash the car, lie on the side of the road panic attack and so she gripped the wheel tighter, focussing on that sensation, watching the road whizz by under the yellow lights. She was also aware that the black figure was sitting in the passenger seat next to her, but to acknowledge that was to acknowledge everything else that had happened, so no, she focussed on the road, on the corners that came quickly, and which caused the large vehicle to tilt and sway as she pressed the accelerator further. "Hazel," it whispered. She barely heard it, she was not here, she was not listening, she was driving. That was her focus.

"No," she whispered as the car went too wide and carved into some lose stones and scree that littered the sides of the road. "No."

She felt a hand resting on her leg, a cold hand, so cold, like an ice cube directly onto her skin –

And then she was in a warm field and Aila was sitting opposite her, *"Hazel, there is no way you-"*

The Land Rover missed its next corner completely, obviously the woman had no concept of driving, and Hazel bounced awake as the car ploughed over hillocks and divots that covered the land. She wrenched the wheel and got the car back onto tarmac.

Ahead a sign pointed to the ferry launch which was three hundred metres away. She floored the jeep and flew into the last corner, forgetting the boat hitched to the back, but the trailer held the road well and she pulled up into the carpark moments later, screeching to a halt and with no concern for accuracy or neatness, she reversed the trailer with the small boat deeply into the frothing sea. In her rearview mirror she could see the lights on the trailer disappear in the black waters. Her passenger was gone. She did look down then into the passenger footwell, hoping to see Ronnie's coat, but, as she had known it would be, it was gone.

No matter.

She eased herself out of the jeep into the freezing gale, her face, hands and exposed left leg turning red instantly. She waded out into the freezing Atlantic Ocean, knee deep, and began to unhitch the boat from the tethers that kept it anchored to the trailer. It was so cold and she knew she didn't have much time. The exposure would kill her. She needed to get to the mainland quickly, even if she got to the ferry master's cabin, that would be enough for tonight, if-

Why were they all naked?

The waves slapped and buffeted her but she got the last clasp undone. Instantly the boat lurched away from her as a wave picked it up but she had a strong grasp of the corded safety rope that threaded itself around the outer layer of the Rib, specifically for reasons such as this.

Her teeth were chattering as she clambered into the boat, the waves lifted and dropped the boat, throwing Hazel forwards and back as she reached for the back of the boat and the engine. She fell backwards, the pain in her ankle was unbelievable but she had fallen onto something sharp and uncomfortable. She twisted and saw she had fallen onto the lifeless corpse of Hamish. Sticks and twigs protruding from his eye sockets, his jaw open wide. She shrieked in horror, kicking herself away – it stank. How long had it been here? In this boat? Why here? She wailed again. The poor thing. Poor Ronnie. Poor Gav. She was shaking. She reached for a guide rope to drag her further away from the thing when its head twitched towards her.

She was wet through now, and the wind was after every last bit of her heat, her hands shook uncontrollably as she climbed to her knees, on all fours, and scrambled over the cylindrical bench that split the boat between front and back, *aft and...what was the other one?* the thing behind her was now mercifully out of view – *don't look at it don't look at it don't look at it* – she clenched her hands several times before trying to grasp the starter cord.

It took seventeen attempts.

Behind her she could hear movement, above the sound of the waves, of something scratching against the rubber hull of the boat. Twice she fell back as the waves hit, panicking and jumping back up, refusing to turn around. Once she heard the bottom grind on stone beneath as the Rib was pulled in all directions, that was a scary moment because if that propeller broke, it was game over. On her last attempt she had yanked the cord so hard that it pulled a muscle in her chest but the motor caught, the engine spluttered and a rather less than impressive engine motor noise could now be heard.

She nodded her head in relief as the Rib began to head out, yet, as they left the shore and the relative tranquillity of the ferry launch, the waves began to grow in size and ferocity. The thing at the front of the boat, the furry, matted horror continued to twitch and jerk, a leg spasming out or its head lurching up and down quickly, too quickly. She refused to look at it, looking out over the front, aware that in her periphery was a thing that should not be, that had no business being in there with her.

Why were they naked?

Hazel was numb, she could barely think, her hands were blue as she tried to see ahead of the next wave, the night was relatively clear but all she could see were the white caps of breakers as they hit again and again and again. She tried to ride them but the engine wasn't close to being powerful enough and the boat was close to capsizing several times. She adjusted the angle of approach, hitting the waves at a diagonal, but this was also futile, taking her further from her course and running her parallel with Muchach, rather than away. Her teeth chattering was painful, the cold and the wind was painful, she shuddered as her body -

Why were they all covered in blood?

Her mind refused to accept what she had seen in that room. She shook her head, trying to physically shake the memories out. Tears were streaming from her face. Freezing water splashed over her again and again. She was freezing cold. Again. She was out of reserves. Her body was giving in, throwing in the towel. *Stop the fight. I give up.* Sobbing, she finally began to give in. She was done. This was it. She had tried. Her ankle was painful. Her soul ached, her heart ached, what was she thinking? Why had she attempted this? She was going to die. She knew this now. No one could survive this. Another wave crashed over the side, covering her in icy water, the thing in the boat skittering and twitching madly, sliding around in the water as the boat tilted. Mercifully there was a rubber seat separating the front and the back of the Rib so she-

What was in those bowls?

She felt detached, watching this small woman in a small boat in the dark getting thrown around by these waves. She knew that the launch was long gone, the safety of the car long gone, her boys long gone, the mainland unreachable, her m-

What had they done to that boy?

She felt something hard press her feet from beneath. Rocks, she was being driven onto the rocks. Sure enough, more hard, unforgiving rocks began to push up from below when suddenly there was an ugly squeal and then a whoosh and the boat was collapsing. She was numb though. She didn't care. New Hazel was on a break. She was tired and the water felt oddly warm as she sank into the

Did he have wings?

The waters churned over her, throwing her along the rocks, she felt bones breaking, skin ripping and grazing, rough rocks thumping and scraping, but it didn't hurt now. Felt that thing fall on her, still twitching. Still warm.

Chapter 17

She opened one eye as a familiar and warming liquid trickled into her mouth. "Shhh Hazel, just drink," murmured Pritchard, he held her head in his lap, gently pouring more water into her mouth. She blinked stupidly. A cave roof was lit by fire. She was warmer. She looked around and saw them all looking down at her. Their faces were ghoulish, caked in blood, dark, as a huge fire roared behind them all, turning them almost into silhouettes. White and yellow smoke billowed from the fire, a rich, deep smoke which she remembered fondly. She breathed deep.

"Hi mum," said Daryl, but she couldn't see him.

He had been holding a head.

"Hi love," she muttered.

"Hi mum," came another voice.

"Hi love," she said.

"Hi mum," came another voice.

"Hi love," she replied.

"Hi mum," said Pritchard looking down on her.

Forcing sticks into places.

"Hi love," she said.

There was silence for a time and she could feel the boy who held her shaking softly. She raised her arm, reaching up to his face. It hurt to do that she noticed. She saw a large bruise on her forearm as she cupped his stubbled face in her hand, squeezed the back of his neck.

"Hi," he gasped again, eyes shining with emotion. "Hi Mum." And a tear leaked out of one eye and landed on her upper arm.

"Hello Mum," said Conal. She could him, large, muscular Conal with his hard looking face but those child's eyes, barely visible in the gloom. Such a sweet boy. She'd look after him.

"Hiya Conal," she whispered. "Help me up please boys," she said and so very gently and so very easily her children helped her to her feet. Sleeping bags slid from her as she rose. She looked down at herself, she was in her yellow panties and white vest. Her body was covered in angry looking bruises and in several places she saw large pads and strapping with small red spots, she must have really hurt herself she decided. She looked to Pritchard and he offered her more of their drink. The fire was so warm and she breathed deeply of the smoke again.

She looked around and saw they were not alone. The cave was full of people, and she smiled at these wonderful folk. These people who had donated their pain and lives so that others could live, so that the island and the planet could live and she wondered that they had come to see her now. She nodded gratefully to them. They did what she could never do.

"Shall we go mother?" asked Conal. She smiled, liking his face and his lovely accent.

"That would be lovely," she replied, reaching for him and stroking his arm lightly. She bent over, wincing at the pain, and then carefully arranged some of the sleeping bags she had been lying on around her, wrapping herself in them. She had bare feet and the ground was cold. She looked again at Pritchard and he gave her some more drink. The walls were covered in white symbols that swirled and danced and told of the history of Lorrsayeth and those that came before her. It was all so simple.

She walked and the pain in her body was sharp. Her back screamed, pain raced up both legs and her neck ached so fiercely but she rode it out until she could take another step. To her side her son Craft held her by the left arm and her son Petey held her right and she smiled at them both in warm gratitude. "My lovely boys," she murmured, patting their arms before taking another step. Again, the pain was acute, but she waited and then took another step.

The crowd around her parted as they made their way to the bright light. The wind grabbed at her, at her hair, her bright coloured robes with down insulation and anti-snag zips blew behind her in the wind as she was helped onto the path and began the ascent.

The stone was unforgiving, it bit and ripped at her feet yet she barely felt it. She could feel her toes, wet with her own blood, but she knew they all suffered the same and it was a minor sacrifice compared to those that the a' tabhann would be making. There wasn't many, not this time and several had already gone forward, but it was a start, a beautiful start.

She looked stiffly around, the pain in her neck so intense, but she had to see, and she wept tears of joy at the multitudes that walked with her. She imagined the pathway turning redder and redder as the crowd made its way up the winding path. Her helpers didn't falter even though their feet must also be receiving the same cuts and piercings that her own were experiencing.

They walked for hours, excruciatingly slow, yet what a beautiful moment, so beautiful she didn't want it to end. She looked up and saw the column of Lorrsayeth reaching so high and a sharp slap of memory rocked her – *she was taking the boys up there soon, they were going to climb it, maybe camp at the-* another stone pierced her foot and she was brought back to the present, thankful for pain. She drank more.

They reached the *Snuadh* and there she waited as the crowd filled into the space. She drank long and deep from the drink proffered to her from the old mother, her mother, her dark skin and yellow eyes soft and warm. There stood the *Dalyn Goffri,* grey hair blowing in the breeze, blue paint covering his body, bones and fabric in his hair and he waited patiently until they had all gathered before beginning his song and Hazel, if that is her name, wanted to be sick. This dirge promoted such vile feelings of illness and horror and yet it is what is needed for the healing time to start. His words are a purge, giving names to all that ails the world, and she knows it will be a long song, for there is much that ails the world and there is not enough *a' tabhann* to cure everything but it is a start, a much-needed start, a start too long overdue, but one that starts the healing.

A young man steps towards her, tears in her eyes, and holds her hand and mouths the words of love and then opens up his stomach in front of her with a sharp stone, eyes glistening in fear, or pain or extasy or awe she doesn't know but she holds him close for he has offered *freth grethalc* and this is such a noble thing he does. The song continues as one after another they offer themselves to *Lorrsayeth* and their blood paints the floor and their screams fill her ears and her heart stops for a sickening moment as a younger boy, floppy blonde hair so very familiar, kneels before her as a larger youth with red hair chokes the life from him, but the words of the song have her now and she is swept up in her love for this boy's sacrifice, such a gesture for his mother.

Finally, the day draws to a close, the sun is fading and many sit on the ledge of *Snuadh,* sitting in the now cold blood, staining their seats with the life of others as those who chose *freth grethalc* sit with them, leaking slowly onto the rocks below.

Far below, in the sea, an older man, a man with a full head of dark hair, is thrown down by his younger compatriots. Large stones are picked up and brought down hard onto him so that he does not resist.

Why does he resist?

And then his arms and legs are pinned in place by these very same stones, legs and arms broken by the weight of such stones.

And they sit there then, listening to the song of the *Dalyn Goffri,* no more *a' tabhann* step forward as the heat leeches from the day, as the sea comes slowly in, rising over the man's legs before lapping at his stomach. It will be hours before the sea claims him. Hazel cannot hear his screams from this distance, not with the song being sung, and there is an itch to be scratched somewhere but-

Why is he screaming?

But those who placed the man in the sea have now made it back to the *Snuadh* and she drinks deeply of their drink and sighs, happy. Old Mother sits with them, she is also happy, and Hazel knows she will not see her again. The healing has begun. She wonders if one day she will be like Old Mother but pushes that thought away too.

For now, everything is right, all is well.

Her children are with her.

The End.

Printed in Great Britain
by Amazon

46558982R00106